ADVANCE PRAISE FOR GILLESPIE FIELD GROOVE

"GILLESPIE FIELD GROOVE is a gripping mystery and a captivating ride through rock and roll history and San Diego's music scene. It's so authentic you can practically hear the fuzz and crunch of Jimi's Stratocaster coming off the page."
    Matthew Quirk, New York Times-bestselling author of RED WARNING and THE NIGHT AGENT (now a Netflix series)

"Rolly Waters is back with a ripped-from-the headlines thriller custom made for music-lovers. Hired to hunt down a missing Fender Strat that may have belonged to Jimi Hendrix, Waters uncovers a series of intertwined mysteries with more twists than a crate full of guitar cables. GILLESPIE FIELD GROOVE is an uptempo page turner that shines a spotlight on the music industry's darkest corners."
    S.W. Lauden, author of BAD CITIZEN CORPORATION and THAT'LL BE THE DAY:A POWER POP HEIST

"Carefully crafted characters. Twists and revelations. Music and murder. A PI who plays guitar or a guitar player who dallies in detecting? Even Rolly Waters isn't sure. Whichever it is, Corey

Lynn Fayman's latest gives you a real insight into what it means to be both. Like Don Quixote wielding a guitar instead of a sword. Awesome."

Pamela Cowan, author of COLD KILL

GILLESPIE FIELD GROOVE is like an easter egg hunt filled with suspense and intrigue that also gives readers a straightforward look into the life of a working musician. I love this series.

Marc Intravaia - RICHIE FURAY BAND; BACK TO THE GARDEN

GILLESPIE FIELD GROOVE

GILLESPIE FIELD GROOVE

COREY LYNN FAYMAN

 KONSTELLATION
PRESS

Konstellation Press, San Diego

www.konstellationpress.com

Editor: Lisa Wolff

Cover design: Corey Lynn Fayman

ISBN: 978-0-9987482-8-3

For my brother Bruce,
Comrade in the rock'n'roll trenches of yore

In Memoriam
Cliff Morse

1

THE CONCERT

The man sat down on the steps, lit up a joint, and watched the cops beat up kids in the parking lot. White kids mostly. Hippies. Young people who wanted to hear Jimi Hendrix. The concert was sold out, but the kids showed up anyway, hoping to get in. He'd seen it before. The crowd outside would get restless. Someone would call in more cops. The kids wouldn't leave, and the cops would start bashing away. The tour would be over in two weeks. No more riots. No more early-morning equipment load-outs, trying to sleep on the bus, mixing uppers and downers to regulate his diurnal rhythms. After the last show, he'd go home, sleep for a week, then start all over again. There was a teenaged girl sitting at the edge of the concrete steps below him. She was crying.

"Lucy," the man said. He looked up from his easy chair. This was his room, his house. He'd put a record on the old turntable. And now the record had ended. The tone arm clicked as it lifted and returned to its rest. The songs on the record held secrets that only he knew.

He took another toke, stood up and walked down to check on the girl who was crying. The lost and lonely kids were there every night too, sitting alone, teenagers trapped in the tragedy of their own adolescence.

"Are you okay?" he asked.

The girl looked up at him, her mascara running like ink from a fountain pen.

"I don't know what to do," she said and started sobbing again.

The man lifted his hand and felt the side of his head, the right side where something had hit him. His hair felt matted and wet. He needed to go to the hospital. He needed to call for an ambulance. Lucy was a nurse. She'd know what to do. He reached for his phone.

A medallion hung around the girl's neck. A love medallion, she called it. There'd been some sort of contest, sponsored by the local radio station. The winner would get to go backstage and give the medallion to Jimi. But the radio station had never cleared the plan with anyone on Jimi's team. The girl and her chaperone, a marketing rep from the station, had been escorted out of the building. The rep, some middle-aged square, was way out of his comfort zone. Disconcerted by his ward's emotional breakdown, repulsed by the fecund presence of dope-smoking hippies and fearing the riot police, he'd abandoned his ward on the steps of the arena, slapping five dollars in her hand and telling her to take a cab home. The girl sat on the steps, clutching the five-dollar bill. She said her parents would kill her if they knew where she'd been. She said she couldn't go home.

As the man reached for his phone, a manila envelope slipped from his lap. He leaned down and retrieved it. The word LUCY had been written in large block letters on the front of the envelope. The photograph inside had been taken a long time ago, before the man in the photo had died. He would give it to Lucy. He reached for his phone again and tapped Lucy's name.

The boss had given him ten minutes for his break, before Jimi went on. He'd used up five of those minutes already, but he couldn't leave the girl here, all alone with squirrelly hippie dudes and cops busting heads. The cops would toss her in jail with the rest. Or maybe something worse. He saw the tour bus parked behind the concrete barrier of the loading dock. He reached out his hand and helped her up.

Lucy didn't answer the phone. She must be working. The man put the phone down. He closed his eyes and leaned his head against the chair. He'd learned, on the road, how to drift off to sleep in an instant. His thoughts faded. A light appeared, rushing toward him. And then he stopped breathing.

2

THE NURSE

Just after two in the afternoon, Rolly Waters sat at a round concrete table in the courtyard of Alvarado Hospital, nursing a cappuccino to which he'd added five drops of artificial sweetener. He was trying to cut sugar out of his diet. The woman across the table from him smiled. Her name was Lucinda Rhodes. She was a nurse at the hospital. Two years ago, Lucinda had seen Rolly at his worst, in the emergency room of a hospital in Brawley where the doctors had treated him for a black widow spider bite. Nurse Lucinda had kept tabs on him through the night, checking his blood pressure, giving him pills, and had fitted him with crutches before he checked out. Rolly didn't remember much else about that night, except that it had been hot in the desert, and everything smelled like fertilizer. He didn't remember giving his business card to the nurse. But Nurse Lucinda had one of his cards in her hand today. She placed it on the table like a bridge player dropping a trump card.

"I don't know why I kept this," she said. "I guess I thought it might come in handy someday. I'd never met a private investigator before. You were funny, not like I thought a detective would be. You flirted with me."

"I did?" Rolly said, hoping he sounded more amnesic than incredulous. "I hope I wasn't out of line."

"I've dealt with a lot worse," said Lucinda. "Besides, I thought you were kind of cute."

"What do you think now?" Rolly said, unable to resist. Lucinda smiled and redirected the conversation.

"You're a musician, right?" she said. "You play the guitar?"

Rolly nodded. He didn't usually drive out to meet potential clients as soon as they called, but his detective work had dried up. The hospital was only a fifteen-minute drive from his house, east on Highway 8 near San Diego State University. He'd gotten to know any number of the local hospitals over the years, interviewing accident victims for their lawyers. Sometimes he'd been in the accident.

"Tell me what you're looking for again," he said. "You said something about your father?"

Lucinda nodded, glanced over at the coffee stand, then back at Rolly. She appeared to be in her late thirties or early forties, a little wide around the middle, with an honest, gentle face. She seemed more down to earth than most of the women Rolly had dated. He wasn't dating Lucinda, though. She was a potential client. He'd gotten too close to a client once, gotten involved with her while working on her case. That was how he'd ended up in the emergency room in Brawley.

"My dad died," Lucinda said. "Last week."

"I'm sorry."

Lucinda stared into her coffee cup, contemplating the black liquid inside.

"He's why I moved here," she said. "From Brawley. It was three months ago. I knew he needed some help. I didn't see my dad much when I was growing up. I lived with my mother after they got divorced. She died ten years ago. Cancer. I don't have any siblings, so my dad was all the family I had left."

"What did your father do for a living?"

"He was in the music business, like you. One of those guys that travels around with bands."

"A roadie?"

Lucinda nodded.

"That's how they met, my mom and my dad. She used to tell me the story all the time. It was at a Jimi Hendrix concert. Here in San Diego. Dad was in charge of those speakers they put in front so the singers can hear themselves?"

"The monitors," said Rolly.

"Yeah. My mom was sixteen. She'd won some contest at a radio station. That's how she got backstage for the concert. She was supposed to meet Jimi Hendrix, but the radio people messed something up, I can't remember exactly what it was, but he wouldn't talk to any of them. Jimi Hendrix, I mean. She met him later, thanks to my dad."

"She met your dad backstage?"

"It was outside, after the show. There was a riot. The police were there. Dad helped Mom get away. That's how she ended up on the band's tour bus. And the rest, as my mom liked to say, was history."

"How old was your dad?" asked Rolly.

"Twenty, I think. Maybe twenty-one. Not that big a difference but . . ." Lucinda shrugged. "Times were different then, I guess."

"Yeah," Rolly concurred. He was not about to throw stones at glass houses. There'd been girls at the clubs where his bands played, girls with fake IDs who were younger than he'd been. He hoped none of the ones he'd taken home had been legally underage, but thinking about it now in his forties made him a little queasy. As Lucinda had noted, times had changed. Some.

"Mom was gone for five days," Lucinda continued. "Her parents didn't know where she was. It made all the papers. This guy at the radio station got fired. Two years later, out of the blue, my dad comes back to town and looks up my mom. She was of age then and they got married. I came along later. I think they were trying to save their marriage by having a baby."

"They wouldn't be the first," Rolly said. Lucinda's story about her parents was interesting and her way of telling it made him like her even more, but he needed to get down to business, keep it professional. "How can I be of help?"

Lucinda reached in the front left pocket of her scrubs and pulled out a photograph. She placed it on the table.

"It's this photograph," she said. "My dad left it for me. I don't know why. I don't even know who the guy is."

Rolly picked up the photograph. It was a black man, no older than thirty. He was dressed in a seafoam-green suit, something a Motown act might have worn in the early seventies. The comparison wasn't far off. The man was a musician, with a white Stratocaster guitar strapped over his shoulder, as if he'd just stepped off, or was preparing to step onto, the stage.

"He's not Jimi Hendrix." Rolly said. "I can tell you that much."

Lucinda frowned.

"I may be from Brawley, Mr. Waters, but I'm not a total hick. I know he's not Jimi Hendrix. The thing is . . . it looks like my dad's guitar. The one Jimi Hendrix gave him."

Rolly leaned back in his chair and reassessed the guitar in the photograph. It looked like thousands of others, but if Jimi Hendrix had touched that Stratocaster even once, it was more valuable than the rest.

"You understand why I thought you could help me?" Lucinda said.

Rolly nodded. He stared at the photo again.

"You think this guy in the photo still has the guitar?"

Lucinda shrugged.

"I don't know. I remember seeing one like it in my dad's apartment when I was a kid. I remember him saying he didn't have much to give me, except that guitar, the one Jimi Hendrix gave him. He said it would be my inheritance."

"Could be a pretty nice inheritance," Rolly said.

"That's what I thought," said Lucinda. She leaned back in her seat and tapped both hands on the table. "I looked up some things on the internet. One of Jimi Hendrix's guitars sold for almost two million dollars."

"Well," said Rolly. "That was the guitar from Woodstock, the one Hendrix used to play 'The Star-Spangled Banner.' I don't think this one would be worth that much . . ."

"It'd be worth something, though, wouldn't it? If it came from Jimi Hendrix."

"Yeah." Rolly nodded. Any guitar Hendrix had touched would be worth a considerable amount to collectors, if it had provenance. That wasn't Rolly's area of expertise, but he knew people who could help him out with the valuation. He'd need to have the actual guitar in his hands, though. This one was only a photograph. And Jimi Hendrix wasn't in the photo.

"Do you have any other documentation or photos?" he asked.

Lucinda shook her head.

"When was the last time you saw the guitar in your dad's possession?"

"Maybe ten years ago." Lucinda shrugged. "I haven't really been through his stuff yet. The church said they could let me into his apartment tomorrow."

"He lived at a church?"

Lucinda sighed. She surveyed the courtyard, then sipped her coffee a couple of times.

"My dad worked at this Russian Orthodox church," she said. "Over in Allied Gardens. He did some maintenance, ran the PA system, stuff like that. They let him live in this little apartment at the edge of the property, rent free, in exchange for his work. My dad was seventy-three, but he couldn't retire. He didn't have any Social Security. Not much, anyway. He was starting to lose it, mentally."

Rolly nodded again, trying not to think about where he'd be

at seventy-three. According to the latest mailing from the SSA, he'd only be pulling in three hundred and twenty-five dollars a month from Social Security when he turned sixty-five. He'd never be able to retire.

"The first thing you should look for is a sales receipt," he said.

"Hmm?" Lucinda said, sounding distracted, as if she'd been thinking about something entirely different.

"When you go through his apartment," Rolly said. "Look for a sales slip. In case he sold the guitar to someone."

"He might have, I guess," Lucinda said. "Dad was always having money troubles. He wasn't the kind of guy who kept accurate paperwork. He always said if you couldn't do business on a handshake with someone then you shouldn't do business with them at all. I think it cost him over the years. Well, that and the drugs. He had substance abuse problems."

"Occupational hazard," Rolly said. "If he worked in the music business. I had to get sober myself."

"How long has it been for you?"

"Twenty years now, I guess, something like that."

"Sober people usually know to the day," said Lucinda. She didn't sound like she was challenging him, just stating a fact. Rolly shrugged.

"My father still drinks too much," he said. "That helps me avoid it."

Lucinda leaned forward again and rubbed her hands together, as if she were washing them.

"Maybe you could come with me tomorrow?" she said. "To my dad's place."

"I'd have to charge you for it," Rolly said.

"How much?"

"Fifty dollars an hour. Three hundred a day. Plus expenses," said Rolly. He liked Lucinda. Her case was already more interesting than most, but he still needed to get paid.

"I can do that," said Lucinda. "Maybe around ten o'clock

tomorrow morning? Just a couple of hours. The church is just down the street from this nightclub you might know. Bump's?"

"Yeah, I know Bump's," Rolly said. "I used to play there sometimes."

"Great," said Lucinda. "I appreciate this. I didn't want to go there alone. I don't have any family or friends here in town I can ask."

Rolly placed the photograph on the table, pulled out his phone and took several pictures of it, checked them, decided they'd do, then passed the original photo back to Lucinda.

"I'll show your photo to some people I know," he said. "Maybe someone's seen this guitar before. They might know who the guy in the photo is, too."

"Are you going to charge me for that?"

"No," Rolly said. He shrugged. "It's on me. I was going to see a guy today anyway."

"Thanks," Lucinda said. "I'll see you tomorrow, at the church. Bring a contract if you need me to sign one."

They exchanged contact information and stood up. Lucinda turned to walk away.

"Wait," said Rolly. Lucinda paused. "Where did you find this photograph?"

"What's that?" she said.

"You said you hadn't been able to get into your father's apartment. Where did this photo come from?"

Lucinda took a deep breath, not quite a sigh.

"We'll have to talk about that, I guess. My dad called me the night that he died. I was working. When I stopped by after work, he was dead. He had an envelope with my name on it in his lap. The photo was in the envelope."

"Was there anything else?"

"No. Just the photo. I put it in my car and called nine-one-one. The paramedics came first, and then the police. They sealed off the apartment. I wasn't allowed to go back in."

"Did you show them the photograph?"

"No. I didn't think it was important."

"What do you mean?" Rolly asked.

Lucinda stared into her coffee cup again. She looked up at Rolly again. Her voice broke.

"The police think someone murdered him."

3

THE MOSTLY

An hour later, Rolly walked into Norwood's Mostly Guitars shop. Rob Norwood sat behind the back counter, grimacing at his laptop computer. It was not unusual to find Norwood grimacing. It was his default facial expression.

"I hate the internet," Norwood said, looking up from his laptop as Rolly pulled up to the counter.

"Anything in particular?" asked Rolly.

"No," said Norwood. "I just hate it in general. The wife says I need to be on Facebook and Instagram and all that stuff, because of the move. So people can find us."

Rolly surveyed the room. It was the first time he'd been in Norwood's new shop, which had relocated from downtown San Diego to the Rolando area, east of the city and close to the university. Downtown real estate had become too valuable for used guitar shops, even if your wife owned the building. The decrepit city block that had once hosted Norwood's Mostly was now a big hole in the ground, soon to become a twenty-story condo tower.

"What're you reading there?" Rolly asked, indicating a comb-bound document on the counter.

"This guy hired me to appraise his guitar collection. For insurance purposes. This is the original appraisal. Campbell Lange was the appraiser."

"Who's Campbell Lange?"

"Top-notch guitar maker. She works at Taybor in El Cajon now. Runs their premier repair and customization department, works with the big shots and rock stars."

"That explains why I've never heard of her."

"This appraisal's fifteen years old," Norwood said, flipping open the first page of the bound document. "The guitars should be worth even more now. There's a couple of real jewels in here if I can confirm their provenance. You remember Intravaia's buddy, right—they found out he'd been playing John Lennon's guitar for the last forty years?"

"Yeah, I heard about that," Rolly said. The story of Lennon's Gibson acoustic guitar that had been stolen from a Beatles concert in England in 1963 and reappeared in the hands of an amateur guitar player in San Diego fifty years later had been the stuff of collectors' dreams. Rolly was on the trail of what might be an even bigger discovery. It was exciting, a lot more exciting than his usual work. "Makes you wonder what you might have in here, doesn't it?"

He surveyed the shop, wondering if Norwood's inventory held any secret treasures like Lennon's Gibson. Had any of the guitars hanging from the walls been touched by a master, been played on a classic recording or toured with a rock star? For Rolly, the value of a guitar was in its playability, its sound, how it felt in his hands. Collectors didn't care about that. They fetishized a guitar's history, looking for signs of the sorcerer's hands, digging for treasure in yard sales and secondhand music shops. Lucinda's father had claimed he owned a Jimi Hendrix Stratocaster guitar. Where had it gone? Was some kid in his parents' garage bashing away at it right now?

"Speaking of collector's items," Norwood said, "I got something interesting for you."

"What is it?" Rolly asked, knowing full well that Norwood wasn't going to tell him. It was a game they played: Norwood asking Rolly to check out unusual additions to his collection, getting Rolly's unfiltered take on the instrument. The guitars were often Frankensteins, significantly modified from their original configurations—homemade electronics or fretboards taken from one type of guitar and attached to the body of another. Rolly didn't feel like playing Norwood's game today but hoped it might improve the shop owner's mood.

"I'll take a gander," he said.

Norwood grinned, stood up and walked out from behind the counter.

"Check this out," he said, lifting an emerald-green, solid-body electric guitar from the wall. He handed it to Rolly, who took a seat on a stool nearby. "What do you think?"

Rolly inspected the guitar. There was no label on it, no manufacturer's branding or badge.

"Looks like a Mosrite," he said. "Maybe a Johnny Ramone or Ventures model."

Norwood nodded.

"That's the idea," he said. "It's not a Mosrite, though. It's all custom."

Rolly played a few chords, adjusted the tuning and ran the guitar through its paces. He inspected the neck, the frets and the tuning pegs. Norwood opened a drawer, pulled out a cable, handed one end to Rolly, then plugged the other into an old Fender Champ amplifier nearby. Rolly inspected the pickups, then played through the amp. He used the selector switch to flip through the pickup positions, changing the sound.

"Plays nice," he said. "What kind of pickups are these?"

"All custom," said Norwood. "The whole damn thing was handmade from scratch."

"Who made it?"

"Campbell Lange."

"That guitar maker you told me about? The one at Taybor who did the appraisal?"

"Yeah." Norwood nodded. "She had a shop of her own for a while."

"It's nice," Rolly said, inspecting the guitar. "How much do you want for it?"

"Five bills," said Norwood.

"Five hundred dollars?"

"No, dumb-ass. Five thousand. Ruby Dean asked me to sell it for her."

"You're still in touch with Ruby?"

"Sure. I was her guitar teacher, you know."

"So was I," Rolly said, which was true, although he'd only had the teenaged Ruby as a student for three months, twenty years ago. Teaching had not been Rolly's forte. He'd shown up drunk more than once, making a less than favorable impression on the future star's parents. He played a few more licks, then sighed and handed the guitar back to Norwood.

"Too rich for my blood," he said.

Norwood took the guitar and hung it back up on the wall.

"Might not be here that long. I'm posting it on my website today. Word will get out."

Rolly surveyed the walls of the shop, the old guitars that hung there, each one with a different history, then reached in his pocket, pulled out his phone and showed Norwood Lucinda's photograph.

"You recognize the guy in this photo?" he asked.

Norwood collected his reading glasses from the counter, took Rolly's phone and inspected the screen.

"Never seen him before," he said, zooming in on the photograph. "Why do you wanna know?"

"New client. Her dad worked in the music business, a touring audio technician from what I understand. He died recently. She wants to track down the guitar in the photo."

"Why?"

"She thinks her dad owned it. She's hoping I can find this guy and ask him about it."

Norwood grunted. Rolly decided not to mention the Hendrix connection. Not yet.

"When was the photograph taken?" Norwood asked.

Rolly shrugged.

"She doesn't know. From the outfit, I'd guess in the seventies."

"Yeah," said Norwood. "That looks about right. You and I were little kids."

"Her dad moved here in the seventies and married her mother. If the picture is from that era, I figure this guy might be from around here too."

Norwood grunted again, narrowed his eyes and moved his fingertips over the screen.

"Looks like the venue was here in town," he said. He showed Rolly where he'd zoomed in on the top left corner of the photo. "That's the KRIP logo."

Rolly stared at the upper right corner where a section of curved sign hung above the stage.

"KRIP the radio station?" he said, noting the elaborate *K* on the sign and the edge of what might be an *R* next to it before it was cut off by the edge of the photograph.

"Yeah. They sponsored a lot of concerts back in the seventies and eighties. Back when they were the first AOR station in town. Killer Rock In Perpetuity."

"What do they play now?"

"Christian radio."

Rolly shook his head in disappointment. Radio sucked. He'd given up on it years ago.

"Lou at Recordman," Norwood said, scratching his chin. "That's who you should talk to."

"I thought he handled folk stuff," Rolly said. The Recordman shop featured the largest collection of vintage folk and blues records in town, perhaps anywhere. Lou, the long-time owner, was a walking, talking encyclopedia of blues, folk and country music history. "The guy in the photo looks like he's playing funk or disco."

"Lou collects a lot of local stuff," Norwood said, handing the photo back to Rolly. "Not just folk records. If the guy in this photo played around town in the seventies, Lou will know who he was."

"Thanks," Rolly said.

"That guitar in the picture," Norwood said, handing the phone back to Rolly. "The Strat. Did your client say anything about it?"

"Like what?"

"Just . . . well, anything."

Rolly thought for a moment, trying to decide what he wanted to tell Norwood. It wasn't easy sometimes, trying to get information from people while also protecting your client's secrets.

"Her father said the guitar was valuable, that he was going to leave it to her."

"How valuable?"

"Pretty valuable," said Rolly. "A collector piece, if what he said is true."

"What did he say?" Norwood asked, getting pushy.

Rolly scratched behind his ear, still unsure how tight-lipped he wanted to be. Norwood could be a big help to him. The trick was to give up just the right amount of information.

"Like I said, my client's dad was in the music business. She says he toured with Jimi Hendrix."

Norwood stared at Rolly for a moment, contemplating this new information.

"Are you saying the guitar in this picture was owned by Hendrix?" he asked.

"That's what my client's father told her," Rolly said. "I haven't seen any documentation. I know her father and mother met at a Hendrix concert. That's the story, anyway. Her father had some substance abuse problems. He wasn't very reliable."

"What's his name?"

"I can't tell you that. Not without my client's permission."

Norwood pursed his lips, weighing Rolly's story. He looked back at the appraisal document on the counter and pulled out his phone.

"Send me that photo," he said. "I might have something for you."

Rolly pulled up Norwood's number, sent the photo.

"What is it?" he asked.

"My client . . . the one I'm doing the appraisal for. I don't have much documentation either, so maybe we can help each other out on this one. Worth a shot, anyway."

"I'm not following you."

Norwood stroked his chin.

"You talk to the Recordman, see what you can find out about the guy in the photograph. I'll talk to my client."

"What about?

"There's a chance—a slim chance, mind you—that he's got this guitar in his collection."

4

THE RECORDMAN

The Recordman store was housed in a bright yellow 1930s bungalow on University Avenue, near tire shops, Asian grocery stores and *mariscos* restaurants. Inside, it was stacked from floor to ceiling with rare and one-of-a-kind recordings from rare and one-of-a-kind acts. Its proprietor, Lou Brendon, had been collecting and preserving audio recordings of all shapes, sizes and styles long before the craze for "classic vinyl" became a twee hobby for Millennials and Gen Xers with disposable income. Lou specialized in long forgotten, or barely known, blues and folk acts from the early days of the record business on to the present, amassing a wide variety of recordings over the years. There was no one else in the store when Rolly entered, an hour before closing time. Lou sat behind the sales counter, going through a stack of 45 singles.

"Hey, Lou," Rolly said. "Remember me?"

Lou Brendon raised his head and looked Rolly over. It had been a long time since Rolly's last visit to the store.

"Creatures, right?" Brendon replied. "Local act. One EP, early 2000s. Grunge Power Pop with a touch of Chicago Blues."

"That was us," Rolly replied. "I'm Rolly Waters."

"Yeah, I remember. You're still playing around town."

Rolly nodded. He pulled out his phone and tapped on the photograph Lucinda had given him.

"Does this guy look familiar to you?" he asked.

Lou took the phone, considered the image, then handed the phone back to Rolly.

"Nope," he said. "I don't know who he is."

Rolly took the phone back and shared his thoughts on the photo, noting the KRIP sign and the era in which he thought the photo had been taken. Lou Brendon leaned back in his chair and scratched his beard, then pointed toward the room off to his right.

"There's a locals' section in there," he said. "Organized by decade, starting in the fifties."

"Thanks," Rolly said. He put his phone back in his pocket, turned and walked into the next room. Racks and racks of record cases filled the room, each case's contents separated by white plastic dividers. Each divider was marked in black felt ink with the category of records behind it. He glanced over the titles as he walked through the room, spotted the locals section and started flipping through the record covers, starting with the most recent, in case anything had been misfiled or misplaced. As he moved back in time, he recognized more and more acts, some who'd been his contemporaries and rivals. For most of them, these records were their greatest glory. None had gone on to national fame. He found a copy of his old band's EP, *Creatures*, lifted it out of the case and read through the back credits. Rolly, Moogus, Derek and Matt. Only Rolly and Moogus still played professionally. Derek was a software engineer now. Matt died in a car accident. Rolly had been driving the car. He put the EP back into the case.

The 1990s passed under his fingers, then the 1980s, without anything of interest. He took his time going through records from the 1970s, checking the front and back of each record to make sure he didn't overlook something. He'd almost made it through the decade when he found what he was looking for. *Otis Sparks. Love Correction.* He pulled out his phone and compared the man in the photo to the one looking out from the record cover. They looked the same. Rolly stared at the face on the album cover for a moment to be sure, then checked the information on the back cover. The credits were listed on top of a background using a second photo of Otis Sparks, looking pensive as he sat on a stool in a wood-paneled recording studio, microphone stands and a drum kit behind him. The songs were listed in order on the back, along with the songwriting credits for each, all assigned to the same names. Sparks and Sledge. Rolly read the credits at the bottom of the back cover. *Produced and recorded at Sledge Sound Studios, El Cajon, CA. Engineered by Gerry Rhodes.* Lucinda's father.

The name of the studio sounded familiar too. He remembered a demo session he'd done with Moogus, years ago at a studio in El Cajon, next to the Gillespie Field airport. He couldn't remember the name of the place, but it might be the same one. He opened the map application on his phone and entered the name. *Sledge Sound Studios.* It was still there, located at the edge of Gillespie Field. He wondered if anyone working there would still remember Otis Sparks and his white Stratocaster guitar. Forty years was a long time, especially in the world of pop music.

He stuffed his phone back into his pocket and took the record out to the front of the store. The album might spark memories from people he interviewed, more so than the photograph.

"I found him," he said, placing the album on the counter in front of Lou.

"Otis Sparks," Lou said, reading the cover.

"You remember him?"

"He's starting to look familiar," Lou said. He flipped the album over and perused the back cover. Rolly waited to see if any enlightenment would be forthcoming. The Recordman frowned.

"That bastard Sledge," he said.

"What's that?"

"Roger Sledge."

"Who's he?"

"You don't remember him?" Lou replied, sounding disgusted.

"No." Rolly shook his head.

"He was Ruby Dean's manager for a while. They got married. And divorced. Sledge Recording Studios, that was his place. He's listed on the songwriting credits, too. Some sort of shenanigans there, I would imagine."

"What do you mean?"

"You know how it is," Lou continued. "This guy Otis Sparks probably wrote all the songs, but Sledge wanted half the credit, took half the royalties. Producer's prerogative. That's how it goes. Especially when guys are getting started."

"You're probably right on that," Rolly said. It was an old trick dishonest producers played on credulous young musicians, adding their own name to the royalty sheet. Some made it part of their contract, while others just turned in the copyright papers and added their name. Either way, the songwriter got screwed.

"Is this guy Sledge still around?" Rolly asked. Lou the Recordman shrugged his shoulders.

"I don't know," he said. "He'd be pretty old now. Might be dead."

"How about the other guy listed there? The engineer. Gerry Rhodes. You know anything about him?"

Lou the Recordman stroked his beard.

"The name sounds vaguely familiar," he said. "But I couldn't say why. You want to buy this?"

Rolly nodded, pulling out a twenty-dollar bill. Lou took the money and gave him five dollars back. An Otis Sparks album wasn't a big collector's item. Rolly picked up the album, flipped it over and looked at the back cover again.

"You said this guy Sledge was Ruby Dean's manager?"

"That's what I remember. She dumped him after she got famous, like they always do."

"Maybe he was taking royalties from her too."

"He made a lot of money, if that's the case."

Lou started sorting through the stack of 45 rpm singles again.

"I played on Ruby Dean's demo tape," Rolly said. He was bragging, but not very much. Ruby's manager, who must have been Roger Sledge, had hired The Creatures to play on her demo sessions, unaware of Rolly's earlier encounters with Ruby, or perhaps overriding any concerns she might have expressed. The pay had been decent, but below union wages. A bunch of L.A session players took over after Ruby signed with the record company, rerecording the songs, making them sound big and shiny, not the bare-bones production that demos often were. The LA guitarist lifted one of Rolly's licks from the demo, but there wasn't anything Rolly could do about it. That wasn't how copyrights worked.

"You got any copies of the demo tape?" Lou asked, looking up from his records.

"I don't think so. Why?"

"It's not really my kind of thing, but it could be worth something to collectors."

"I don't remember much about the sessions," Rolly said. The only thing he'd cared about at the time was the money. They'd had no idea Ruby would do so well. "I think we recorded it at Sledge's studio. It was one of the last gigs I did before I took my . . . hiatus."

"Your what?"

"Nothing." Rolly sighed. He'd need to sit down with a calendar to figure out the exact dates. The year before the car accident had been a pretty heady time for The Creatures. They were the most popular band in San Diego. They'd opened for national acts and could sell out small theaters. They got hired to play on Ruby's demo tape, among others. And they'd just signed a two-album deal with Columbia Records. Then it all went to hell, and he was left alone in a guilt-ridden jungle of his own making. He hadn't picked up a guitar for two years after Matt died. Didn't play a single note.

"Thanks for your help," he said. He pulled out a business card and placed it on the counter. "Let me know if you remember anything else about Otis Sparks."

"Sure thing," Lou replied, his attention on his stack of records. Rolly headed toward the door.

"Wait a minute," Lou said. Rolly paused and turned to look back at him. Lou had Rolly's business card in his hand. "You're a private investigator? That's why you're looking for this guy?"

Rolly nodded. "Yeah. A client showed me the photograph I showed you. Gerry Rhodes, the recording engineer listed on the back of this album, gave my client the photograph. My client wants to find the guitar that's in the photograph."

"Have you asked this Rhodes guy about it?"

"He died. A few days ago. I don't know the whole story. The police are looking into it."

"Huh." Lou the Recordman stared at the opposite wall, sorting through his thoughts like a crate of old records.

"What is it?" Rolly asked. Lou's eyes turned from the far wall back to Rolly.

"It's really weird," he said. "But when I saw you were a detective, this thought just popped into my mind. About that Otis guy."

"What is it?"

"I don't remember exactly what happened, but I think someone shot him. Or he shot somebody else. I think Sledge was there, too."

5

THE REHEARSAL

Rolly sat in his car on the opposite side of the street from the industrial park where Sledge Sound Studios was supposed to be located. He wasn't sure it was still there. A sign on the building said "Stryzaga Flight School." He'd rung the bell, but the thug who'd answered hadn't been particularly friendly, meeting Rolly's inquiries with a flat and forbidding "no" while adding an occasional "we are closed" or "you go now" to the mix. Rolly wasn't an expert on accents, but the man sounded Russian or Eastern European.

At least he had a name now, to go with the man in the photograph. Otis Sparks. He'd called Lucinda, asked her if she recognized the name, but she drew a blank. They might learn more when they went through her father's apartment tomorrow, find some bit of information that got them closer to Otis, wherever he was, alive or dead. If Otis Sparks had been involved in a shooting like Lou Brandon remembered, there'd be a police report. A story in the newspaper. That would take some more research.

A small plane, some sort of Cessna or Piper, took off from the airfield, located on the other side of the building. It buzzed overhead and turned west toward the sunset. There were several cars in the parking lot, two of which were notable. One was a Range Rover, brand new, fully equipped, top of the line. Someone in the building could drop $100k on a car. A more modest Ford Ranger sat parked next to the Rover. Rolly recognized the truck from its personalized license plate: DRUMASS. The license plate, and the truck, belonged to Moogus, his long-time drummer. If Moogus was inside the building, there was probably still a recording studio in there as well. Unless Moogus had signed up for flying lessons. Rolly pulled out his phone and texted him, hoping his peripatetic drummer could call off the watchdogs and help Rolly get in.

As he waited for Moogus to respond, he ran a search for Roger Sledge on his phone. There wasn't a lot to read—one minor entry on Wikipedia and a one-screen web page for Sledge Sound Studios describing it as an artist management and production company. There was no phone number listed, so Rolly filled out the contact form and sent in a request, identifying himself and asking to speak to someone about a former employee, Gerry Rhodes.

The Wikipedia entry on Roger Sledge provided some basic biographical information, with two paragraphs dedicated to Sledge's involvement in establishing the career of Ruby Dean. Rolly tapped on the Ruby Dean link and read through her page as well. It provided more details on the relationship, including Sledge and Dean's short-lived marriage. According to the article, Dean had filed for divorce from Sledge five years after their wedding, citing physical and emotional cruelty as well as sexual assault. A settlement had been reached before the case went to court.

Light flashed through the cab of his car. He looked up to see a man and a woman exiting the front door of the building. The woman looked to be in her twenties, a blond glam doll in stiletto heels and oversized sunglasses, but she disappeared into the Range Rover so quickly his view was more an impression than a definitive assessment. The goon he'd dealt with earlier closed the door after her, walked around to the driver's-side door and started the car. Rolly slunk into his seat so the man wouldn't see him as the Range Rover pulled out onto the street. He debated his options, wondering if he should follow the SUV or hang tight. He decided to stay and see who else left the building. Before long, Moogus was hauling his drum cases out the door and loading them onto the back of his truck. Some other musicians, none of whom Rolly recognized, also exited the building and loaded their gear into their cars. There was no sign of anyone who might be Roger Sledge. He honked as Moogus drove out of the lot, but Moogus was looking the other way and turned down the street. Rolly picked up his phone and tapped his name.

"Hey, bud," Moogus answered.

"Hey," said Rolly. "What're you up to?"

"Just left rehearsal and on my way home."

"Who're you playing with?"

"Svetlana," said Moogus.

"Who?"

"This Russian chick. Her name's Svetlana. Serious hottie, but she can't sing worth a damn. It'd be one thing if all she needed was a little pitch correction, but this chick can't even come in on time. Fortunately, it'll be over soon."

"Why's that?"

"We're doing a showcase at Music Box tomorrow night. Private event, invite only, industry types. I'll be done after that. Thank God. It's torture."

"It must pay pretty well for you to stick around this long."

"I'd kill myself if it didn't. What's on your mind?"

Rolly wasn't sure what he should ask Moogus. They'd known each other so long, it was best to shoot blind and see if anything ricocheted back.

"I saw your truck. I'm out in East County, near Gillespie Field."

"What're you doing out here?"

"Working a case. I'm parked on the street outside this place that used to be Sledge Recording Studios. I saw you drive out, but you didn't see me."

"You in the old Volvo?"

"I got rid of the Volvo. It was falling apart. Bought a used Subaru Outback. Anyway, I was hoping to talk to somebody who works at the recording studio, preferably someone who's been there a while. I rang the bell, but the guy who answered the door didn't exactly welcome me in."

"Must have been Sergei," Moogus replied. "He's a hard-ass. It's not really a recording studio anymore, not like when we did those sessions for Ruby. There's a room where we rehearse that's got a PA, but the rest is a flight school or something. It's a weird vibe."

"What do you mean?"

"There's these other guys, kind of like Sergei, hanging around all the time. They got that same look. Security guys. Bodyguards. Goons."

Rolly considered the new information. He'd hoped the recording studio would still be in business, that they'd documented their recording sessions over the years and could search through the archives for Otis Sparks. He'd hoped they might have an address or a phone number, or at least know whether Otis was alive or dead.

"You should talk to Roger Sledge," Moogus said, breaking into Rolly's thoughts. "He was Ruby Dean's manager. I think he still owns the building."

"You've seen him there?"

"A couple of times. Svetlana's his protégé. His new act. He says she's going to be bigger than Ruby. I don't see that happening."

"Was that his Range Rover?"

"Nah. That's the guy in the wheelchair. They call him Uncle

Dmitri. It's a weird vibe. Like I said, I'll be glad when this is over. You could try Joan."

"Bonnie's Joan?" Rolly asked. Detective Bonnie Hammond was his one solid connection in the San Diego Police Department. They'd helped each other out on cases before. Joan was Bonnie's longtime companion.

"Yeah," Moogus replied. "Joan's the production manager for a lot of clubs now, including the Music Box. Sledge'll be there tomorrow for Svetlana's concert. He arranged the whole thing. Maybe Joan could put you on the guest list or something."

"Thanks. I'll give her a call."

"Listen, if you do show up tomorrow, don't talk to me or act like you know me."

"Really?"

"Yeah, really. I'm not being paranoid. Actually, I am. I don't know. You can ask me all about it after tomorrow."

Moogus disconnected. He had a way of blasting through life without apology or doubt. It was disconcerting to hear him express misgivings or doubts. Something was off. Rolly searched through his contact list, found Joan's number and gave her a call, left a message. As he finished, another car, an older Toyota Prius, pulled into the parking lot. It drew up parallel to the building that housed the flight school and Sledge Studios, then stopped, straddling the white lines between two parking places. Someone jumped out of the passenger side and ran to the front door of the building, then ran back to the car, which then zoomed out of the parking lot and down the road. Rolly didn't get a good look at its occupants, but the license plate on the back of the Prius was *PJL1234*. He waited until the light at the intersection turned green, watched the Prius turn left and drive out of view, then climbed out of his car and walked back into the parking lot. Something had been pasted on the front of the door.

It was a decal, circular, about six inches in diameter, with the same initials that had been on the license plate—*PJL*

spelled out in white block letters on a purple background. He
pulled out his phone, brought up the camera and took a photo
of the sticker. He doubted it had anything to do with his investigation, but it wouldn't hurt to have the photo handy. The
vandalism felt like a protest, a political statement. He surveyed
the parking lot. Security cameras were mounted on the corners
of the building. Unless the cameras were scarecrows—hollow
boxes designed to intimidate would-be criminals—the owners
would have seen the incident. They would also have seen Rolly.

He walked to his car, climbed in and started the engine,
then checked his rearview mirror and saw a patrol car
approaching. The cop flashed its lights and pulled in behind
him. Rolly sighed, rolled down his window and waited, both
hands on the upper part of the steering wheel. It wasn't the first
time the cops had shown up at one of his stakeouts. It wouldn't
be the last. The officer climbed out of his car and walked down
the sidewalk toward Rolly's Outback.

"Good afternoon, sir," he said, stopping two steps away from
Rolly's door. "License and registration, please."

Rolly reached for his wallet, extracted his license and the
car's registration, then passed them out the window for the
officer to inspect.

"Thank you," the officer said. "Please wait here."

"I'm not going anywhere," Rolly said. The officer returned
to his patrol car. He'd punch in Rolly's license and registration
number, searching for records of any previous malfeasance.
He'd get a couple of hits, too, but they were old ones, from
Rolly's drug and alcohol days. Rolly hadn't recorded a DUI in a
long time. He didn't drink anymore. That part of his life was
over. The policeman returned.

"Thank you, Mr. Waters," he said, handing back the license
and registration. "Do you know why I stopped you?"

"No idea," said Rolly. "There shouldn't be a problem. I'm
parked on a public street."

"I notice you have a pair of binoculars there on the seat,"

said the officer.

"Tools of the trade. I'm a private detective." He showed the officer his license.

"Have you seen anyone else parked nearby?" the officer asked.

"No," Rolly said, shaking his head. "Just me."

"We got a call, said a man was masturbating in his car, near a playground with children."

Rolly winced. Whoever had made the call had it in for him. It was the kind of report that would make cops hyperventilate.

"There are no kids around here," he said.

"There's a day care center down there," the officer said, pointing down the street to a set of playground equipment surrounded by a chain-link fence. It was at least a hundred yards away.

"This doesn't seem like a very good spot for leering at children," Rolly said.

"Why do you have those binoculars?"

Rolly sighed. "Why would I set up here peeking at little kids through binoculars when I can get child porn on my computer."

"Do you look at child porn on your computer?"

"What? No. Of course not. I'm just saying, Officer, that it's a ridiculous idea. I haven't done anything. I'm a private investigator and I was waiting here to see if anyone else came out of that building over there."

The policemen glanced across the street.

"Who are you looking for?"

"No one. Not now. The person I was looking for wasn't there. As a matter of fact, I was just getting ready to leave."

"Well," the officer said. "Your information checks out. No priors for anything like that. I expect someone was playing a joke on us both. You can go."

"Thank you," said Rolly. The joke hadn't been funny. He wondered if Svetlana's chauffeur, Sergei, had spotted him as they left and put in a call to the police. Maybe the occupants of the Prius had decided to make trouble for him. Or possibly, there was someone still inside the building who'd seen Rolly on the security feed and decided to make his life uncomfortable. His investigation felt different now, more dangerous. Moogus's misgivings felt like a warning.

6

THE ANNOUNCEMENT

Rolly dumped the remains of his La Posta burrito in the trash and returned to the kitchen table, tapped the keyboard on his laptop to wake up the computer and sighed. Life had been good lately. He'd changed his diet, lost ten pounds over the last six months. He'd purchased the Subaru Outback to replace his ancient Volvo wagon, the only car he'd owned since wrapping his Volkswagen bus around a tree years ago. The old Volvo had been a kind of security blanket, the safest car on the road at a time when his life seemed like a dangerous joke. He'd stopped drinking and cleaned up his act. His days had become steadier. A relaxed regimen of detective work and nightclub gigs brought in enough money to put some of it away, enough for a five-year-old Outback, anyway. But Lucinda's case felt more dangerous than he'd originally thought it would be. It had torn a ragged little hole in his contentment.

He wasn't planning to quit. He wanted to help Lucinda. They'd only just met, not counting the Brawley emergency room, but something about her made him like people better. Maybe it was her experience with an alcoholic father that made him feel a bond. The possibility of tracking down a Jimi Hendrix guitar was a great enticement, as well. If any PI was the right match for this case, it was he. He sighed again, accepting his fate, and searched the name of the man in the photograph Lucinda had given him, the man on the album cover—Otis Sparks. One little internet search wouldn't kill him. He could stop anytime. That's what he told himself, the same way he used to think he could stop drinking.

Most of the results that came back were related to the album he'd purchased at The Recordman, including two copies for sale on eBay. He continued through the search pages. A link at the bottom of page two led him to a website that included a short biography of Sparks and several more photographs. There were links to MP3 files there as well, songs from the album that someone had posted. Rolly clicked on one of the songs and gave it a listen. Sparks had a smooth soul voice and the song had a funky low-key vibe, like J. J. Cale had crossed paths with Bill Withers. Sparks's guitar playing, assuming it was Sparks on guitar, was understated and in the pocket, loose and teasingly rhythmic. Rolly felt a kinship with the man already. Otis could sit in with his band anytime. If he was still alive.

His phone buzzed. He read the text message. Joan from the Music Box. She told him to come by the club after seven o'clock tomorrow. He'd get a chance to hear Svetlana and decide if she was as bad as Moogus claimed, but, more importantly, he'd have an opportunity to talk to Roger Sledge.

Someone knocked on the door, three light raps that he recognized. He stood up, walked over and opened the door. His mother, Judith, stood outside, dressed in a loose off-white sweat suit. She looked frailer than usual. He felt sure she'd lost weight over the last few months, but her energy seemed as omnipresent as ever. She was getting older. It was normal for old people to shrink.

"Good evening," his mother said, flashing a gentle smile.

"Hi. You want to come in?"

"Yes, thank you."

Rolly opened the door farther. Judith walked in. She spotted the laptop open on the table.

"Are you working?"

"Just doing some research," Rolly said. "I started a new case. You remember a couple of years ago when you brought me home from the hospital in Brawley?"

"How could I forget? That was quite an adventure."

"My new client is the nurse who took care of me in the emergency room."

"I remember her. She was a lovely young woman. Calm and professional. She explained everything and helped set me at ease."

"Her father died. I'm clearing up a few things about the estate."

"Did he leave her some money?"

"No. Well, maybe. I can't really go into the specifics."

Rolly wondered if he'd already broken his client's confidentiality by telling his mother who she was. He hadn't mentioned Lucinda's name, so it wasn't much of a breach. "What's going on with you?"

"Oh, nothing. I just wanted to talk."

"Have a seat," Rolly said. His mother arranged herself across the table from where Rolly had been sitting. He took his seat again and closed his laptop, indicating to his mother that she had his full attention, but he was still thinking about Otis Sparks. Something at the bottom of the page had caught his eye just before his mother knocked on the door. He made a mental note to go back and read it more closely after she left.

"I haven't seen you much lately," his mother said.

"Work's been pretty regular. I'm playing three nights a week."

"Are you happy with that?"

Rolly nodded.

"It's just that . . ." his mother continued. "I know you used to worry about playing too much."

"This is just about right. Between that and my day job, I'm making a decent living."

"Do you like your new car?"

"It does the job. And it should last a while."

"Yes," said his mother. "Those Subarus are very dependable from what I've heard. I'm glad you replaced that old Volvo."

She glanced away from him and surveyed the room.

"Anything new in your collection?" she asked, noting the guitars that hung on the walls and the cases stashed in the corner.

"Nothing new," Rolly said. "I'm trying to be more frugal in that department. No new guitars unless I sell one of the ones I already have."

"I've been thinking about something," his mother said.

Rolly braced himself. If his mother said she'd been thinking about something, she'd expect him to have an opinion on whatever it was. It might be about changing the drapes or something more substantial. He wondered if her recent weight loss was more serious than she'd claimed. He nodded and waited while she found the words.

"I think it's time we refurbished your flat," his mother said.

"What do you mean?" Rolly said. He'd heard his mother perfectly well, but he needed a moment for the idea to sink in. A hundred different thoughts entered his head. "You don't have to do that for me. I'm fine with the place as it is."

"I know, dear, but . . . we need to start thinking about the future, after I'm gone."

"Is something wrong? Are you ill?"

She waved her hands at him, swatting at his worries like flies.

"The doctor says it's nothing to worry about. It's my thyroid. I'm taking pills and everything's fine."

"Is that why you've lost weight?"

His mother cleared her throat and looked past Rolly's left ear at the kitchen cupboards behind him.

"I should've told the doctor earlier. I thought fasting would help. It's all right now. Everything's fine."

"I wish you'd told me."

"It's nothing dear, really, but it did get me thinking. I'd like to get things in order before something more serious comes along. We've talked about this before."

Rolly nodded. His mother had talked about making changes and upgrading his flat since the day he'd started living there fifteen years ago. He'd never expected it to happen.

"Can you afford to fix the place up?" he asked.

"Don't worry about that," she said, swatting at the worry flies again. "The city's changed the rules about granny flats. They've got these incentives now, tax breaks and such. It's the right time to do this."

His mother's pragmatism and business sense surprised Rolly sometimes, her infatuation with gurus and spiritualism, vegetarianism and holistic medicine counterbalanced by a kind of Midwestern practicality. She wasn't asking for his opinion. She'd already made up her mind. Which didn't surprise him.

"Well," he said. "What does that mean for me? I suppose I'll have to move out for a while."

"Yes," said Judith. "Hopefully only a couple of months. You can stay in the big house with me."

Rolly leaned forward and rubbed a spot between his eyebrows, as if massaging his brain.

"You can move back in when it's finished," his mother said. "It will be a lot nicer. The property taxes will go up, I suppose. I might have to increase your rent."

Rolly continued rubbing the spot on his forehead. He had a sweetheart deal with his mother for the granny flat. They'd never signed any kind of lease. Any other renter in the area would be paying three times as much for a similar space.

"It would only be a slight increase," his mother said,

reading his thoughts. "You're doing so much better now. Financially. I think it's time."

Rolly nodded. He stopped rubbing the spot and gave his mother an acquiescent smile.

"When do you want to get started?" he asked.

"I need to hear back from the contractor, but probably sometime next month. We're going to remodel the kitchen completely. You can't really do any serious cooking in here. We'll work out a plan for your move."

"Okay."

"Thank you, dear." His mother smiled. "I knew you'd understand." She rose from the table. "Don't stay up late worrying about this. It's going to be for the best. When I'm gone you can move into the big house and rent this one out, have an income from it."

Rolly nodded and smiled. His mother departed. He sat at the table, ruminating on the changes the remodel would bring. He didn't relish the idea of living under the same roof as his mother, in the big Victorian house on the other side of their shared driveway. The granny flat had always provided just enough privacy, a way he could pretend he, an adult in his forties, wasn't really living with his mother. Under the current arrangement there was just enough separation between them that they could lead their own lives. He didn't know if it was possible for them to live under the same roof without driving each other crazy. They might make it a month, but they'd never make it two, and construction projects always seemed to go on longer than promised. The rental rates in San Diego were over the roof, but it might be time for him to find his own apartment.

He put the thought aside for later, opened his laptop computer and read the two paragraphs at the bottom of the web page, the ones he'd only glanced at earlier. They explained why Otis Sparks had only completed one album. Otis Sparks was dead. He'd been shot and killed a long time ago, back in the mid-seventies, just as The Recordman Lou Brendon remembered. Rolly leaned back in his chair, rubbed his eyes and exhaled deeply, then returned to the computer and clicked on a Contact link he found on the page. He filled out the form, including his phone number, and asked whoever had created the website to give him a call. He read the last two paragraphs again, just to make sure he'd read the story correctly.

Otis Sparks had been shot and killed at Roger Sledge's recording studio. And the man who'd killed him was Lucinda's father. Gerry Rhodes.

7

THE APARTMENT

Lucinda paused outside the door of her father's apartment, a small bungalow similar to Rolly's granny flat. It sat in the corner of the parking lot of the Russian Orthodox church in the Allied Gardens neighborhood, halfway between Rolly's house and the hospital where he'd first met with Lucinda. It was just after ten in the morning.

"Is everything okay?" Rolly asked.

Lucinda nodded and gave him a tight smile.

"Not really," she said. "It's strange. I have this feeling that he's going to be in the house, that somehow he isn't dead. He'll be sitting there in his La-Z-Boy, leaning back with his headphones on, smiling and listening to a record. I felt like he was safe here, that he'd conquered his demons."

She sighed.

"We had a pretty complicated relationship. Because of his drinking. And the divorce from my mom. I loved my dad, but I couldn't count on him. When he was drunk he'd go silent, just brood in his chair. He was better, I think, more communicative, once he stopped drinking. I talked to him at least once a day. You always wonder what might have been different, I guess."

She pulled a key from her pocket, then hesitated, working her way through regret or sorrow or anger. Maybe all three at once. Both her parents were gone. Rolly's mother and father were both alive. Gratitude, closure, acceptance—all the things therapists talked about still seemed possible to him. Lucinda had only memories.

"You want me to go first?" he asked, holding out his hand.

Lucinda handed him the key.

"Thank you," she said.

Rolly fit the key into the lock and opened the door. He stepped over the threshold, flipped on the lights and surveyed the room. The drapes were drawn. The musty smell of old carpeting drifted up to his nose. Lucinda stepped in behind him.

"You okay?" Rolly asked.

"Yeah," she said. "I'll be okay."

"Where do you want to start?"

"Over there," Lucinda said, pointing to the wall where a turntable sat on top of a cabinet. The cabinet shelves were filled with record albums.

"Your dad stayed old school," Rolly said.

"He's got some shoe boxes down there, next to his records. That's where he keeps . . . kept his photos and documents. His memorabilia. You see 'em?"

Rolly walked to the cabinet, knelt down, and retrieved a pair of shoe boxes at the end of the bottom shelf. He glanced at the record on the turntable.

"Ruby Dean," he said.

"What's that?" said Lucinda.

"The record your dad was listening to. It's Ruby Dean's first album."

"Oh. She sang that blue flame song, right? 'Blue flame burning down in my soul'?"

"Yeah," said Rolly. "That was her big hit."

"What's it called?"

"It's called 'Someday.'"

"My dad used to listen to that song a lot. After my mom died. He said that song had been written for them."

Rolly plopped the boxes down on the kitchen table where Lucinda had cleared a space.

"Literally or figuratively?" he asked.

"What?"

"Your father said the song was written for them. Did he mean it literally?"

"Oh. I think he meant it *felt* like it had been written for them. He did work in the music business, though. I never really thought about that. You think Ruby Dean wrote that song for my dad and my mom?"

"I know your dad worked at the studio where Ruby recorded her demo album. I played on those sessions for Ruby."

"Did you meet my dad?"

Rolly shrugged. If Gerry Rhodes had recorded the session, Rolly didn't remember him or any interaction Gerry might have had with Ruby. The band went home once they'd finished recording. They didn't stick around for the mixing session. That wasn't their job. He didn't remember them playing "Someday" on the demo session. Ruby must have written it later.

"I don't remember your dad, if he was there," he said. "But I don't remember a lot of things."

Lucinda looked at him a moment, as if assessing his sobriety, then lifted the lid on one of the shoe boxes.

"What exactly are we looking for?" she asked.

"Anything that connects your dad to that white Stratocaster in the photograph you gave me. A receipt, a note, something that confirms your dad as the owner. Second, anything that connects your dad to Jimi Hendrix. Even if we find the guitar, we'll need some provenance."

"Something like this?" Lucinda asked, passing a withered yellow card to Rolly. He took it from her, looked at the printing on the card. It was a backstage pass for a Jimi Hendrix Experience concert in Houston on February 18. There was no year listed, but the name Gerry Rhodes was handwritten in the space for the holder's name. Rolly smiled.

"That's a good start," he said. "Let's see what else we can find."

"There's more of them," said Lucinda. "With different cities and dates."

"Even better," said Rolly. He found a photograph in the box he was going through, a wedding photo of the bride and groom. He showed it to Lucinda.

"Oh, look at that," said Lucinda. "I haven't seen that picture in years. That was my mom and dad's wedding day." She sighed. "Now they're both gone."

Rolly continued to flip through the photos and documents. There was nothing about a white Stratocaster. He found a photograph of Gerry Rhodes in a studio control room, standing next to a stick-figured young woman in her late teens or early twenties. She was dressed in torn jeans and her hair was long and straight, without the luxurious curls she'd sport on her album covers.

"Looks like your dad did know Ruby Dean," he said, showing Lucinda the photo.

"That's her?"

"That's her. Before her makeover. There's some writing on the back. *To Gerry. Someday. Love Ruby.*"

"Wow," said Lucinda. "Maybe my dad did have a personal connection to that song."

"Sounds like it," said Rolly, wondering if Gerry had a more intimate relationship with Ruby than just being her sound engineer. Gerry Rhodes looked old enough to be Ruby's father. Then again, Ruby had married her manager, Roger Sledge, who had been born twenty years before she had. According to Wikipedia.

"I could probably get in touch with Ruby and ask her,"

Rolly said. "Like I said, I played on her demo tape. I was her guitar teacher, too, for a while."

"Really? You taught her how to play the guitar?"

Rolly nodded. Rob Norwood had one of Ruby's old guitars in his shop, which meant he had Ruby's phone number. Rolly wasn't sure how, or even if, Ruby would remember him, but he'd played on her demo and given her guitar lessons for three months. It was worth a shot. Norwood might plead his case for him if he needed backup.

"I think I can get in touch with her," Rolly said. He waved the photograph of Lucinda's father with Ruby. "Can I keep this to show her?"

"Of course," Lucinda said.

They continued to search through the boxes. There were more photos of Gerry Rhodes backstage with various rock stars, holding other guitars, but none of them were of much interest to Rolly's investigation. There was no documentation of a white Stratocaster being bought or sold, either. No photograph of Jimi Hendrix handing a white Stratocaster to Gerry Rhodes. Things were never that easy.

Nor was there any guitar in the house, Stratocaster or otherwise. If Gerry Rhodes had owned the white Stratocaster that Otis Sparks held in the photograph, he must have hidden it somewhere, sold it or had it stolen. Lucinda's father had been a drunk and drug addict. Careless and reckless. He could've made up the whole story about the guitar. There were the backstage passes, though. Gerry Rhodes had been part of a Hendrix tour. That part of the story was true. He'd been close enough to the master to touch his guitars. Maybe he'd tuned them, cleaned them or packed them away after the concert. That was enough to keep looking. Rolly continued to flip through the box, but he didn't find anything else of interest. Lucinda finished going through hers as well.

Rolly took the boxes and returned them to the shelves. He paused and looked at the record on the turntable. Ruby Dean's record. Side one with her hit "Someday" on it. It was a well-written song, a shiny pop-rock recording, with Ruby's voice cracking and aching in just the right places, a classic torch number that lounge singers would be covering for years to come. Rolly pulled out his reading glasses, leaned over and read the label, looking for the songwriting credits that were listed in parenthesis below the title. He wondered if Gerry Rhodes might have written the song, which would also explain Ruby's inscription to him on the back of the photo. His hunch didn't pan out. Rhodes wasn't credited. The songwriters were listed as Dean/Sledge. Just like on Otis Sparks's album, Roger Sledge took half the credit. There was a long, sad history of rock-and-roll managers taking a share of the royalties for their artists' work. Roger Sledge had been Ruby's manager. Rolly wasn't surprised he'd taken writing credit too. Songwriting and publishing were where the real money was in the music business, at least where it used to be before internet streaming.

"He might have some other stuff in the bedroom," Lucinda said behind him. "We should look in there."

"Sure," Rolly said. Maybe they'd get lucky and find the guitar hidden in a back corner closet or stashed under the bed. It wasn't impossible. Rolly kept three guitars stored under his own bed.

Lucinda and Rolly walked back to the bedroom. They looked under the bed, and in the closet, but there was nothing of interest, only old clothes and dust bunnies. Someone knocked on the front door.

"I'll get it," Lucinda said. "It's probably Detective Hammond. She said she was going to stop by."

"Bonnie Hammond?" Rolly asked.

"I don't remember her first name."

"San Diego Police Department? Short blond hair, blue eyes?"

"Yeah. You know her?"

Rolly nodded.

"Does she know you hired a private detective?" he asked.

"No," Lucinda said. "Is that a problem?"

"Probably not. But you should tell her right away. I'll be out in a minute."

Lucinda left the room and went to answer the door. Rolly sat down on the bed, switched on the reading light and checked the books on the nightstand—a Bible, an autobiography of record producer Glyn Johns, and a true crime book about the Russian mafia in the United States. The guitar seemed far away now, perhaps a figment of Gerry Rhodes's imagination, a story he'd told his daughter to try to impress her, a drunkard's fantasy that had never been true.

He picked up the Bible and flipped through it. People often hid items of personal value in their Bibles, thinking of it as a kind of protection, but it was one of the first places both cops and crooks looked. Drunks who'd found Jesus seemed particularly susceptible to that kind of thinking, but Gerry Rhodes wasn't one of them. There was nothing hidden in his Bible.

Out in the living room, Rolly heard Bonnie's voice, asking Lucinda if there was anything missing or if she'd remembered anything else that might be of value. It sounded like the investigation was ongoing, that the police still had enough questions to keep the case open.

He picked up the Glyn Johns book and read the back cover blurbs. It sounded like an interesting read, but he needed to focus on the task at hand. He placed the book back on the nightstand and opened the book about the Russian mafia. A business card had been inserted to mark a page. He glanced over the two pages on either side of the bookmark, looking for anything Gerry Rhodes might have deemed worthy of interest, but nothing was noted. He checked the card Rhodes had used to mark his place. *Afrocraft Co-op.* There was an email address and phone number on the card.

Out in the living room, he heard Lucinda explaining to Bonnie that she'd hired a private investigator to help with her father's estate. He heard her tell Bonnie his name, heard Bonnie say she'd like to talk to him, then heard them walking toward the bedroom. Sometimes Bonnie was open to working with him. Sometimes she was a pain in the ass.

He looked at the business card again, flipped it over to see if there was anything on the back, then glanced back toward the door. He had about two seconds before Bonnie arrived and started giving him a hard time. He slipped the card into his coat pocket and replaced the book on the nightstand.

On the back of the card, in handwritten capital letters was a name he'd seen before. *OTIS.*

8

THE TRAIL

"Let's go for a walk," said Detective Bonnie Hammond. They were standing by her patrol car in the parking lot of the church. Lucinda Rhodes had just left. She needed to get to work at the hospital.

"Where are we going?" Rolly asked. Bonnie was rarely forthcoming, using her taciturn manner to elicit questions from him, making him do the work. She waved her hand toward the far corner of the parking lot, where it looked out over the canyon below.

"There's a trail along the canyon ridge. I understand Mr. Rhodes walked there often."

"How'd you learn that?"

"It's called police work," Bonnie said. She pointed at the commercial park that bordered the church property. "I did some interviews yesterday, showed Mr. Rhodes's photograph to folks in the neighborhood. A guy in the bar said Rhodes was in there the night he died."

"The bar? You mean Bump's Tavern?"

"Yeah. You know the place?"

"I've played there a few times," Rolly said. Bump's was a

dingy, if not quite seedy, establishment, a poorly lit haven for serious drunks. Lucinda seemed sure her father had been on the wagon. Perhaps she'd been wrong about that.

"Was Rhodes drinking?" Rolly asked. "Did the autopsy find any alcohol?"

"Alcohol clears the body in about twelve hours," Bonnie replied. "His body wasn't discovered until late the next day, so they wouldn't have found anything even if he was drinking."

Rolly felt a sadness creep into his thoughts, for Lucinda. She'd seemed sanguine about her father's sobriety. He knew it would pain her to find out otherwise. He knew because he'd done the same thing to his parents and friends for years, fooling them, feigning temperance. It seemed easy at first. When their suspicions finally surfaced and he could see the pain in their eyes, hear the strain in their voices, it was too late. He couldn't stop.

Bonnie set out across the parking lot. Rolly hustled to catch up.

"I forgot to ask Lucinda," he said. "How did Rhodes die?"

"Epidural hematoma," Bonnie replied.

"Which means?"

"Bleeding inside the brain, most likely due to a blow to his head."

"You think someone hit him?"

"Don't know. We can't find any evidence of where he might've hit his head in the house. No marks, no dents, no blood. I'm thinking maybe it happened somewhere out here."

"Would he be able to walk home after hitting his head like that?"

"That's how hematomas work. You get knocked on the head, recover from the initial shock and start to think you're okay. But your skull's bleeding inside, putting pressure on the brain. If you don't get treatment right away, it's usually too late."

They arrived at the corner of the lot. The canyon fell away

to their right. A narrow dirt path snaked along the ridge behind the back exits of the commercial buildings.

"Keep an eye out," Bonnie said.

"I got it," Rolly said, assuming she was concerned for his safety. Bonnie wasn't as tough as she pretended to be. Years ago, on patrol, she'd found him passed out in an alley. She'd taken him home instead of to jail.

"I mean let me know if you see anything out of the ordinary," Bonnie said.

"Oh. Will do."

They continued along the trail. Bonnie paused to scrutinize a set of boulders below.

"Maybe he fell and hit his head on those rocks," Rolly said, trying to read her mind.

"That's what I'm thinking," she said, pointing. "This trail could be treacherous in the dark. I'll have a look."

Rolly waited as Bonnie made her way down the slope and examined the area. She inspected a large smudge on one of the boulders, then returned to the trail.

"Is it blood?" Rolly asked.

"Looks like it could be. I'll get our lab folks out here."

Rolly scanned the slope of the canyon as they continued down the trail. Had a drunken Gerry Rhodes stumbled on his way home and hit his head on the rock? Had someone pushed him over the edge? If someone pushed him, had they also stolen the Stratocaster guitar? An object below caught his eye.

"What's that?" he asked, pointing at a dark blue rectangle entangled in a clump of low-lying bushes twenty feet below them. Bonnie squinted and peered down the canyon.

"I'll take a look," she said.

She stepped off the lip of the canyon, braced herself against the slope and made her way down. Rolly waited. He saw no reason to climb down the slope with her. Bonnie was far more athletic than he was. He watched as she reached in her back pocket, retrieved her evidence gloves, put them on, leaned down and grabbed the blue rectangle. She inspected it, then looked around for other items of interest. She didn't find any and started to climb back up the slope.

"What it is it?" Rolly asked. Bonnie didn't answer until she'd made her way to the top.

"It's a deposit purse," she said, showing him the brass-zippered vinyl bag. "Like merchants take to the bank with their cash receipts."

"That could have come from any of these places," Rolly said, indicating the row of businesses.

"There's an ATM up the street," Bonnie replied. "Maybe there's a receipt."

She unzipped the bag with her gloved fingers, reached inside and pulled out a slip of paper.

"It's a cocktail napkin," she said, showing the item to Rolly. "From Bump's Tavern. Somebody's written on it. 'Two thousand dollars.'"

"You think it's connected to Gerry Rhodes?" Rolly asked.

"I don't know," Bonnie replied. "I'll have it checked for fingerprints, just in case."

"Maybe someone robbed him and hit him on the head."

"Maybe. But if this napkin is a receipt, it means the money was already deposited or transferred to someone else. Someone he met at Bump's. There's a lot of things that could've happened. Maybe he tripped, fell into the canyon, dropped the purse in the dark."

"If it was even his purse," said Rolly.

"Which is why I need to get it checked for fingerprints."

"What about Bump's?" Rolly asked.

"What about them?"

"You could ask them about the napkin. If they're missing any money or that purse."

Bonnie considered Rolly's idea for a moment, then shook her head.

"Better to wait until I can confirm if Rhodes was carrying

this. It'll give me more leverage when I talk to Bump's. This might just be a number somebody scratched on a napkin, not a receipt."

Bonnie surveyed the canyon again, looking for other items of interest. She didn't find any.

"Let's head back," she said. "With any luck, I can get someone in the lab to look at this today. I'll try to talk to someone from the church first."

"What for?"

"Churches can take in a lot of cash every week. Donations from passing the hat. Mr. Rhodes worked at the church. Maybe he deposited their cash donations in the bank every week."

"You think Gerry Rhodes might've spent church money at Bump's?"

"I don't know. I'm just testing ideas."

They made their way back down the trail to the church parking lot. Rolly hoped, for Lucinda's sake, that her father wasn't embezzling money from the church, that he wasn't a drunk and a thief. The validity of the Hendrix guitar story now seemed less likely, as well. They arrived at their cars. He waited while Bonnie placed the blue pouch in an evidence bag. He knew from experience he should wait until she'd dismissed him and got the last word in. Bonnie tossed the evidence bag into the trunk, closed the hood and turned back to him.

"Good spot, by the way," she said. "I didn't think you'd actually be useful."

"Then why the hell did you want me to go with you?" Rolly retorted.

"For the company, of course," Bonnie replied. She always gave Rolly a hard time, even when he'd managed to be competent. "Anything else you want to tell me?"

"Like what?"

Bonnie leaned back against the car and crossed her arms. "I understand from Ms. Rhodes that you're looking for a guitar her father used to own?"

Rolly nodded.

"That's why she hired me."

"You think this guitar was valuable enough for somebody to kill Mr. Rhodes?"

"You think someone killed him?"

"Can't say they didn't," Bonnie replied. "Not yet, anyway."

"Well," Rolly said. "If the guitar is what Lucinda thinks it is, the answer is yes, it might have been valuable enough for somebody to rob and kill him. It's also possible he sold it to someone. Or that it never existed."

"Maybe that's what the two thousand dollars on the back of that napkin is about," Bonnie said, scratching her chin.

"Maybe," said Rolly. He decided not to tell her the guitar would be worth a lot more than that if it had really belonged to Jimi Hendrix. The two thousand dollars might have been a down payment, of course, a reserve fee. He couldn't discount any possibilities. He hoped the guitar was someplace safe. In storage. That they just hadn't found it yet.

"Got any leads?" Bonnie asked. She wasn't ready to let him go.

"Only one," said Rolly. "Lucinda showed me a photograph of this guy her father worked with, Otis Sparks. It's from a long time ago. Sparks was a musician. He's holding a guitar that looks like the one she remembers."

"Have you been able to locate Mr. Sparks?"

"He's dead," Rolly said. "Gerry Rhodes shot him to death."

"Holy shit," Bonnie said, lifting herself from the car.

"It was a long time ago. Thirty-five years. I'm trying to get in touch with a guy named Roger Sledge."

"The music promoter? He's still around?"

Rolly nodded.

"Gerry Rhodes worked at Sledge's recording studio. Otis Sparks recorded his album there. Sledge's name is all over the album. I figure he might remember something about the guitar."

"Good luck with that," said Bonnie. "That Sledge guy's an asshole."

"You've met him?"

"Joan used to work with him. Back when she was freelance. When we were first dating. She told me a few things."

"Like what?"

"Nothing," Bonnie said. She glanced at the church, as if looking for someone else she could talk to.

"What'd Joan tell you?" Rolly asked.

"It's old history," Bonnie said. "Joan had to deal with a lot of that stuff, when she got started in the concert business. She was the only woman on the crew sometimes. A lot of guys hassled her."

"Including Sledge?"

"Yeah."

"What'd he do?"

"Oh, the usual. Talking about her body, her looks, like he had some right to do it. Pressuring her to sleep with him. Taking a grab at her now and then."

The left corner of Rolly's mouth twitched. What was it with some men? He hadn't always been a perfect gentleman, but his transgressions had been one-offs, misjudgments of a situation emboldened by youth and alcohol. It wasn't a way of life like it seemed to be with some guys. Men who refused to take no for an answer, jerks trying to compensate for their own fears and self-doubt. Rolly had accepted his personal inadequacy a long time ago. It was how he'd become an adult.

"Anyway," Bonnie said. "That's neither here nor there. Do you know anything else about this Sparks guy Rhodes killed?"

"Like what?"

"Was he married? Did he have any kids?"

"There's a little write-up on Wikipedia. I didn't see anything about family."

"I'll look him up in our database, pull the records and see what's there."

"You think Gerry Rhodes's death might have something to do with Otis Sparks?"

"You never know," Bonnie said. "Could be somebody out there still carrying a grudge."

"Sparks died in 1984. That's a long time to carry a grudge."

"Like I said, you never know."

"But you know something, don't you?"

Bonnie cocked her head to one side, contemplating her response.

"I spotted the money purse," Rolly said. "I should get a reward."

Bonnie brought her head back to center and unfolded her arms.

"That guy in Bump's Tavern," she said. "The one who saw Mr. Rhodes there the night before he died? He saw Rhodes talking to a middle-aged Black woman. He couldn't identify her. He'd never seen her before."

9

THE CO-OP

The Afrocraft Co-op was on Market Street, set back from the street in an old house located in a commercial block of Sherman Heights just east of downtown San Diego. Rolly parked his car, pulled out the card he'd found in Gerry Rhodes's Russian mafia book and checked the name on the back of the card again. It still said *OTIS*. What connection could a man who'd died almost forty years ago have to the store? Had the missing Stratocaster passed through its doors? Someone had scrawled *OTIS* on the back of the card for a reason. He climbed out of the car and walked into the shop.

The woman behind the front counter wore a flowing print smock and a purple-and-gold turban around her head to match.

"Good afternoon," she said in greeting. "Welcome to Afrocraft."

"Good afternoon," Rolly said. "Are you the owner?"

"Yes."

The woman drew herself up, preparing to dismiss Rolly if he was salesman or solicitor. She was taller than he was by an inch or two, which, along with her flawless dark skin and the elegant dashiki she wore, suggested a certain regal confidence. The reading glasses that dangled from the gold chain around her neck suggested she might be older than she first looked, north of forty. Even fifty. She fit the description of the woman who'd been seen at Bump's nightclub with Gerry Rhodes.

"My name is Rolly Waters. I'm a private detective," Rolly said, showing her his identification. "A man named Gerry Rhodes died recently. I'm doing some work for his estate. Have you ever met Mr. Rhodes?"

"Why do you ask?" the woman said, her eyes narrowing in suspicion.

Rolly showed the card he'd found in the book on Rhodes's nightstand.

"I was going through Mr. Rhodes's belongings and found this card from your shop."

"I see," said the woman. "I don't think I know him, not by name."

"He wasn't a customer?"

"Not that I can remember. Can you describe him?"

"Older. In his early seventies. White. He lived out in Allied Gardens, next to the Russian Orthodox church. And a bar called Bump's Tavern."

The woman shook her head.

"He doesn't sound like my usual clientele."

"He wrote a name on the back of your card," Rolly said. He flipped the card over to show the woman. "Otis. Does that mean anything to you?"

The woman gave the briefest pause before answering. She still seemed wary.

"Isn't there an elevator company called Otis?" she said.

"Yes, I think there is. But I don't know why Mr. Rhodes would write down the name of an elevator company on the back of your card."

The woman nodded, concurring. Rolly glanced around the shop, hoping to find a way to connect, to get her to trust him.

He had to admit it didn't seem like the kind of store a man like Gerry Rhodes would frequent. There was jewelry and clothing in the store and some paintings on the walls, all of it African-themed. In the back corner, he spotted a small display of traditional African instruments.

"I see you've got a djembe back there."

"Yes. You know something about African music?"

"I'm a musician myself. A guitar player. This person, Gerry Rhodes, he was in the music business too. On the production side. A roadie and sound engineer. I'm wondering if maybe that's why he came in. Maybe he was looking for a specific instrument."

"I suppose that's possible. But I still don't remember him."

"Okay if I take a look?" asked Rolly, indicating the instruments in the corner.

"Help yourself."

Rolly strode to the back of the store. He picked up the djembe, tapped a couple of times on the drumhead and checked the price tag: $150. He didn't know what the going price was for a djembe, but it seemed reasonable.

"I have a friend who's an expert in these things," he said. "Marley Scratch?"

"Yes, I know Marley," said the woman at the counter. "Those are his instruments."

"What do you mean, they're his?"

"This isn't a store per se. It's a co-op. Different people are selling different items in the store. I give them a space to display their wares and take a cut of whatever they sell."

"I see," said Rolly. "Does anyone else work here besides you?"

"Some of the co-op members, the people selling things, also work here. We try to fit their shifts around everyone's schedule."

"So someone else might have given Mr. Rhodes that business card?"

"Yes. That's certainly possible."

Rolly considered the information. It seemed likely that the woman Rhodes had been seen with also gave him the card from the store. It might be a different woman than this one.

"Does Marley Scratch ever work here?" he asked.

"Sometimes, though to be honest, Marley doesn't put in as many hours as others do."

"Marley has his fingers in a lot of pies."

"He certainly does." The woman shrugged. "But I'm glad to have him as part of the group."

Rolly walked back to the front counter.

"Can I show you something else, Ms. . . .? I'm sorry, what's your name?"

"Worrell," she said. "Mavis Worrell." She sighed, as if hoping she wouldn't have to put up with the interrogation much longer. Rolly pulled his phone out of his pocket and showed her the photograph of Otis Sparks.

"This is a photograph from thirty-five, forty years ago," he said. "Do you recognize the man in it?"

"Why do you want to know about him?"

"Well, like I said, I'm working with Gerry Rhodes's estate. This photograph was important to him for some reason. Gerry Rhodes also had your business card with this man's name on the back. Otis Sparks. We're trying to locate a guitar like the one he has in the picture."

"You think this Sparks person stole the guitar because he's Black?"

"No, no," said Rolly. "Not at all. It's just that we'd like to track down the guitar so we can prove, or refute, that it belonged to Mr. Rhodes at the time of his death. And your business card is the only real connection I've found so far."

"Why is the guitar so important?"

"My client believes it may be valuable. A collector's item. But we can't really determine that until we find the guitar."

"I see," said Mavis. There was something in her voice that seemed different, less resistant to Rolly's inquiries. He waited.

"You're the one who sent me the email, aren't you?" she asked.

"What's that?"

"Last night. From the website. You sent me an email asking about Otis."

Rolly took a moment to process what Mavis had told him. He remembered reading through Otis Sparks's website last night, filling out the *Contact Us* form.

"That's your website?" he asked.

Mavis nodded.

"So you do know something about Otis Sparks?" Rolly said to make sure.

"Yes," Mavis replied. "I'm his younger sister. Mavis Sparks is my original name."

Rolly considered this new bit of information, and decided to ease back on the throttle and let Mavis tell him whatever story she wanted to tell. He could sort out the important parts later.

"I'm sorry about your brother," he said. "I didn't know what had happened to him until I read your website last night."

"It was a painful time in my family's life. I don't like to talk about it."

"I understand. It's just that . . . on the website it says Gerry Rhodes killed your brother?"

"That's right. Rhodes shot my brother."

"Why?"

Mavis sighed.

"Self-defense. That's what they said. I never believed it, not for one minute. My brother never hurt anyone. He was a good man, gentle and decent. But he was a Black man in a white man's space. The police only got one side of the story. From the owner of the studio."

"Roger Sledge?"

"Yes. He was Otis's manager."

"Why was your brother at the studio? Was he recording there?"

"Otis wanted out of his contract. He thought Mr. Sledge was ripping him off. I think he was, too, but I can't prove it. Not now, anyway. Otis was just another dead Negro to the police. A gangster. They said the shooting was justified."

Rolly considered the story. Sledge wouldn't be the first manager accused of cheating his clients. He wouldn't be the last one, either. Mavis said her brother was kind, but a man's outrage could easily come to the fore if he felt he was being ripped off or disrespected. Angry words might have been spoken. Tempers might have risen to the point where someone pulled out a gun. Gerry Rhodes, it would seem. Once that gun appeared, anything could have happened, almost none of it good. Mavis may have felt cheated by her brother's death, but that didn't mean it was murder. It wasn't Rolly's burden, either. His job was to chase down a Stratocaster.

"Why didn't you tell me you knew Gerry Rhodes," he asked, "if you knew he killed your brother?"

Mavis looked at him and sighed.

"It was painful," she said. "I was in high school when Otis died. I was a teenager. I worshipped my brother and then he was gone. My parents were devastated. They tried for years to get the case reopened. It ruined their lives. My father and mother. Now they're both gone."

"I'm sorry," said Rolly.

"It changed my life, too," said Mavis. "I've tried to make up for it, to honor them all with my work."

"You mean this shop?" Rolly said, waving a hand at the merchandise.

"This isn't my job," Mavis said. "Not really. It's more of an experiment, a side project to give Black artists and craftsmen an outlet to sell their wares. It's an extension of my academic career."

"You're a teacher?"

"A professor," Mavis said, in a tone that indicated she considered her occupation above that of mere teachers. "I run the Black Studies program at Grossmont College."

"You're a busy woman."

"I try to be," said Mavis. "I guess if there's anything good that came from my brother's death, it would be that. I found a mission in life, a seriousness I don't think I would've had otherwise. I applied myself in school, gave my parents something to be proud of, to help relieve the pain of what happened to my brother. They were proud of me, too, when I got my PhD."

"As they should have been," Rolly said. "I never got very far in college myself. Only a couple of semesters."

"Yes, well," Mavis said. "It's not for everyone. You seem like an intelligent man."

"You learn a lot playing in bands." Rolly smiled at his little joke. His smile was his only dependable weapon. It helped people like him. And trust him. But the smile had to be real, spontaneous, not just a ploy. People could tell when you were faking that kind of thing. His smile was real because it was true. "I read a lot, too."

Mavis picked up the photograph, looked at it again, then placed it back down on the countertop.

"Any other thoughts?" Rolly asked.

"I do remember something," Mavis said. "It was about a week after my brother died. Roger Sledge came to the house. He said he was there to collect Otis's things—musical stuff. Cassette tapes, records, stage outfits. Musical instruments."

"Any chance one of the instruments was that guitar?"

"I don't know. I hid in my room. I was upset to see Mr. Sledge in my house. My mother took me aside and explained how those things weren't really my brother's, that he hadn't paid for them, that he had debts he owed to Mr. Sledge."

"I see," Rolly replied. This was the first bit of information he'd received that hinted at where the guitar might be. With

Roger Sledge. Someone had seen Gerry Rhodes at Bump's Tavern, talking to a middle-aged Black woman. Rhodes and Mavis Worrell might both have legitimate grievances with Roger Sledge. Perhaps they were working together, looking for ways to find some personal justice.

"Have you ever been to a place in Allied Gardens called Bump's? It's a bar."

"I'm a Muslim, Mr. Waters," Mavis Worrell said in a voice that sounded like Rolly had accused her of all the deadly sins. "I don't drink."

Rolly nodded, deciding not to press the matter. She hadn't said no.

10

THE MUSIC BOX

Rolly arrived at the Music Box nightclub at seven thirty to give himself time to scope out the situation before the music started. True to her word, Joan had put him on the guest list. He had no trouble getting in. There were fewer people than he expected in the club, most of them huddled in small groups around high-top tables that ran the length of the walls leading to the stage, chatting and drinking as they waited for Svetlana to appear. He did a quick walk-through, looking for her manager, Roger Sledge, but didn't see anyone who fit Sledge's description. The audience at the tables all looked the same—muscular white men wearing leather jackets and expensive collared shirts, glam-doll women in short skirts and stilettos. Most of them looked younger than thirty. There was an older man sitting in a wheelchair at a table front and center of the stage, dressed in a well-tailored suit. A sign on his table said "Reserved." A younger man walked to the table, set down two drinks and took a seat. Rolly recognized him as Svetlana's chauffeur, the one Moogus called Sergei, the thug who'd chased Rolly away from Sledge's studio and, possibly, reported him to the police.

Sergei's demeanor suggested the old man in the wheelchair was his boss.

Rolly's phone rang. It was Joan.

"Where are you?" she asked when he answered the phone.

"Down on the dance floor," said Rolly.

"You'll need to come up to the booth. Only invited guests on the floor."

"Okay," he said and hung up the phone. He walked back to the front of the club, stopping at the bar before heading up the stairs to the sound booth.

"Club soda, please," he said to the bartender. "With a lime."

The bartender pulled out a glass, filled it, added a lime and passed it over to him.

"On the house," she said, when Rolly started to reach for his wallet. She stared at him a moment. He stared back. The bartender looked familiar, but something about her seemed out of place. Her eyes were too penetrating, her body too stiff for a bartender. A caution light came on in Rolly's mind. He resisted the urge to ask if they'd met before. The bartender turned and walked away without any acknowledgment. Rolly climbed up the stairs to the sound booth.

Joan was waiting there when he arrived. They'd first met years ago when Joan had handled the mixing duties at the now defunct Bacchanal nightclub in Kearny Mesa. Rolly, Moogus and their band, The Creatures, had been regulars at the Bacchanal. They, and all the boys who played the club, lusted after the curvy sound girl with the smoky voice, but few, if any, had much luck, though Moogus had once managed to bed her. Their rendezvous was still a mystery to anyone who knew them both. Some claimed Moogus had made up the whole story. Soon after, Joan and Bonnie moved in together, and they'd stayed together ever since. Joan's youthful curviness had given way to the thicker solidity of domestic contentment.

"You running the board tonight?" Rolly asked.

"No," Joan said. She nodded toward the window overlooking the stage. "The sound guy's down there resetting a monitor. What's up with you?"

"Just came out to hear the music. Moogus is playing with the band."

"Yeah, I thought I saw that doofus down there at sound check. Why are you really here?"

"What do you mean?"

"Have you heard this singer before?"

"No." Rolly shrugged. "Is she any good?"

Joan took a quick look at the stairway to make sure no one was coming.

"Not my place to say, but . . . I think you'll be disappointed."

"That bad, huh?"

Joan's phone buzzed. She glanced at it, then placed it back in her pocket. Rolly looked out toward the stage.

"Bonnie said she ran into you this morning," Joan said.

"Yeah, we talked for a little bit," Rolly said, surveying the room. "I've got a case that's connected to hers."

"Is that why you're here?"

Rolly turned back to Joan.

"It's part of the reason," he said.

"I met him, you know," Joan said. "Gerry Rhodes. Back when I got started. I worked the deck for him on some shows. There was something sad about Gerry, but he was always nice to me. A sweetheart. Can't say the same for his boss. I don't know why Gerry kept working for that guy. He was a pig."

"You mean Roger Sledge?"

"Sledge the Squid. That guy was the handsiest bastard I ever dealt with. Always grabbing at me, violating my personal space, getting me in a corner. It was exhausting."

"Bonnie mentioned something about that. I've never met the man myself."

"Yeah, well, you're a guy. You wouldn't have to deal with it. As far as I know, he saved all that stuff for the girls. I feel sorry for his assistant. She's around here somewhere."

"Did you ever report him?" asked Rolly.

"Who was I going to report him to in those days? I put up with a lot of crap from guys when I got started in this business. Sledge was the worst of the bunch. I call him The Squid. It was like he had tentacles. I dreaded working his shows. There was no me-too stuff back in those days. Not enough women in the business."

Rolly nodded. He wondered if he'd been one of those guys. There were some choices he wasn't proud of, but they were mostly offstage, relationships that were less than equitable. He could be as persistent as anyone when pursuing a woman who'd brought on his lust, but he never grabbed any of them without some invitation. Any jerk could do that. Getting an invitation was part of the dance. Hassling a woman while she was working wasn't a good idea either, especially if that woman was responsible for how your band sounded onstage. Audio techs could really screw you over.

"Apparently, Sledge is Svetlana's manager," Rolly said.

"Yeah. First time I've seen him in a while. Brought back some unpleasant memories."

"Is he still harassing you?"

"No," said Joan. "He stopped doing that a while ago. I thought maybe Gerry got him to back off."

"What else do you remember about him? Gerry, I mean."

"Not much, just that he was super-cool and competent. I learned a lot watching Gerry work. Bonnie told me about him shooting that guy. I had no idea. It's hard to believe he could do something like that. He was so chill, never blew up at people when they screwed up. Bonnie says his daughter hired you to go through all his stuff?"

Rolly nodded.

"Do you remember Gerry owning a white Stratocaster?" he asked.

Joan shook her head.

"Not that I remember. But I hadn't seen him in twenty years.

Why?"

"His daughter says he used to have one. She thinks it's valuable, says it's gone missing. That's why I wanted to talk to
Sledge."

The sound man returned to the booth, nodded at Rolly,
then seated himself behind the audio console.

"We all set, Jimmy?" asked Joan.

"It was just a fuse," said Jimmy. "I replaced 'em all. We're
ready to rock."

"You let them know, right?"

"Sorry. I thought you were going to do that."

Joan looked at her watch, then over at Rolly.

"The band'll be going on in a minute. You'll have to wait
until after the show if you want to talk to Sledge."

"I'll hang out here," Rolly said. "If that's okay with Jimmy."

"Rolly Waters can hang out in my booth anytime," Jimmy
said, looking over at Rolly and cracking a smile.

Rolly tried to remember if he'd met Jimmy before, but he
couldn't think of the occasion. A lot of people in the local music
scene knew Rolly. A lot of people had seen him perform. He
didn't remember most of them. That's how the business
worked.

"All right," Joan said. "I'll head down there and let them
know it's showtime."

Someone stopped outside the doorway just as Joan turned
to leave, a small woman with spiky hair.

"Mr. Sledge wants to know if we're ready," she said.

"I was just heading down to let him know."

Joan started toward the door. The other woman glanced
over at Rolly, sizing him up.

"Are you on the guest list?" she asked.

"No," Rolly said, and he pointed at Joan. "I'm just here to see
her."

"No outside guests. Those are the rules."

"Club business," said Joan. "He'll stay up here. Your boss

won't ever see him."

The short woman narrowed her eyes, then nodded her head.

"Okay," she said. "I think I'll stay up here too."

Joan glanced back at Rolly.

"Sure," she said. "I'll let them know that we're ready."

Joan headed down the stairs. After she was gone, the other woman turned to Rolly.

"What's your name?" she asked.

"Rolly Waters," he said. "What's yours?"

"Christy Carpenter. I'm Mr. Sledge's personal assistant. Don't I know you from somewhere?"

"I don't think we've met before," Rolly said.

"You seem familiar."

"I'm a musician. I play in a band."

"No, that's not it."

Rolly shrugged. He reached in his pocket, pulled out a business card and handed it to her.

"What's this?" she asked.

"Self-promotion. I'm a private investigator. In case you or your boss ever needs one, you'll know who to call. How long have you worked for Mr. Sledge?"

"About a year," the woman said. "Are you the guy that was hanging around the rehearsal hall yesterday? Sergei said some guy kept ringing the doorbell."

"Where's this rehearsal hall?"

"Out east near Gillespie Field."

Rolly remembered the cameras outside the building. He was better off telling the truth.

"Yeah. That was me."

Christy didn't get a chance to ask any more questions. The band hit the stage and started playing a loud, aggressive vamp. Rolly and Christy turned to watch. An older man with fleshy cheeks, a potbelly and hair that couldn't possibly be his own stood at the microphone, the band vamping behind him.

"Ladies and germs. Welcome to the show," he said. "I'm Roger Sledge. Tonight I'd like you to give it up for an exciting new act, on her way to the top, Sledge Productions recording artist Svetlana!"

The crowd, what little of it there was, applauded. Rolly had a feeling they'd been handpicked, restricted to those who'd be friendly. Sledge left the stage as Svetlana walked on. She gave him a kiss on the cheek as they passed. The crowd cheered some more, though it was mostly the women in the audience making the noise. The men were less enthusiastic, which seemed odd given the singer's appearance. Svetlana looked at least six feet tall, wearing a miniskirt and black leather boots, fishnet stockings and a tantalizingly unbuttoned blouse. Her face looked sharp and severe, with cheekbones like razors. It was a dazzling package overall. Then she started to sing.

Rolly grimaced. Moogus and Joan had warned him. Svetlana's caterwauling was awful, out of tune and out of time. It might pass if she showed any real commitment to her performance, but she didn't look particularly thrilled to be onstage. Her only movement consisted of swinging her arms around like a wounded duck. Rolly glanced over at Christy, checking her reaction. Sledge's assistant stared defiantly at the stage, clenching her jaw as if grinding her teeth.

Joan came back to the booth. Rolly didn't want to raise Christy's suspicions, so he said a few words and headed down the stairs and toward the exit. He doubted he'd be able to speak with Roger Sledge before the concert was over. And it would be too painful to wait through the rest.

He passed the bar on his way out, placed his empty glass on the counter and gave a farewell wave to the woman behind the bar. It wasn't until he was outside that he remembered where he'd met her before. It was almost a year ago. She'd sat across from him at a table in a bare room at Coast Guard headquarters, grilling him with questions. Agent Goffin. She was as an FBI agent.

11

THE APPOINTMENT

As he sat down on his sofa the next morning, Rolly wondered if he'd done something different with the coffee. It tasted better than usual. He checked his watch. Just after eight thirty. He thought about picking up a machaca burrito for breakfast from the La Posta taco shop but knew he should eat something healthier. Cereal and a banana. A hefty portion of the ten pounds he'd managed to lose had come from cutting down on visits to the taco shop where he'd order machaca, carne asada, or barbacoa wrapped in huge flour tortillas. He'd managed to reduce his overall burrito consumption to only one a week.

He checked his cell phone. No missed calls. No emails of importance. No messages. He could start the day clear, on his own terms. Days like this were sometimes the hardest to get started. He finished his coffee, closed his eyes, leaned back on the sofa, and tried to remember the dream that had woken him.

Jimi Hendrix had been in the dream. That was the main thing he remembered. Jimi was onstage while Rolly waited in the wings to go on next. Which didn't make sense. Rolly wasn't even born when Hendrix died and even if Jimi had lived to a ripe old age, he'd never be the opening act for someone like Rolly. Jimi would have been a headliner forever.

In the dream, Jimi walked offstage and said something to Rolly. "You're up." That's what Jimi had told him. He'd said something else too, but Rolly couldn't understand it. Then Rolly ran onto the stage to start his big number, and no one was there. The seats in the auditorium were empty. Just before he woke up, he heard Jimi backstage, laughing at him.

Someone knocked on the front door, three light taps, as always. He rose from the sofa, unlocked the door and let his mother in. She carried a white bag from the bakery a few blocks away. The warm smell of butter and flour infiltrated his nose.

"I brought you a cheese danish from Bread & Cie," she said, shaking the bag. "Are you able to have breakfast with me?"

"Sure," Rolly said. His cold cereal would have to wait until tomorrow. "Have a seat. You want any coffee?"

"No coffee for me," his mother said, taking a seat at the table. "Do you have any tea?"

Rolly shook his head.

"No tea. You want milk?"

"Cow's milk?"

"Milk milk."

"No thanks," his mother said, looking nauseated at the thought. "Water will do."

Rolly grabbed a glass from the cupboard, filled it up with tap water, then refilled his coffee cup and returned to the table. His mother had placed the cheese danish on top of a napkin in front of his seat. He took a bite of it, felt the ambrosial smoothness and buttery crunch in his mouth. He'd go light on lunch today.

"You're not upset, are you?" said his mother. "About my plans for this house?"

Rolly hadn't given his mother's construction project much thought. He'd almost forgotten about it. The realization that he'd need to move soon invaded his sunnier thoughts. The second cup of coffee didn't taste as good, either.

"No," he said. "I'm not upset. A little surprised, but not upset. When do you think this will happen?"

His mother looked vaguely ill again.

"Well, you see, I just got a call from the contractor," she said. "His schedule changed. He wants to know if he can start work on Monday."

"*Next* Monday?"

Rolly's mother nodded.

"Yes, I know it's short notice. I've been meaning to show you the plans. They're going to redo the kitchen, replace the old ceiling and move your back wall out three feet to give you more room. You can't live here when they're working."

"I wish you'd given me more time to plan for this."

"Yes, I'm sorry, but like I told you, the construction people got a window in their schedule. It'll only take a few weeks. I'd like to get it done soon."

Rolly looked at his mother. Her voice seemed frail and muted, the usual bright energy somehow diminished.

"Is something wrong, Mom?" he asked. "Are you feeling okay?"

"It's nothing," she said, looking even more stricken. "Just a little procedure."

The coffee turned to dark oil in Rolly's gut.

"What kind of procedure?" he said.

His mother waved her right hand like a fluttering moth searching for light.

"It's my thyroid. They're going to remove it. One side, anyway."

"How long have you known about this?"

"I just decided to get it done yesterday. I was having a hard time swallowing. The doctor explained it all to me; it's not a big deal, really. I don't want you to worry about it."

Rolly stared at his mother for a moment. The fact that she'd consulted a doctor was both reassuring and concerning. Judith Waters didn't smoke, barely drank alcohol and, aside from the occasional morning croissant, ate a diet that rabbits would kill for. She walked at least two miles a day. He felt blindsided by her news.

"Well," he began, sorting through his thoughts. "Are you sure this is the right time to take on a construction project?"

"It's the perfect time," she said, her voice forged in steel. Rolly knew that tone. His mother had planned this announcement, rehearsed the whole thing. She wouldn't listen to anything he had to say, not until later, when she was in a more reflective mode. It had to be what it had to be.

"Okay," he said. "I'll move my stuff into the big house as soon as I can."

"Thank you, dear."

They finished their breakfast. Rolly's mother cleaned up the crumbs while he poured himself a third cup of coffee. He tried not to worry about his mother's health or finding a time when he could pack up and move, but the floor seemed less stable under his feet.

After his mother left, he moved back to the sofa and considered his next move. He had a client to work for and a mysterious guitar to track down. He thought for a moment, then lifted his phone from between the couch cushions, found Max Gemeinhardt's number in his address book and tapped the name to start the call. Max had been Rolly's sponsor and mentor in the investigation business. He was retired now, but still advised Rolly on legal matters and, if the situation called for it, served as Rolly's lawyer. Max knew a lot of people in the business and had deep connections to San Diego's legal community—paralegals, lawyers and judges.

"What's up?" Max said, answering his phone.

"You know anything about a guy named Roger Sledge?" asked Rolly.

"The music guy?"

"Yeah."

"I heard he was kind of an asshole, but that's about it."

"I was wondering about his divorce. From Ruby Dean."

"She's that singer, right?"

"Yeah. I thought you might know one of the lawyers who handled their divorce."

"You want her side or his?"

"I guess hers would be my first choice, but I'd take either one. It's an estate case. I'm trying to track down some personal property. A guy who worked for Sledge. Gerry Rhodes."

"You try talking to Sledge?"

"Sure. So far, it's a no-go."

"I'll run a search on the Superior Court website, see what I come up with."

"Great. Thanks."

"Anything else on your mind?"

Rolly considered telling Max about his mother's surgery, then decided against it. His mother would tell Max herself if she wanted to. They were old friends and, perhaps, for a short time when Rolly's parents were getting divorced, lovers. Rolly had never asked either of them to confirm it. He never would.

"No," Rolly said. "Everything's fine."

"Good. I'll talk to you later."

Rolly disconnected his phone. Less than a minute later, Max had texted him the phone number for someone named Stan Gabriel, who was Sledge's lawyer. Rolly tapped the number and added it to his address book. His phone buzzed with an incoming call. The phone's display read "Sledge Productions." He answered.

"Hello?"

"Mr. Waters?"

"Yes."

"This is Christy Carpenter. Mr. Sledge's personal assistant. We met last night at the Music Box."

"Yes," said Rolly. "I remember."

"Mr. Sledge would like to see you. Do you have any time today, say around two o'clock?"

"Let me see," said Rolly, surprised by the sudden summons, pretending to check appointments in his calendar. "I think I can do that. Where does he want to meet?"

"At his residence. 1787 Hacienda Place in Fletcher Hills."

Rolly tried to remember what he'd told Christy Carpenter last night, how he'd introduced himself. He remembered giving her a business card, saying something about calling him if Sledge ever needed a private detective. He hadn't said anything about Gerry Rhodes or a white Stratocaster guitar.

"Did Mr. Sledge say why he wants to see me?"

"The Sledge Productions office was vandalized yesterday," she said.

"I don't know anything about that."

"We know you were there, Mr. Waters. We've identified you on the videotape. You walked onto the property shortly after it was vandalized."

Rolly sighed. He hated security cameras. By the time you knew they were there, it was too late to do anything about it. Now was the time to stop messing around and go on the offensive.

"Okay," he said. "I admit it. I was there. I wanted to ask Mr. Sledge about an individual I'm investigating. Some goon got in my way. Goons piss me off."

"I see," said Ms. Carpenter. "Did you see the vandalism occur? Did you see who did it?"

"If you're talking about the person who pasted a sticker on the front door, I saw the whole thing," said Rolly, realizing he had a valuable card in his hand, even if he couldn't identify the perpetrators. "I can tell you what I saw, but I'd like Mr. Sledge to answer my questions first, about this individual I'm investigating."

"What is this individual's name?"

"Gerry Rhodes. He died recently, but I know he used to work for Mr. Sledge."

"I see. And those are your terms?"

"Yep."

Rolly heard a rustling of paper on the other end of the line, a loud voice in the background. Carpenter returned to the line.

"Mr. Sledge accepts your proposal. Please arrive promptly at two o'clock."

"I'll be there," said Rolly. He tapped the phone and ended the call before Carpenter could say anything else.

12

THE IMPRESARIO

Rolly waited for the security gate at Roger Sledge's house to roll back, then drove his Outback into the driveway, parked near the front door and climbed out of the car. Sledge's assistant, Christy Carpenter, opened the front door.

"Good morning, Mr. Waters," she said. She wore a pair of blue jeans and a Hole T-shirt. The left side of her jet-black hair was gelled in a stiff peak with a stripe of light blue down the middle. The right side had been cut razor short, making her look more like an alt-rock drummer than a personal assistant, but the music business had always been more forgiving and colorful than, say, accounting or law.

"Good morning," Rolly said, distracted by Christy's hair. He wondered how much maintenance it required, if Christy went to a stylist or did it herself. Either was plausible.

"Mr. Sledge is on the phone," Christy said as she led him through the foyer and into the living room. "He'll be with you in a minute. Can I get you anything—coffee, water?"

"No thanks, I'm fine," Rolly said. He walked to the picture window on the opposite side of the room and looked out.

Sledge's house stood on a ridge overlooking Gillespie Field and the city of El Cajon. He watched as a small plane rose from the airfield and banked into the brown haze above. Searching the near edge of the airfield, he spotted the control tower and a building he thought was Sledge's recording studio, where he'd been yesterday. There was a telescope on a stand nearby for anyone who wanted to take a closer look at the world below.

"Nice view," he said.

Christy looked out the window, following Rolly's gaze.

"You get used to it," she said, sounding unimpressed. Rolly leaned over to look through the telescope and adjusted the eyepiece.

"How do you like working for Mr. Sledge?" he said.

Christy paused for a moment, considering her answer. As Rolly adjusted the eyepiece, the sign on the side of the building came into focus: "Styrgaza Flight School." Sledge had pointed his telescope at his old recording studio. Someone had, anyway.

"It's been interesting," Christy said. "Seeing this side of the music business."

"Which side is that?" Rolly lifted his eye from the telescope and looked at Christy.

"Oh, you know, the business stuff," she said. "The contracts and negotiations."

"Yeah," said Rolly. "I've mostly avoided dealing with that stuff."

"You were a guitar player, right?"

"Still am."

"You're still in the business?"

Rolly shrugged.

"Not THE business," he said. "I play clubs here and there."

"Ruby Dean told me you were a big deal at one time."

"Did she also tell you I was an incompetent guitar teacher?"

Christy chuckled and shook her head.

"No. I don't think she said anything about that."

Rolly was about to ask Christy how well she knew Ruby

Dean when Roger Sledge walked into the room.

"Rolly Waters!" he bellowed like an ebullient moose. "How the heck are you?"

"Can't complain," said Rolly moving over to shake Sledge's hand. "Have we met before?"

"Oh gosh," said Sledge. "It must have been a half dozen times or so, back when I first started managing Ruby. You played on her demo tape, didn't you?"

"I think so," Rolly replied. "But I don't remember a lot from those days."

Sledge laughed. He indicated for Rolly to take a seat on the sofa, then grabbed a high-backed chair from the corner of the room, placed it in front of Rolly and sat down. The chair was taller than the sofa, forcing Rolly to look up at Sledge. It was a cheap and tired power play Rolly had seen more than once. Alpha male power maneuvers didn't intimidate him. Unless, of course, they included some sort of weapon.

"Now, what can I do for you?" Sledge asked.

A woman walked into the room before Rolly could answer. It was Svetlana, the aspiring singer, slumming in a yellow silk pantsuit and low heels. She seemed as surprised to see someone new in the house as Rolly was to see her. She stopped to scrutinize the new guest.

"What man is this, wolfie?" she asked. Sledge stood up and walked over to her.

"This is Rolly Waters, sweetheart," Sledge said. "He's a guitar player."

"You want for the band?"

"No, no. He's got other business with me," Sledge replied, then turned back to Rolly. "You're not looking for a gig, are you, Waters?"

"I'm pretty booked up," Rolly replied, which wasn't entirely true, but playing in Svetlana's band was not on his wish list.

Sledge returned his attention to Svetlana.

"Where are you going?" he asked.

"I am going to business," she said. "To see Uncle Dmitri."

"Okay," Sledge said, leaning in toward her. Svetlana kissed him on the cheek and turned for the door. Sledge slapped her butt. Svetlana looked back at him, a butane torch in her eyes, then turned down the flame.

"You are such bad boy," she said, her lips halfway between a smile and a sneer. She waggled a finger, turned and walked to the front door, opened it and walked out, slamming the door with some force. Sledge watched her go, then turned back to Rolly.

"What do you think of that?" he asked.

"She's . . . a very attractive young woman," Rolly said, still processing his astonishment. Svetlana was Sledge's new Ruby Dean, in every way. Except for talent. Roger Sledge reasserted his place on his chair, puffed up and pleased with himself.

"Never count yourself out, Mr. Waters," he said. "Not many guys my age get a piece of ass like that without paying good money for it."

Rolly suspected Sledge was paying one way or the other, but it wasn't his job to poke holes in another man's vanity. He turned to the subject at hand.

"Gerry Rhodes," he said. "He used to work for you?"

"Sure. What about him?"

"Mr. Rhodes died a few days ago."

Sledge's assistant, Christy, moved to the table in the corner and sat down, listening attentively. Sledge cleared his throat.

"I'm sorry to hear that," he said. "We'd lost touch."

"Mr. Rhodes's family has hired me to track down an item of personal property they think has gone missing."

"What is it?"

Rolly pulled out his phone and showed Sledge the photo of Otis Sparks. "I'm looking for this guitar."

Sledge recoiled at the photo, then glared at Rolly.

"What kind of bullshit are you selling, Waters?" he said, his voice constricted and angry.

"Excuse me?" Rolly said.

"I know a grift when I see one," Sledge replied. "Where did you get that photograph?"

"My client gave it to me."

"Your client. That wouldn't be Mavis Worrell, would it?"

"No," said Rolly, deciding not to reveal he'd spoken to Mavis. "It was given to me by a member of Mr. Rhodes's family. If you can't identify the guitar, I thought you might know the man's name."

"You already know who he is," said Sledge. "Don't you?"

"I believe his name is Otis Sparks."

Sledge clamped his mouth into a thin line before responding.

"Now you listen, Mr. Waters," he said. "I want you to give Mavis Worrell a message. Tell her I'm going to sue her for harassment if she tries something like this again. It was self-defense. The police exonerated Gerry. And me."

"I don't understand," said Rolly, deciding not to reveal what he knew about Sparks. Sledge stared at him a moment before relenting.

"Mavis Worrell thinks I was responsible for her brother's death. She's always blamed me. It happened in my studio, but I didn't shoot Otis. Gerry Rhodes did. I was there. I saw the whole thing. It was self-defense, like the police said, but Mavis has always had it in for me, thinks I ripped her brother off."

Christy Carpenter's phone buzzed. She checked the screen and stood up.

"Excuse me, Mr. Sledge. The maids are here."

"Let the little bitches in." Sledge nodded at Christy. She left the room. Sledge turned back to Rolly.

"Mavis Worrell is Otis Sparks's sister. She teaches Black studies or women's history, some revisionist bullshit like that. I don't remember which college. She's got a real problem with men, especially white men."

Rolly nodded. Mavis hadn't shown any hostility when he

talked to her, just the usual hesitation he had to deal with when asking people questions. If Sledge raised Mavis's temperature, it was probably because he was an arrogant asshole. A white male asshole, to be sure. A larger-than-usual group of that subspecies seemed especially prevalent lately.

"Listen," said Sledge, using a less aggressive tone. "It was tragic what happened to Otis. It was unfortunate. It was all a big misunderstanding. He shouldn't have broken into the studio like that."

"What happened?"

"I was Otis's manager. This was before Ruby. Otis got it in his head that I was cheating him somehow, that I'd stolen money from him. He came to the studio one night when Gerry and I were working and started yelling at me, telling me how he was going to kick my ass if I didn't come up with some money real soon. He was coked up and out of his mind. To tell you the truth, I think Gerry was on drugs too. He only meant to scare Otis, make him back off. He pulled the trigger somehow and then Otis was dead."

Sledge paused for a moment, caught up in an emotional memory or at least acting that way.

"I don't think Gerry ever got over what happened," he said. "He discovered Otis, you know, brought him to my attention. Gerry was never the same after that. His drug problem got worse."

A noise in the hallway interrupted their conversation. Christy arrived with two young women in tow. The women were pushing a tall cart like the kind hotel maids used. Both of them were dressed in blue jeans. One wore a Joan Jett T-shirt. The other wore an X T-shirt. Punk and alt-rock music fans, just like Christy.

"Excuse me, Mr. Sledge," said Christy. "Where would you like them to start today?"

"Well, not in here," said Sledge. "I don't want to carry on a conversation with that damn vacuum going."

"I'll have them start in the kitchen," Christy said.

Sledge waved his hand, trying to brush the women out of the room.

"Go away now," he said. "You're my personal assistant, not my nanny."

Christy's mouth twitched, but she didn't say anything. She led the maids out of the room, presumably to the kitchen. The maids slouched away like insulted cats. Sledge watched them go, then turned back to Rolly.

"Hard to get good help these days," he said.

"I wouldn't know." Rolly shrugged.

"Can I ask you something, Mr. Waters?"

"Yes?"

"What happened to women? Young women, I mean."

"Umm?"

"They used to care about looking attractive. They didn't slouch around like this bunch. No effort. No makeup. Ugly, ugly, ugly. It's like a badge of honor with them."

Rolly felt uncomfortable with the turn the conversation had taken. Perhaps Sledge was testing him, probing to see how he leaned in the war of the sexes. Rolly wasn't about to give Sledge that satisfaction. He wouldn't give him an argument, either. Arguing with angry old men was rarely constructive.

"I didn't know that part of the story," he said. "About Gerry Rhodes and Otis Sparks. I'm looking for the guitar in that photograph."

"Why?" Sledge asked.

Rolly hesitated a moment, apprehensive about revealing Lucinda's claim. It wouldn't be easy to get another interview with Sledge. He decided to go for it.

"Gerry Rhodes's family say he used to own a Stratocaster like this," he said. "It was played by Jimi Hendrix. I wondered if it's the same guitar Otis Sparks has in the photograph."

"Well, why didn't you just start with that?" said Sledge. "I have that Hendrix guitar in the basement."

13

THE PREDICAMENT

R oger Sledge escorted Rolly to the kitchen. The two maids were mopping the floor and scrubbing the range. Sledge pressed a button on the wall. An elevator door opened. The two men entered the elevator and rode down to the basement.

"I've picked up a lot of guitars over the years," Sledge said as the elevator clattered around them. "I got a lot of them for a song, from future rock stars, before they were big, when they needed some money. One of the fringe benefits of my years in the industry. I got a guy looking at the collection right now, doing an appraisal."

A wobbly thought floated through Rolly's mind like a feather, but he had no time to see where the wind took it. The elevator door opened. Sledge led him into a bright room with a large-screen TV, a wet bar and what looked to be about a dozen guitars hanging on the walls. There was another man in the room, inspecting a guitar that lay on the pool table.

"What're you doing here?" Rob Norwood said, looking up at them.

"I live here." Sledge laughed.

"He means me," Rolly said. "I've singlehandedly kept Rob in business for years."

"Hardly," Norwood said. "We both gave Ruby Dean guitar lessons back in the day."

"Well, hell, Mr. Norwood," Sledge said. "Why didn't you tell me that before? That little girl was my meal ticket. Her first record paid for this house."

Rolly's wobbly thoughts blew back toward him. Norwood's appraisal. Sledge's guitars. The connection was there. The Stratocaster might really exist. He looked around the room, giving the guitars a once-over. An eight-by-ten glossy photograph of each guitar's previous owner had been mounted below the guitar. Ruby Dean's photo was there, along with some mid-level guitar heroes—big-game trophies for Sledge's man cave.

"Is that it?" Rolly said, pointing at a white Stratocaster with a photo of Jimi Hendrix below it.

"That's the one," Sledge replied, with a smug grin. "My 401(k) plan. Assuming Mr. Norwood here can provide the expected valuation."

Rolly glanced over at Rob Norwood, who looked like something had curdled inside him. Even for Norwood it was a sour-milk face.

"Did you check out that picture I sent you?" Rolly asked him. "Is it the same guitar?"

Norwood tugged on the silver loop earring in his left ear.

"It's similar, for sure," he said. "Did you identify the guy in that photo?"

"Yeah. His name's Otis Sparks. He's dead."

"Any connection to Hendrix?"

"Gerry Rhodes is the connection. That's who I'm working for. His family, I mean. Rhodes worked for Mr. Sledge at one time. Mr. Sledge was Otis Sparks's manager. Before Rhodes came to work for Mr. Sledge, he was a roadie for Hendrix. I'm not sure how the guitar made it into Mr. Sledge's collection, but that's the connection."

The two men looked over at Sledge, expecting him to follow up on Rolly's report. He didn't. Sledge looked like a man who'd been dealt a good hand and was trying to hide it. The next steps could be tricky.

"Did you buy the Hendrix guitar from Gerry Rhodes, Mr. Sledge?" Rolly asked.

"It wasn't exactly a sale," Sledge replied. "I'd advanced Gerry some money. He didn't have it when the loan came due, so I let him pay me with the guitar instead."

"How long ago was this?"

"Maybe fifteen years ago."

"Do you have any paperwork that proves Mr. Rhodes sold it to you?"

"You calling me a liar?"

"No. But a receipt would be nice. I could show it to Mr. Rhodes's family, let them know where the guitar is, that it was legally obtained and they have no claim."

Sledge gave Rolly a peevish look.

"Are these folks going to come after me if I don't have some damn paperwork?"

Rolly shrugged. As the saying went, possession was nine-tenths of the law. He didn't have any reason to doubt Sledge's story. Apart from the fact that Sledge was a jerk.

"I have the IOU somewhere," Sledge said. "If you want to see it."

"Any documentation would help," Rolly replied.

Sledge glanced at his watch.

"I need to go now, Mr. Waters," he said. "I'm meeting with my lawyer. I'll ask my assistant to look for the IOU. You can wait here with Mr. Norwood."

"Thanks."

"No problem," Sledge said with an unnerving grin. He pointed to a corner of the room and laughed. "Just remember. I've got eyes on you both. Don't try any funny business."

Norwood gave a feeble laugh. Rolly looked to where Sledge

had pointed and spotted a security camera tucked in the corner just under the ceiling. Sledge disappeared into the elevator and Rolly returned to the pool table. Norwood rubbed the graying soul patch below his lip.

"This client of yours, who is she?" he asked.

"What makes you think it's a woman?"

"Knowing you for the last twenty years."

Rolly grinned. Norwood had always been a perceptive grouch. He could've been a detective, if he hadn't married a rich woman and had the opportunity to turn his guitar fixation into a business. Some guys had all the luck.

"It's Gerry Rhodes's daughter," Rolly said. "But don't tell Sledge."

"I'm not telling that jerk anything. Not yet."

"What do you mean?"

"This woman, the guy's daughter, does she have any other proof he owned this guitar? I mean, c'mon, a Stratocaster played by Jimi Hendrix? That's like the holy grail. I've done some research. I can't find it listed anywhere. I can't find any photos of Jimi playing the thing."

"What does the previous appraisal say?"

"Not much. Campbell Lange played it safe and gave a range of value. Sledge is pushing me to give it a higher assessment, but I need better provenance, something that connects Hendrix to the guitar. I'm not going to sign off on this thing if I don't see some documentation."

"I found something that might help," said Rolly. "It's a back-stage pass with Gerry Rhodes's name on it. From a Hendrix concert in Houston."

"Now we're talking," Norwood said. "Can you make me a copy?"

"I think so. I'll need to check with my client."

Rolly turned and looked at the Stratocaster on the wall, noted its center position amongst the other guitars, the jewel of the collection. He'd seen hundreds of Stratocasters like this one, played a few himself over the years. For collectors, the wear and tear on a guitar were what made it special, the way it had been gripped, stroked and manipulated by the people who played it. That's what made it magical, a totem, a fetish. Otis Sparks. Jimi Hendrix. He glanced back at Norwood.

"Have you tried playing it?" he asked, resisting the desire to take the guitar down and get it into his hands. He understood now why Christians preserved the vestiges of saints. If Hendrix had touched the guitar, held it in his hands, it was like a holy relic of rock-and-roll history.

Norwood walked over to the display, lifted the guitar from its hook and handed it to Rolly.

"You know you want it," he said.

Rolly took the guitar, sat down on the couch and inspected it. Even without Jimi's imprimatur, he knew the guitar was worth more than most used Stratocasters.

"It's pre-CBS," he said.

"What makes you say that?" Norwood asked.

"The small gold logo on the headstock. CBS used block letters in black. Right?"

"You're not as dumb as you look," Norwood said. "The serial numbers check out."

Rolly played the guitar, pulling out some Hendrix-style riffs, getting a feel for it. The action was smooth all the way up the frets. Some guitars felt good in your hands from the start. This was one of them. He wondered if Jimi's hands had really held the guitar, if there was still some voodoo magic in it. If so, someone else had played it since Jimi. Jimi was left-handed and the strings had been set up for a right-handed player. Otis, perhaps. The elevator clanked in the corner of the room. He handed the guitar back to Norwood, who put it back in its place. The elevator door opened. Christy Carpenter stepped out and walked over toward them.

"I've copied that document you requested, Mr. Waters," she said, handing Rolly a sheet of paper. It was a photocopy of a written note, an IOU for two thousand dollars from Gerry Rhodes to Roger Sledge, dated at the bottom with both men's signatures.

"There's nothing here about a guitar," he said.

"What's that?"

Rolly pointed at the Hendrix guitar on the wall.

"Mr. Sledge told me he forgave this IOU in exchange for that guitar," he said. "But there's nothing about a guitar in this document."

"I'm sorry," Christy said. "That's the only thing I could find." She turned her attention to Norwood.

"Will you be taking your lunch break soon, Mr. Norwood?" she asked. "It's just that the maids would like to get in and clean."

Norwood checked his watch and shrugged his shoulders.

"Sure," he said. "I can take my break now."

"Thank you," said Christy. She turned back toward the elevator. "I'll let them know."

After she'd left, Norwood placed the guitar that was on the pool table back in its display case. He picked up his jacket and keys.

"Was there something else you wanted to tell me?" Rolly asked.

"It can wait," Norwood replied. "Let's take this outside."

Rolly slipped the copy of Gerry Rhodes's IOU into his pocket and followed Norwood into the elevator. When it opened on the ground floor, the two maids were waiting with their cleaning supply cart parked between them.

"It's all yours, ladies," Norwood said, smiling as they passed the two women. The maids gave them a perfunctory smile, like people did on an elevator. Christy Carpenter escorted the men to the front door.

"I'll check with Mr. Sledge about that document," she said. "Let me know if you need anything else."

Rolly thanked her. The two men walked out to the driveway.

Norwood paused by his truck, glancing back at the front door to make sure it was closed.

"What is it?" Rolly asked, moving in closer to Norwood to keep their conversation private. Norwood sighed and looked around the driveway, searching for the words he wanted to say.

"Something's up," he said.

"What do you mean?"

"I found something weird on the guitars," Norwood said.

"What is it?"

"They're stamped. With someone's initials. At first I thought it was just the Ruby Dean guitars. Those were all custom made. But I found it on two others as well. A Les Paul and a Gretsch. Same mark. Different locations. Someplace you wouldn't normally see. In the hollow bodies, like Ruby's, it's inside, at the waist. On the solid bodies it's under the neck bolt."

"What about the Hendrix Strat?"

Norwood shook his head.

"That one's okay, but the other ones—those marks aren't in the original appraisal. I've read through the thing a half-dozen times. Campbell Lange doesn't mention the marks anywhere."

Rolly considered Norwood's predicament.

"Maybe she just missed them," he said. "You said they were hard to find."

Norwood folded his arms and leaned back against his truck. He glanced at the front door, checking to make sure no one was watching.

"It's not like her to miss something like that. She's a perfectionist."

"Have you talked to her?"

"I left a message for her a couple of times. At Taybor. She hasn't called me back."

"Probably just busy."

Norwood pulled out his keys and opened the driver's-side door of his truck.

"I don't like the way Sledge is pressuring me. He's in a hurry, wants me to finish this thing asap, even offered me a bonus if I could have it done by the end of the week. He won't tell me why. I think he might have a buyer or something. Let me know if you come up with anything else that would help with that Stratocaster. It's the big one, if I can find a way to authenticate it."

"I'll let you know," Rolly replied.

Norwood climbed into his truck, started the engine and put it in gear. Rolly knocked on the window, realizing Norwood's predicament might be useful to his investigation. Norwood rolled down his window.

"What is it?" he asked.

"The initials on the guitars," Rolly said. "What are they?"

"*PJL*," Norwood replied. "In small block letters. The same on each one. *PJL*."

14

THE LAWSUITS

Rolly spread a dot of mayonnaise on a flour tortilla, placed one slice of processed turkey on top of it, added two leaves of romaine and folded the tortilla. Lunch. He brought it to the kitchen table, sat down, took a bite, then opened his notebook. He looked at the photo of Otis Sparks with the Stratocaster. Then he looked at the copy of the IOU that Gerry Rhodes had written out to Roger Sledge for two thousand dollars. The same amount had been written on the Bump's cocktail napkin Bonnie found yesterday in the canyon. The matching numbers might just be a coincidence. There was no guitar listed on either item.

PJL. That wasn't a coincidence, but he didn't see how it had anything to do with his case. Norwood had found the three letters hidden on Sledge's guitars, but the Hendrix Stratocaster didn't have the mark. Someone had pasted a *PJL* sticker on Sledge's studio door. Whoever had pasted the sticker drove away in a Prius with the license plate *PJL1234.* He could ask Bonnie to look up the license plate, but she'd want to know why. He wasn't sure he had a good enough reason. He could go to the DMV and get the information as well, but he wasn't sure it would be worth the wait.

His phone rang. Max Gemeinhardt.

"Eleven lawsuits over the last twenty-five years," Max said, when Rolly answered. "All settled out of court."

"What's that?"

"Roger Sledge. You asked me to check his legal record, right?"

"Right," Rolly said, grabbing a pen to make notes. He'd forgotten about his earlier conversation with Max.

"Anyway," Max continued. "There are eleven lawsuits on the books. None of them went to trial, so there's no proceedings. He also filed for bankruptcy three times. And there's his divorce settlement with Ruby Dean."

"Any criminal cases? Any arrests?"

"None that I found. Did you hear something?"

"Not exactly. Someone was shot and killed in Sledge's recording studio back in the eighties. Sledge was an eyewitness."

"These are civil cases, not criminal. The plaintiffs are all women. They're listed as miscellaneous civil petitions."

"What's that mean?" Rolly asked.

"I talked to some people," Max said. "From what I heard about the guy I'm thinking sexual assault, sexual harassment, hostile work environment, coercion—stuff that would be tough to prove in a criminal case, but evidence enough for a civil judgment. Two of the cases involved minors."

"How do you know that?"

"They're listed by their initials, not their full names. That's usually what that means."

"He was sexually harassing minors?"

"Can't say for sure, but that's what it looks like. He's in the rock-and-roll business, after all."

"What's that mean?"

"Didn't Jimmy Page take some fifteen-year-old girl on tour with him?"

"Yeah," Rolly said. The Baby Groupies. A gaggle of underage girls from LA who slept with rock stars back in the 1970s. David Bowie, Steven Tyler, Mick Jagger, Ted Nugent. The girls had been willing and no one had said anything. No one objected. Was whatever Sledge had done any different? Perhaps so if the two girls had sued him. Maybe it only worked if you were a rock star.

"You never slept with any teenagers, did you?" Max asked. "When you were older, I mean, when you were playing the clubs."

"Not that I know of," said Rolly, his eyes darting toward the front door, hoping his mother wasn't about to walk in. "There were girls at the clubs, of course. But they had to have a driver's license to prove they were over twenty-one."

"They might have used fake ones."

"I try not to think about that," said Rolly, rubbing his temples. "Can we change the subject?"

"Yeah. Sorry," said Max. "I shouldn't talk. I was dating girls in their twenties when I was fifty."

"Those women were legal adults," Rolly said. "They made their own choices. Bad ones, in your case, but their own."

Max chuckled.

"Anyway," he said. "I downloaded the cover page of the initial filings from Superior Court and emailed you the PDFs. That'll give you the names. You owe me eleven dollars."

"I'll buy you a beer at the next Padres game."

"You need anything else?"

"I'm good for now, thanks," Rolly said and hung up. He scrolled through his contacts, found Lucinda's name and tapped on her number. He wanted to tell her what he'd learned so far, about the Stratocaster in Sledge's basement and the IOU from her father to Sledge. He wanted to talk to her, too, trade quips and maybe flirt with an adult woman, hoping to clear his thoughts of sexual harassers, misbehaving rock stars and underage girls. Lucinda didn't answer. He texted her, suggesting they talk later so he could report the latest developments.

He opened his laptop and checked his email, finding the attachments Max had sent him. He read through the names of plaintiffs and wrote them down in his notebook. There was only one lawyer listed for Sledge: Stan Gabriel.

Someone knocked on the door. He opened the door to let his mother in. They took a seat across from each other at the kitchen table.

"What's that?" his mother asked, indicating his notebook with the names of Sledge's legal accusers.

"Some names Max gave me. I just got off the phone with him," Rolly said. "He says hi." Which wasn't true, but his mother would expect Max to say hi.

"Quite a list," said his mother. "Who are they?"

"Plaintiffs," said Rolly. "Eleven women. They all sued the same guy. Not together, but separately."

"Why did they sue him?"

"Don't know exactly. The records are sealed, confidential. They all made deals of some sort. Max thinks it might indicate a pattern of sexual harassment."

"Are you working for Max?"

"No."

"Then what are you doing with the list?"

"Just a hunch. It's tangent to a case I'm working on. It's a long story."

"I see," said his mother. "Well, anyway, I've talked to the contractors. They'll start on Monday. I'm sorry, but it's the only way we can get this done soon."

Rolly sighed and nodded, checking his cell phone to make sure what day it was. Wednesday. It would only take him a day to move all his stuff and settle in. Two more days to see what he could do for Lucinda. Then move on the weekend.

"What about the furniture?" he asked. "I can't bring that with me. It's really yours, anyway."

"I think we should get rid of it."

"You don't want to keep any?"

"Not really. I picked up all this stuff from Goodwill. We'll give it back to them, then go shopping at IKEA. Spruce up the place with new furniture."

Rolly didn't want the place spruced up. The secondhand furniture and worn carpet were a reminder of the condition he'd been in when he first started living there, getting back on his feet after he'd stopped drinking. After the accident. The decor was run-down and scruffy. He didn't want it to look fresh.

"I'll let you make those decisions," he said. Shopping for furniture was way outside his comfort zone and going to IKEA with his mother sounded like an interminable headache. On his own, he might be able to walk through the store and choose the first thing he liked, but his mother would need to inspect every piece of furniture and discuss its pros and cons before buying it. His mother didn't respond. She seemed distracted.

"I had to deal with that once," she said. "It was awful."

"What's that?"

"Sexual harassment."

"Only once?" said Rolly. "Some women I know would say you got off easy."

"Oh, I know," said his mother. "I'm not talking about the whistles and the leering and the day-to-day stuff we've all had to put up with. This was more complicated."

"Who was it?" said Rolly.

"Well, that was part of the problem," said his mother. "He was your father's superior, two ranks above him. I stopped going to events if I knew he'd be there."

"Did you talk to Dad about the guy?"

"Yes. It was hard for your father too. This man had a lot of say over his career. In retrospect, I think it's one of the things that drove us apart."

"I don't think you ever told me about this. What did the guy do?"

Rolly's mother shifted in her seat, running through her old memories.

"It started at parties, social events. At first, he'd just tell me how attractive I looked. Then he got more aggressive about it. When your father made captain and was assigned to sea duty, the man started calling me, showing up at our house. He'd corner me at social events, invite me out on his boat, and act offended if I put him off. I started to dread seeing him. There was no way to report him. Navy wives had no power at all."

"How long did this go on?"

"A year, maybe a year and a half. I wanted to be a good wife and support your father, but it started making me physically sick, knowing I'd have to be in a room with this man. I stopped going to social events, anywhere he might be."

Rolly shook his head and clucked his tongue in sympathy. He was still learning things about his mother and father, the pressures and tensions they'd faced, the things that had driven them apart. You never knew what would happen between two people when they got married. That was the folly of marital bonds. And the strength.

"Sorry you had to put up with all that," he said.

"Yes, well," said his mother. "It was all water under the bridge until this 'me too' stuff started happening. It triggered some memories, that Weinstein fellow especially. As you get older, you think things might have changed for the better, but it's the same old story."

"Women have more power now," said Rolly. "Sometimes. I think."

"Let's hope so," said his mother. "Are you going to call all the women on that list?"

"Maybe. I think I know one of them."

"Well, be kind," said his mother. "Whoever you talk to. It's not easy going through memories like that."

"I'll be good," Rolly said. "Thanks for telling me what happened to you. I had no idea."

"Yes, well," his mother said, rising from the table. "I don't mean to burden you. At least those women on your list were able to sue."

"It's something, I guess," Rolly said, wondering how much Sledge had paid each of the women to stay quiet, if he'd paid them. It might have cost Sledge dearly, but he didn't seem to have learned much from the experience.

His mother stopped at the door. "Remember. The contractors will be here on Monday."

"I got it," Rolly said. His mother left the house. He looked back at his notebook, the list of names he'd taken from the court filings, lingering on the one name he recognized. Joan hadn't mentioned it the other night at the Music Box, but she'd sued Roger Sledge. Maybe that was the reason Sledge had stopped harassing her.

15

THE ATTORNEY

Roger Sledge's lawyer, Stan Gabriel, sat behind the Plexiglas wall of a DJ booth, in the back corner of the Bottleneck Brewpub, grooving to the noisy attack of King Crimson's first album, *In the Court of the Crimson King*. Gabriel had apparently done well as an attorney. He owned the brewpub. He could do whatever he wanted with it, including building a DJ booth so he could spin records for patrons.

Rolly sat at the bar, nursing a club soda with a slice of lime, nibbling bits of cheese and thinking about rich men and their toys. Fancy boats and fast cars, wine cellars, expensive guitars. Stan Gabriel looked to be in his sixties, with long, frizzy gray hair pulled back in a ponytail. The DJ booth was his plaything —a rich, aging beatnik reclaiming his youth.

His phone buzzed. It was a text message from Lucinda. *Working till 8. Maybe after?* Rolly sent back a thumbs-up. They could figure out where and when later.

King Crimson roared to its rousing finish. Stan Gabriel took a break and headed toward the bar, ordered something called a Socks and Sandals Pilsner, then turned to look at Rolly.

"Do I know you?" he asked.

"Rolly Waters." Rolly extended his hand.

"You were in a band or something, weren't you?" Gabriel said after they shook.

"I still play guitar around town a bit," Rolly said. Gabriel nodded, turned to pick up his beer glass and took a sip, then placed it back on the counter.

"The Creatures," he said. "That was the name of your band. You were kind of a big deal."

"We did pretty well locally," said Rolly. "That was a long time ago."

"You're not drinking beer," Gabriel said, indicating Rolly's glass of clear bubbles.

"Wish I could," said Rolly. "Looks like you've got a pretty good selection."

"Most of the local heavy hitters plus a range of weekly taps. If you don't mind me asking, what brought you in here? You don't drink beer and I doubt it's the cheese plate."

"I wanted to talk to you," Rolly said. He reached in his pocket and pulled out a business card. "I'm a private investigator."

Gabriel took the card and looked it over.

"I'm off the clock," he said. "Call my secretary and set up an appointment."

"She told me I'd find you here."

Gabriel shook his head as if he might need a new secretary.

"This won't take long," Rolly said. He pulled out his phone and showed Gabriel the photograph of Otis Sparks and the Stratocaster guitar. "Do you know who this is?"

Gabriel reached in his shirt pocket and extracted a slim case, opened it and put on a pair of reading glasses. He leaned in and stared at the photograph.

"Otis Sparks," he said, sitting back and removing his glasses. "That was his name. He's dead."

"Yes, I know," Rolly said.

"So why do you need me to identify him?"

"I'm interested in the guitar," Rolly continued, beginning to doubt this would be a useful line of inquiry. If he brought up Roger Sledge, Gabriel might claim attorney-client privilege and refuse to answer anything that he asked.

"What about it?" asked Gabriel.

"I'm working for the estate of Gerry Rhodes."

"Gerry's dead?"

Rolly nodded.

Gabriel stared across the bar as if contemplating the beer selection listed on the wall.

"Gerry Rhodes killed Otis Sparks," he said, almost robotically. "I guess you know that."

"Yes. It's the guitar that I'm interested in. Gerry Rhodes's family thinks he owned the guitar in this photo, but Roger Sledge has this guitar in his collection. He says he purchased it from Mr. Rhodes, part of an agreement that settled a debt."

"That doesn't surprise me. Gerry was often in debt."

"How well did you know Mr. Rhodes?"

"He worked for Roger. I haven't seen him in ages. I didn't know he was dead."

"It was only a few days ago."

Gabriel took a long swig of his Socks and Sandals and wiped his lip.

"I still don't know what you want from me," he said.

"Mr. Sledge showed me the IOU from Gerry Rhodes, the one that paid for the guitar. As his lawyer, I thought you might know something about it."

Gabriel shook his head.

"Anything Roger's told me is privileged," he said. "I don't handle his finances, thank God. I'm only his attorney."

"You filed his bankruptcy papers," Rolly said. Gabriel might not be Sledge's accountant, but he must know something about Sledge's finances. Gabriel's name was listed on all the court filings Max had sent him.

"That's different," Gabriel said. "That's a court proceeding. Any agreement that Roger and Gerry made for a guitar, that's on their own dime. They'd hardly need me for that."

Rolly looked at his cheese plate. The corner of a Gouda slice had turned hard and brown. He wasn't getting anywhere with the questions he'd asked so far. Maybe there wasn't anywhere to get. He'd hoped to find something that would give Lucinda a claim on the guitar.

"I don't like the guy," he said.

"What's that?"

"Roger Sledge. I don't like him."

"Join the club." Gabriel laughed. "I don't like him either. I don't have to. I'm his lawyer."

"You've handled a lot of cases for him."

"Yes."

"I noticed a lot of women had sued him."

"I have no comment on that."

Both men took another sip from their drinks. Rolly felt defeated, but Gabriel seemed to have accepted defeat a long time ago. Lawyers took defeat for a living. Often a good living.

"The escape artist," Gabriel said, as if he'd been thinking the same thing. There was honor in defeat, but no joy. There was always some level of pain. "That's what Roger likes to call himself. It's my job to help him escape. That's what he pays me for. Filing bankruptcy to escape his debts. Working out settlements with aggrieved parties to avoid trials. That's how the game works. You're a private detective. You should know that."

"I don't make enough money to think about it that way," Rolly said. Gabriel chuckled.

"You see that DJ booth?" he said, pointing to the corner of the room. "That's my escape. I was a real DJ once, back in college, at the student radio station. It was the best time of my life. I started looking for jobs in the business, you know, big-time radio, FM and AOR stations. Clear Channel and big corporations had taken over the business by then. The on-air jobs were for shock jocks and sheeples who played songs from their pre-approved list. I went to law school instead. I make a good living and now I get to DJ, at my place, play any record I feel like."

"I can appreciate that." Rolly nodded his head. He played any song he wanted to, in the band. Not giving a damn could be quite satisfying.

"You handled Sledge's divorce, didn't you?" he asked, following up on that thought. "When he split up with Ruby Dean?"

"Like I said," Gabriel, "I help Roger escape. Although in that case, I'd say it was Ruby who escaped."

"What do you mean?"

Gabriel took a long chug on his beer, placed the glass back on the bar and stared at the listings of today's beer selections written in chalk above the back bar.

"Would you want to be married to Roger Sledge?" he asked.

"No. Was it a complicated divorce?"

"I can't tell you the details, but Roger went scorched earth on the assets. He wasn't willing to give Ruby anything. Eventually she just wanted out. She even let Roger keep her guitars."

"I saw Ruby's guitars in his collection. I didn't know they were spoils of war."

"I learned a lot about Roger then. More than I'd like to know, really."

"Anything you want to share?"

Gabriel shook his head.

"At this point I'll have to claim attorney-client privilege, Mr. Waters. I've probably said too much already."

"I understand."

The two men looked at the listings of beer on the back wall. Grapefruit Sculpin. Speedway Stout. Arrogant Bastard. A lot had changed about beer since Rolly had drunk his last Budweiser, fifteen years ago. A lot had changed about Rolly, too.

"What about Ruby's copyrights?" he asked.

"What's that?"

"The songs she wrote. I noticed that Sledge gets half the credit."

"Ruby kept her share of the royalties after the divorce. And Roger kept his. That was one of the few things they agreed on. Fifty percent each, just like before. I remember those numbers. I filed the original papers with the copyright office. You know that 'Someday' song? That one's still paying his bills."

"You think Sledge really had anything to do with writing it?"

Gabriel shrugged his shoulders.

"Doesn't matter. That's how it was filed. Unless one of them willingly gives up a share of the ownership, that's how it will stay."

Rolly considered the fine points of the music industry, the nooks and the crannies where people got lost or tossed away. It was a cutthroat business. One document, one signature, could free or enslave you the rest of your life.

"Gerry Rhodes had that song on his record player when he died," he said. "'Someday.'"

"Gerry still had a record player?" Gabriel smiled. "I guess we had something in common."

"He said that song had been written for him. 'Someday.'"

"That's how a lot of great songs work, isn't it? We feel like it's been written for us."

"I got the sense it was more literal. There was a photograph of Gerry with Ruby in his apartment. Ruby had signed it on the back with a note that said, 'Someday.'"

Gabriel shrugged his shoulders.

"I wouldn't know anything about that."

"How well do you know Ruby?" Rolly asked.

"Not very well," Gabriel replied. "I sat in depositions with her for a year, but I haven't heard from her since the divorce.

Understandable. I wouldn't want to talk to me either after something like that."

"You can't call her up and say hi?"

Gabriel laughed, but it sounded more like a sigh.

"No," he said. "Roger put the screws to her, and I twisted them in. Not the shiniest episode in my legal career. Did you know Ruby? You must have been playing in town when she came along."

Rolly smiled.

"Sure. I gave her guitar lessons. For a little bit. I played on her demo tape."

"Sounds like she owes you one."

Rolly's phone rang. It was Joan. He answered.

"Can you come by the house?" she asked.

"What's up?" Rolly asked back.

"I need to talk to you. Bonnie will be here."

"What's this about?"

"There's a few things I didn't tell you about Roger Sledge."

16

THE DISCUSSION

Bonnie and Joan's house was a 1920s fixer-upper they'd purchased in Golden Hill, when the area was "in transition," as the real estate agents liked to say. Pride of ownership. The two women had been renovating the place for the last four years. They sat on a pot of gold now.

Joan opened the front door and led Rolly into the living room. Bonnie stood behind the couch, next to the dining room table. She was out of uniform, wearing a pair of worn-out jeans and a gray Pendleton shirt. She looked fatigued, maybe even ill, but that might be the way she always looked at home. Rolly usually dealt with Bonnie in her professional capacity, when she'd put on the uniform, locked and loaded.

"You want anything to drink?" Joan asked. "Water or something?"

"I'm fine," Rolly said. "What's going on?"

"You wanted to know about Roger Sledge. I'm going to tell you the whole story."

Joan looked over at Bonnie.

"C'mon, Bon," she said. "Have a seat."

Bonnie didn't move an inch.

"Why are we even talking about this?" she asked.

"I found the guitar I was looking for," Rolly said, inserting himself into the tension he felt between the two women. "Sledge has it in his collection. Gerry Rhodes owed him money. Sledge says he paid off his debt with the guitar."

"From what I've heard," Bonnie said, "Mr. Rhodes owed a lot of people money."

"Which is not unusual for someone with substance abuse issues," Rolly said.

"No."

"Here's the thing," Rolly continued. "The IOU he signed over to Sledge was for two thousand dollars."

Bonnie moved from the table and sat on the sofa with Joan.

"That's the same amount we saw on the napkin from Bump's," she said.

"Yeah, I've been thinking about it. It could be just a coincidence," Rolly said. Two thousand dollars was not a distinctive number. He'd really feel he was onto something if the matching numbers had been less round, say nineteen hundred thirty-five dollars and twelve cents, but the match was still worth keeping in mind.

"What's this have to do with me?" Joan asked.

"Nothing, probably," Rolly said. "I just wondered why neither of you told me about your lawsuit against Sledge."

Joan and Bonnie exchanged glances.

"It was not a good time in our relationship," Joan said. "There was a lot of stress."

"Because of the lawsuit?"

Joan nodded.

"I wanted to take Sledge to court, but Bonnie thought I should settle. She said if there was a trial, his lawyers would try to make me look like a slut, bring up my relationships. I was, you know, kind of wild and fluid back then, trying out different things. Bonnie was worried they'd put her on the stand."

"I hadn't come out yet at work," Bonnie said. "I wasn't ready."

"I get it," Rolly said. Bonnie had probably been right. Turning a woman's sexual history against her had been a tactic of lawyers since the beginning of time.

"Was it a decent settlement?" he asked.

"Not really," Joan said. "But it helped keep Sledge off my back."

"He stopped hassling you after that?"

"Pretty much." Joan nodded. "I kept working his shows, with no problems. Gerry Rhodes might've had something to do with that, too. He kept an eye on things, gave me jobs that kept me away from his boss. Gerry was a good guy, even when he was drunk."

Bonnie rubbed her chin absentmindedly, doing her own processing.

"Not the kind of guy you'd expect to shoot his best friend," she said.

"What's that?" Rolly asked, confused by the non sequitur.

"I pulled the case files on that shooting case," Bonnie said. "When Mr. Rhodes shot and killed Mr. Sparks at Sledge's studio. I read Rhodes's deposition. He didn't remember anything except waking up with the gun in his hand. The rest of the story came from Roger Sledge. He was the only eyewitness. He said there were two men. Sparks and somebody else. An accomplice."

"Did they ever find the other guy?"

"No, but I looked through the call roster for that night. Somebody called in about a man running across the tarmac at the airport and climbing over the fence. It was around the same time as the shooting."

"Did the cops follow up on that?"

"No one got a good look at the guy. There wasn't much they could do."

"You think this guy might've had something to do with the shooting?"

Bonnie shrugged.

"I think it's an interesting coincidence," she said. "I found out something else, too. Otis Sparks had a sister."

"I know," Rolly said. He pulled out his wallet, retrieved Mavis Worrell's business card and handed it to Bonnie.

"She runs a shop in Sherman Heights," he said. "Her name is Mavis Worrell."

"Afrocraft Co-op," said Bonnie, reading the card and processing Rolly's new information, contemplating chewing him out. Rolly had planned to tell Bonnie about Mavis Worrell. He just hadn't gotten around to it yet. He waited to see how angry she'd get.

"I told you there was a Black woman at the bar that night," Bonnie said, sounding mildly peeved but no more. "Talking to Gerry Rhodes."

"Yeah. You told me. I asked Mavis about that. She's Muslim. She doesn't drink."

"You don't have to drink to go into a bar."

"True." Rolly grunted. Mavis Worrell hadn't exactly answered his question about visiting the bar. She'd played the religious morality card instead of answering the question.

"We got a partial on that change purse," Bonnie said. "The prints matched Gerry Rhodes."

Rolly pulled on his earlobe as Bonnie pulled out her phone, took a photo of Mavis Worrell's business card and handed it back to him.

"I talked to that witness again," she said. "The one who saw Gerry Rhodes at the bar. With the Black woman. The witness said Gerry did something unusual that night, something he'd never seen him do before."

"What was it?"

"He had a drink. Four drinks, maybe five. According to my witness, Gerry Rhodes would come into the bar every night and order a shot of whisky. He'd stare at the drink on the bar but never touch it. It would still be there, a full glass, after he left."

"He fell off the wagon," Rolly said. He'd never tested his own sobriety so publicly and formally, but he understood the ritual Rhodes had created for himself. If you could resist for five minutes, defeat that first lurking impulse, you were halfway to victory. One test. One day at a time. And then one day, the road in front of you forked and you couldn't resist taking a detour. Something had changed for Gerry Rhodes that night at Bump's Tavern.

"There's something else, too," Bonnie said. "This witness says Rhodes gave an envelope to the bartender every night. I asked the bartender about it. He says he doesn't know what was in the envelope. He doesn't ask questions, just puts the envelope in the safe every night. And the next day it's gone. That two thousand dollars on the napkin could be some sort of receipt for the envelope."

"This is getting a bit Felonius Monk," Rolly said, wondering if Gerry Rhodes had been party to some criminal malfeasance. "I just want to figure out the guitar thing."

"You'd better be careful. When a guy who delivers sealed envelopes to a bar on a regular basis ends up dead . . ."

"Yeah. I know," Rolly said, wondering if he or Lucinda were in any danger. "Who owns the bar?"

"A company called Stryzaga Holdings."

Rolly remembered the name on the flight school sign on Sledge's building.

"There's a similar name on the outside of Sledge's building," he said. "At Gillespie Field. Stryzaga Flight School."

"I'll look into it," Bonnie said. They fell silent, each thinking their separate thoughts.

"So that's my Roger Sledge story," Joan said, breaking the silence. "Now you know the whole thing."

Rolly stood up to leave.

"If it's any consolation," he said, "you weren't the only one who sued Roger Sledge for sexual harassment."

"Doesn't surprise me at all," Joan said. "How many are there?"

"A lawyer friend of mine found eleven cases. Can't be sure they were all the same thing, but . . ."

"I'm pretty sure they were all the same thing," Joan said, shaking her head.

"And there's probably more who didn't sue him," Bonnie chimed in.

"Yeah," Rolly said. "Well, thanks for talking to me."

Bonnie stood up as he turned toward the door.

"I'll see you out," she said.

Joan stayed on the sofa. She seemed withdrawn, focused on some thoughtful quandary. Rolly hoped he hadn't brought up something too painful. No one felt nostalgia for their past fears and anxieties, but sometimes they felt a need to raise their voice. Bonnie opened the front door and followed Rolly out to his car.

"There's something else you should know about," she said as Rolly jangled his keys and reached for the driver's-side door. He paused and leaned across the top of the car.

"What's that?" he asked. Bonnie leaned across the car from the other side and lowered her voice.

"This is between you and me," she said. "You can't tell Joan. You can't tell anybody, ever. The real reason I didn't want Joan to take Sledge to court, why I didn't want to appear on the stand. You swear not to tell anyone?"

"Scout's honor." Rolly nodded and waited while Bonnie organized the story in her head.

"It pissed me off," she said. "All that stuff Joan was dealing with, with Sledge. He was really a jerk, grabbing her ass, making remarks and stuff, aggressively cornering her. I wanted to confront the guy, but Joan didn't want me to do anything. She thought she'd lose her job if she complained. Sledge was in charge. He was her boss. She really wanted to do concert work, learn the ropes. It was a great opportunity. But she was miserable. I had to do something."

"What'd you do?"

"I was on patrol back then, only a couple of years on the force. Single patrol. I found Sledge's business address and parked my cruiser out there one night. I saw him leaving in his car, pulled him over when we got to a quiet spot. I told him to get out of the car, made him spread-eagle with his hands on the roof. I ... Christ, why am I telling you this?"

"I get the idea," Rolly said. Bonnie had saved his life more than once. He owed her for that. "I won't tell anyone."

Bonnie hadn't finished, though. She could be as reticent as anyone he'd ever met, but today she needed to own up to her mistakes. It was a rare reversal in their relationship. Rolly was on the other side of the confessional screen.

"I've always tried to be a good cop," Bonnie said.

"You're a damn good cop," said Rolly. "Always have been. Even if you do give me a lot trouble."

"It's usually for your own good."

"I know."

Bonnie crossed her arms, then uncrossed them, trying to find a comfortable position. Rolly waited. He knew this was important.

"I've never done anything like that, before or since," Bonnie said. "I abused my power. I might have lost my job if anyone had found out."

"What did you do?"

"I took out my gun, when I was behind him and he was grabbing the roof. I stuck it up his ass and told him that he was going to talk to his lawyer and offer Joan a settlement, that if I heard anything else about him hassling my girlfriend, I'd ... I'd find him again and shoot him in the balls."

It was Rolly's turn to whistle. Bonnie had always been intense, but this one took the cake.

"I guess it worked," he said. He chuckled, dumbfounded by Bonnie's confession. "He stopped hassling her."

"I didn't need to do that," Bonnie said. "I didn't need to go that far."

"Did Sledge say anything after you put the gun up his ass?"

"No. But I think he peed in his pants."

17

THE NIGHTCLUB

Bump's Tavern was the kind of strip-mall venue The Blasters had celebrated in their song "Flat Top Joint." The ceiling was low, even lower when you stood on the stage. Guitarists had to be careful not to bring their guitars up over their head or they'd risk ramming the headpiece into the ceiling, dislodging the acoustic tiles and raining dust, chalk and probably asbestos down on their heads. Rolly had long ago abandoned any Pete Townshend leaps or showy guitar moves, so the low ceiling wasn't a problem. He didn't drink anymore, either, which made him less likely to forget himself and do something stupid.

Bump's clientele leaned toward an over-fifty set that liked beer and classic rock. Rolly hadn't played the club in years, but J.V. Sideman's guitar player was sick, and Sideman had called Rolly to sit in. It was an easy way to make a hundred bucks and, perhaps, learn something about Gerry Rhodes's last night at the bar. He'd been happy to give up his plans for the evening— packing for the move to his mother's house. He sent a message to Lucinda, suggesting she could stop by the club after her shift, but she hadn't responded.

Moogus sat behind the drums and Sideman's bass player, Bruce, was solid as a rock. All professionals. No attitude. Not onstage, anyway. Rolly knew every song on Sideman's set list, most of them shuffle blues or sixties soul hits. The band was halfway through its third set and the audience had been lively and attentive. But the over-fifty crowd needed their beauty sleep and the crowd had dwindled to a handful of people. A few late arrivals kept the band going.

One of those late arrivals was Svetlana, the blond-haired siren with the faulty whistle. She arrived with her chauffeur, Sergei, and the man in the wheelchair who'd sat front and center at the Music Box concert. Rolly assumed their appearance had something to do with Moogus, but when the band took a break, Svetlana beckoned to him.

"I am Svetlana," she said, extending an elegant, well-manicured hand. Her fingernails were a purplish red. At least they looked that color in the dingy club lighting.

"Rolly Waters," Rolly said, shaking her cool porcelain hand. "I think we met yesterday."

Svetlana's face went as blank as a department store mannequin.

"I came to see Mr. Sledge yesterday," Rolly said. "At the house. You were just leaving."

"Oh yes," Svetlana replied, sounding unconvinced. "I must be glad to see you."

"And I'm glad to see you." Rolly didn't know if he should feel offended or gratified that he'd made so little impression. Younger women rarely paid any attention to him anymore. Not since he'd passed forty.

"I mean, what is to say . . ." Svetlana continued, trying to find the words in English. "I mean it is good for me to see you. To hear someone who plays music as you do."

"Thank you," Rolly said, deciding it was a compliment.

"I am singer but I would like to play the guitar also. Like Ruby Dean."

"Yeah, Ruby's great," Rolly said, wondering if Svetlana knew about his connection to Ruby Dean and was angling for an introduction, which he couldn't, and didn't want to, provide.

"This is my uncle, Dmitri," Svetlana continued, indicating the man in the wheelchair, who gave a curt nod. "And this is my driver, Sergei."

The chauffeur, Sergei, looked at Rolly with pinpoint eyes, as if sighting a target.

"We have met," Sergei said. "At the flight school. I tell you to leave."

"Yes," Rolly said. "That was me. I was looking for Mr. Sledge."

"For why do you want Mr. Sledge?" Sergei asked.

"It's not important," said Rolly. "I was able to find him at home."

The chauffeur continued to study Rolly with narrow slate-gray eyes.

"Sergei," Uncle Dmitri said, as if calling off a dog. Sergei glanced over at Svetlana, and she at him. Some secret message passed between them and died. Uncle Dmitri turned his attention to Rolly.

"Forgive my assistant, Mr. Waters. He is very protective of my niece. As you know, Mr. Sledge is her manager."

"And her husband."

"Yes." Dmitri sighed like a reluctant uncle. Rolly felt as if he were being herded into a trap by three jackals.

"Sergei was pilot, you see," Dmitri continued. "In Russian air force. He flies MiG fighter planes. Like many pilots, he has eyes of the hawk. He must always watch if someone is friend or foe."

"You don't need to worry about me," Rolly said, giving them his best smile. "I'm always friendly."

"I agree with my niece," said Dmitri. "You are a fine guitar player. I am glad we came to hear you tonight. That is a Fender Telecaster you are playing, is it not?"

"Yes," Rolly said, glancing back at the stage and wishing he were on it. "I have several guitars."

"How do you choose which guitar to play for each occasion?"

"Intuition, I guess." Rolly shrugged. "The Telecaster seemed right for tonight."

"Mr. Albert Collins, he played such a guitar," Dmitri said, "A Telecaster."

"Yes," Rolly repeated, surprised by the old man's familiarity with the Ice Man. Dmitri explained further.

"I am a connoisseur," he said. "Of the blues guitar. You would not expect this from a man such as me, would you?"

"I don't expect it of anyone." Rolly shook his head, expressing a small measure of wonderment. The old guy might be okay. "I don't meet many people who've even heard of Albert Collins, let alone know what kind of guitar he played."

Uncle Dmitri smirked, pleased with his demonstration of cultural refinement.

"Your playing reminds me of Albert Collins," he said. "I hear Freddie King too, and perhaps Peter Green."

"I'm flattered by the comparisons," Rolly said. "You're quite an aficionado."

"You are not as genius as any of them, of course," Dmitri continued. "But you are very good. I enjoy your performance. So did my niece. Is that not correct, Solnyshkuh?"

Svetlana nodded enthusiastically. Rolly wished Svetlana sang better in case he was called upon to return the compliment. From what he'd heard so far, the only vocalist he could compare her to was some slurry blend of Pia Zadora and Yoko Ono.

"Sergei here, on the other hand," said Dmitri, tilting his head toward his assistant, "I believe he finds your music to be like torture. He would rather be in one of those clubs with the DJs and dancing and lights."

Sergei didn't respond to the old man's gibe. Rolly could

sense the fighter pilot underneath, steely, no-nonsense, implacable. A hard nut to crack open. Not that Rolly wanted to do any cracking. Uncle Dmitri was in charge of the conversation. He was the big dog. His niece and his assistant were supporting players, contemplating their drinks and waiting to see where his wind blew.

"Is your guitar worth a great deal?" Dmitri asked. Rolly shrugged.

"Not really," he said. "It's a 1950s reissue. I modded it a bit, replaced the original pickups with Seymour Duncans and had the frets sanded down to improve the action."

"How much would you say the guitar is worth?"

"Maybe a thousand dollars." Rolly shrugged. "Tops."

"Would this be a good guitar for my Svetlana?"

Hearing her name, Svetlana lifted her gaze from the table and acted like she was interested in the conversation again.

"Well . . ." Rolly said, glancing between Dmitri and his niece while he searched for a diplomatic answer. "I've modified this one for my personal playing style. I'd probably choose something else for a beginner. You can pick up a new, and perfectly good, Telecaster for under a thousand bucks."

"Price is no object," Dmitri replied. "Not for my Svetlana. She has told me there is a guitar she would like me to buy for her. The Ruby Dean signature model made by the Taybor Guitar Company."

"That's an acoustic guitar," Rolly said. "Electric acoustic, I think. Not like a Telecaster."

"Yes. That is what I tell her, but she insists she must have this guitar. Because it is from Ruby Dean."

"Ruby Dean is my exemplar," Svetlana chipped in. "She writes own songs and plays the guitar. She is beautiful, too. Like a musical goddess."

Rolly nodded, checked his watch and glanced back toward the stage. He didn't want to pick sides in an argument between Svetlana and her uncle. Svetlana had a long way to go before she got close to Ruby Dean's level, except in the looks department.

"You should ask Mr. Sledge," he said, wondering if Sledge had any communication with Ruby these days. Probably not. "He managed Ruby. He might have an opinion on what guitar Svetlana should play. Or even if she should play."

"Mr. Sledge works for me," Dmitri said, asserting his authority in the matter. "I am paying the bills."

Rolly nodded. Svetlana had talked her rich uncle into financing her dream. And Sledge had bamboozled the old man with razzle-dazzle stories of the music business, happy to take him for the money. Dmitri didn't seem like a fool, though. He must be aware of Svetlana's vocal limitations. He did it for love and for family. Rolly had fallen into their orbit and needed to find his escape velocity. He came up with an answer he hoped would release him.

"There's no perfect guitar," he said. "Everyone's different. You have to try some things first. It's really a personal choice."

Dmitri gave another smirk, acknowledging Rolly's answer, but still unsatisfied.

"You are a clever *chelovek*, Mr. Waters," he said. "I would like to ask you to assist my Svetlana in the purchase of a new guitar. You will pick the best one for her."

"I'm not sure . . ."

"I would pay you for this service, of course," Dmitri continued. "So that it is not a burden for you. You are a musician. I know you must make a living."

Rolly considered the offer a moment. Yes or no, either answer would create problems. He decided on the one that included money.

"Okay." He nodded. He glanced at the stage again. The band had started to assemble. "I need to get back now. We can talk later."

He turned and made his way to the relative safety of the stage, feeling the three sets of eyes staring at him, burning like lasers into his back. He strapped on his guitar and turned on his amp. It was good to be back up onstage. It was a place he felt safe. He glanced over at Moogus sitting behind the drums. Moogus raised his eyebrows and leaned his head in toward Rolly.

"Be careful, buddy," he said. "That bunch is trouble."

Sideman counted off and the band launched into "Barefootin'" by Robert Parker. Fortunately for Rolly's peace of mind, Svetlana and her retinue left before they played the last song of the night, a version of Sam & Dave's "I Thank You" that lived in the space between the original and ZZ Top's version. He packed up his guitar and walked to the bar, where he asked for a club soda with lime. His phone buzzed. He picked it up, checked the message. It was from Lucinda.

Can't make it tonight. Had to work overtime. Want to go flying with me tomorrow?

18

THE PILOT

Archibald's Café sat on the southwestern edge of Gillespie Airfield in El Cajon, not far from Roger Sledge's former recording studio. Rolly and Lucinda sat at a corner table on the café's patio, looking out at the Cessnas and Pipers and small turboprop airplanes that were parked on the apron. A chain-link fence separated the café from the aircrafts. A gate with a keypad allowed those who knew the code to enter and leave the café via the airfield.

"How's the food here?" Rolly asked, contemplating the over-sized menu he held in his hands. It was ten thirty in the morning, the witching hour between breakfast and lunch. He didn't do brunch.

"Terrible." Lucinda laughed. "But there's plenty of it."

Rolly decided to split the difference and take his chances with the breakfast sandwich on an English muffin. He placed the cumbersome menu on the table and scanned the area while he waited for Lucinda to indicate she was ready to order. The airport's control tower stood two hundred feet behind them, its glass-encased control room overlooking the café. A red biplane hurtled down the runway and juddered into the sky. Lucinda placed her menu on the table.

"You sure you don't want to go up with me?" she asked.

"Maybe another time," Rolly said. "I'm kind of busy today."

"I'm only going up for an hour. Just getting in some flight time to keep my skills up. I got my solo license last month. It's different from flying on a commercial jet. It's beautiful and peaceful up there."

"So you've told me."

The waitress arrived and took their orders. Lucinda reached across the table and began rearranging the packets of sugar and sweeteners.

"What'd you find out?" she asked, organizing the packets by color. "About my dad?"

"I've got good news and bad news," Rolly said. "The good news is I might've found the guitar you were looking for. The bad news is someone else owns it. He has a strong claim on it, anyway. Your father owed money to this guy. He used the guitar to pay off his debt."

Lucinda leaned back in her chair and sighed. She sipped her iced tea through a straw.

"I can't say I'm surprised," she said, shrugging her shoulders. "Dad was always running out of money. Especially when he was drinking and doing drugs. Who's this guy he sold it to?"

"His name's Roger Sledge,"

"I've heard that name," she said. "Didn't my dad used to work for him or something?"

Rolly nodded.

"I talked to Mr. Sledge," he said. "He showed me the IOU from your dad. For two thousand dollars."

"When did he sign the IOU?" Lucinda asked.

Rolly searched his memory.

"Nineteen ninety-seven, if I remember right."

"That's after my mom and dad got divorced. Was there a sales receipt?"

"No," Rolly said. "I learned something else that might be related."

"What's that?"

Rolly paused for a moment, trying to think of the best way to tell Lucinda her father might've fallen off the wagon.

"Your dad was at a bar called Bump's the night before he died," he said. "It's just down the street from his apartment. The police found a cocktail napkin from Bump's with a number written on it. Two thousand dollars. The same amount as the IOU your father paid off with the guitar."

"You think he was trying to buy it back?"

"No idea," Rolly said. "It could've been anything. It's not an unusual number."

Lucinda slumped back in her chair.

"Was he drinking?"

"That night, yes. Other nights, no."

"What does that mean?" Lucinda said, sounding cross with him. "Just tell me what happened."

Rolly paused. He didn't want to be the bearer of bad news, but that's what he was. Detective work was sometimes that way.

"Your father went into the bar every night," he said. "Gave the barman an envelope and ordered a shot of whisky. He'd stare at the whisky for a few minutes and then leave. Never touched it. Like he was testing himself. Except that night. That night he drank the shot and had several more."

Lucinda fiddled with her silverware, processing the information.

"What was in the envelopes?" she asked.

"We don't know. The barman puts the envelopes in a safe."

Rolly considered the possibilities. Gerry Rhodes conducted some sort of regular business with Bump's, delivering envelopes. If there was money in the envelopes, it might explain the number on the cocktail napkin. It was a receipt. But none of that explained why Gerry Rhodes fell off the wagon that night.

"Your dad talked to someone at the bar that night," Rolly said, remembering the details of Bonnie's report. "A middle-aged Black woman. Does that ring any bells with you?"

Lucinda shook her head.

"No," she said. "He would've told me if he was seeing some-one. He couldn't keep a secret like that. He was in hock most of his life, to one person or another. Maybe he owed the woman money."

They paused for a moment as the waitress arrived with their food. Rolly took a bite of his egg sandwich, peeled off the top piece of toast and garnished the eggs with a shake of Tabasco. He was going to drop a bomb on Lucinda. The explo-sion might hit her hard.

"Did you know your dad shot and killed someone?" he asked.

"What?"

"It was a long time ago. Thirty-five years ago. It was ruled self-defense."

Lucinda put down her fork and stared at the planes outside the fence.

"I remember hearing something like that from my mom," she said. "I rarely saw my dad back then. We lived out of state. I asked him about it later, when I was grown up, but he said nothing like that ever happened to him, that my mom was confused. Who was it he killed?"

"The man in that photograph you gave me. His name was Otis Sparks."

"Why did Dad shoot him?"

"Sparks broke into the Sledge's recording studio one night when Sledge was his manager. Your father was there. Sparks was angry with Sledge and threatened to kill him. There might have been someone with Sparks. A friend or some muscle."

"Isn't Roger Sledge the guy my dad sold the guitar to?"

Rolly nodded. He took a few more bites of his sandwich

while Lucinda digested the new information. She sighed and wiped a tear from the corner of her left eye.

"Was my dad on drugs when he shot the guy?"

"I don't know," Rolly said, which was true. Bonnie hadn't found anything about drugs in the report, but given Gerry Rhodes's history, it seemed likely.

"Do you think Jimi Hendrix really owned that guitar?" Lucinda asked. She seemed defeated, aggrieved. "You think my dad was lying to me about that too?"

"We'll find out soon enough," Rolly said. "Sledge is having his collection appraised. I know the guy who's doing the appraisal. I sent him a copy of your dad's backstage pass. He said he'd let me know how the appraisal comes in. He might want to talk to you."

Lucinda nodded. They ate in silence for a moment, thinking separate but perhaps similar thoughts. Rolly looked out past the fence and watched as a man inspected a private jet, ducking under its shadow and fiddling with something under the wings. The man moved into the sunlight and climbed up the stairway into the jet.

"It's Sergei," he said.

"What's that?" Lucinda asked.

"That man who just got in that jet," Rolly said. "I've met him before."

"You mean the Gulfstream?" Lucinda said, pointing in the direction of the jet. Rolly nodded.

"Nice plane," said Lucinda. "Those things can do over five hundred miles per hour. I hope I get a chance to fly a jet someday."

"This guy was fighter pilot in the Russian Air Force," Rolly said.

"Is that his jet?"

"It belongs to his boss, I think," Rolly replied. Sergei was Uncle Dmitri's chauffeur and Svetlana's keeper. He might also fly jets for his boss. Dmitri had the money and Sergei had the training. Sergei left the cockpit and climbed down from the jet, headed back toward the warehouse behind it, opened the door and went in. Rolly looked over the landscape, getting his bearings, and decided that Sergei had gone in through the back door of the flight school, Sledge's old studio. He remembered the name on the front of the building.

"Do you know anything about the Stryzaga Flight School?" he asked, turning back to Lucinda.

"I stopped by there once," said Lucinda. "They didn't seem interested in giving me lessons. Is that guy a flight instructor?"

"Could be," Rolly said, rubbing the stubble on his chin. "He works for this old guy in a wheelchair. Dmitri. Dmitri's niece wants to be a pop star. Her name's Svetlana. Dmitri's paying Roger Sledge to be her manager. She's married to Sledge."

"What does this have to do with my dad?"

"Nothing. Probably. I don't know. Maybe."

Lucinda stared at Rolly a moment, as if reevaluating his mental fitness. As it turned out, she was thinking about something else.

"Listen," she said. "I know this might be inappropriate, but would you be willing to go on a date with me? It wouldn't be like a date date."

"What is it?"

Lucinda poked her hash browns with a fork. "There's this hospital thing, a fund-raising banquet. This other nurse can't make it and asked me to go in her place. I'd like to do it, but I don't want to go by myself. I don't know anybody in town I could ask. I've only been here a few months. Between working at the hospital and taking care of my dad, I haven't had much time for getting out and meeting people. Going on dates."

As a declaration of romantic interest, it didn't amount to much. Rolly resisted the impulse to make a smart remark and went with his standard response.

"I try not to date clients, at least while I'm working for them."

"I could pay you, like it's part of the job."

The stakes had been raised, but something didn't feel right. Lucinda appeared to be a well-functioning adult who could handle being alone at a party. She didn't need a chaperone.

"It's just that . . ." Lucinda said, the tone of her voice suggesting she needed to come clean. "There's this doctor at the hospital who's been bugging me to go with him. I told him I was bringing a boyfriend. I can't show up alone. He'll be on to me."

Rolly nodded.

"When is the banquet?" he asked.

"Saturday. It's a lunch thing. I could pay you."

Rolly ran through his mental calendar. He still hadn't packed for his move to his mother's house. But he'd make an excuse for a maiden in distress.

"He's a good doctor," said Lucinda, explaining her predicament in more detail. "He's even kind of good-looking, but he's a pain in the ass. Anytime we're in a room together, with no one else there, he asks for a date, telling me how great he is in bed."

"Have you spoken to your supervisor or HR?"

"I've only been there three months. He's been there ten years. I don't feel like I've got any leverage, you know?"

"Yeah, I understand," said Rolly. She was right. Rank and experience would weigh in the doctor's favor. Lucinda would go on record as a troublemaker. He nodded. "I'll do it. You don't have to pay me."

"Thank you," said Lucinda. "I'm just hoping that if he sees me with someone, maybe he'll lay off."

"You want me to flash my PI credentials at him?"

"Ooh." Lucinda laughed. "That might be good. He'll think I'm having him investigated. I'll send you the details. I really appreciate this."

That decided, the two of them returned to their food. Lucinda asked Rolly about his musical career, and why he'd become a detective. He told her most of the truth, about the car accident that made him stop drinking, how he'd fallen into the private-eye business because of the accident, working in Max Gemeinhardt's office and then getting his license. Lucinda seemed genuinely interested. Rolly was glad he'd agreed to attend the banquet. She was a good one. There weren't many of them around, fewer every year for an aging rock musician. He'd given up on settling down with someone, but if a woman like Lucinda was still available, there might be hope. He'd go to the banquet. They could consider a real date once their business was over.

Rolly looked up as a man in a gray jumpsuit entered the patio through one of the gates. He caught the man's eye and they stared at each other a moment. The man turned away and went into the café. Rolly had met him before. The man's name was King. FBI agent King.

19

THE CHURCH

Rolly pulled his Subaru Outback into the parking lot of St. Nicholas, the Russian Orthodox church down the street from Bump's nightclub. He turned off the engine, sat for a moment and considered the odds of encountering two FBI agents, working undercover, in the same week. Agents Goffin and King were a team he'd dealt with before. Were they investigating Roger Sledge, Dimitri or both men? And, most importantly, did Gerry Rhodes's death have any connection to their investigation? Did the FBI know about the envelopes Gerry delivered to the bartender at Bump's every night? Did they care? He decided his best course of action would be to call in to the local FBI office and try to set up a meeting. He was on the agents' radar now, anyway.

That was for later. Right now, Rolly wanted to learn more about Gerry Rhodes's final days. Rhodes had worked at the church, lived on the grounds. Someone there must have had regular contact with him, someone who might have noticed changes in his mood or behavior. Rhodes might have sought counsel with the church's priest.

Rolly climbed out of his car, walked to the front door,

tugged on the ornate handle and entered the church. As houses of religion go, it was modest, with a vaulted wood ceiling and rows of wooden pews. Behind the pulpit, a wide wooden cabinet featured iconographic paintings of the holy family and saints embellished in gold leaf. He walked down the center aisle and paused as he reached the front pews.

"Hello?" he called. His voice echoed back from the rafters. "Is anyone here?"

The room was quiet. He called out again. Something clanked beyond the open doorway off to his left. He heard footsteps and waited to see what kind of creature had stirred from its nest. A man appeared in the side doorway, attired in black. He looked to be in his early sixties, bald, with pinkish skin and a long gray beard.

"May I help you?" the man inquired, his voice revealing a light tremor. "I'm Father Orloff. I am the bishop here."

"My name's Rolly Waters," said Rolly, retrieving his business card. "I'm a private investigator. I wanted to ask you about a man named Gerry Rhodes. I understand he lived on your property."

"Yes, Mr. Rhodes," said the bishop. He glanced at the card Rolly had given him. "We shall miss him here at St. Nicholas."

"Did you know him personally?"

"Oh yes, I hired Mr. Rhodes."

"What did he do?"

"He took care of the audiovisual system, set up the public address system in the community room for special events. He was a janitor and a bit of a handyman, fixing things that needed to be fixed. Electrical. Maintenance work."

Rolly nodded. It was no different from what he'd heard from Lucinda.

"Did he show any signs of drinking or drug abuse?" he asked.

"Why do you ask?" asked Father Orloff.

"Mr. Rhodes had a history of alcoholism."

"Who are you working for, Mr. Waters?" Orloff said. "Why are you so interested in this man?"

"His family hired me to handle Mr. Rhodes's estate," Rolly said, which was a bit grandiose, but close enough to sound feasible. Gerry Rhodes didn't have enough of an estate to require handling, not by professionals, anyway.

"I see," the bishop said, though Rolly could tell he didn't buy the story. "Mr. Rhodes was a repentant man. He told me some of his history, about his sins. He told me he'd freed himself from drugs and the bottle. I saw nothing in his behavior that would indicate otherwise."

"He was a good employee?"

"Oh yes. A quiet and mild-mannered man, always eager to do what needed to be done."

"What would you say if I told you Mr. Rhodes went to the bar up the street regularly?"

The bishop frowned.

"I would say that's unlikely," he declared. "I never saw Gerry drunk. He was a repentant man."

"Did he have money troubles? Did he mention any debts?"

The bishop shook his head.

"Again," he said, "nothing that I'm aware of."

"You don't know anyone he might've owed money?"

"No."

Rolly paused and surveyed the room.

"It's a beautiful church you have here."

"It is not elaborate, but it is enough. The faith of our parishioners is strong."

"You mentioned a community room?"

"Yes, there is a separate community room, as well as some offices in back for the clergy and other employees."

"Did Mr. Rhodes have an office?"

Father Orloff stroked his gray beard.

"He had a desk in the storeroom."

"Could I see it?"

Orloff stroked his beard again, contemplating how much access he was willing to provide to a stranger. He looked at Rolly's business card again.

"I was not aware Mr. Rhodes had any family," he said. "He never spoke of them."

"One child," said Rolly. "His wife passed some years ago."

"And it is his progeny who have hired you?"

"Yes," said Rolly. "I am looking for something very specific, something Mr. Rhodes claimed to have owned, before his passing."

"What is this thing?"

"A guitar. An electric guitar."

Father Orloff raised his eyebrows in surprise. It wasn't the answer he'd expected or probably even imagined. He continued to contemplate Rolly's business card.

"And you think Mr. Rhodes might've stored this guitar here?" he said. "At the church?"

"I don't know," said Rolly. "If he didn't, he might've left some information about it. I wouldn't be doing my job if I didn't check for it here."

"Very well," said Father Orloff. He led Rolly through the side door, then down the hall before he paused in front of the storeroom, which was about twice the size of Rolly's closet at home. The storeroom was lined with shelves of toilet paper, light bulbs and other necessities. A section of one of the lower shelves had been cleared for a makeshift desk and a rolling chair. A two-drawer metal file cabinet sat under the desk.

"This is where Mr. Rhodes worked," Father Orloff said. "As you can tell, there's no guitar here."

"What's in the file cabinet?" Rolly asked.

"Contracts, manuals, warranties, that kind of thing," Orloff said.

"Do you mind if I look?"

"Help yourself."

Rolly entered the room, knelt in front of the filing cabinet, and opened the top drawer. He flipped through the hanging files but found nothing of interest. The lower drawer proved equally insignificant. All business. Nothing about the man who had worked there. Rolly stood up and surveyed the shelves.

"What's that?" he asked, pointing at what looked like a shoe box in the corner of the top shelf.

Father Orloff looked at the box, pondered its existence for a moment, then shook his head.

"I don't know," he said.

"Okay if I . . .?"

"Yes, yes," said the father, sounding impatient. His regular schedule had been interrupted by an interloper who had already taken up too much of his time.

Rolly reached into the corner, went up on his toes and tried to grab the shoe box, but it was still inches away. He tensed his legs and jumped, adding a couple of inches to his reach. His fingers caught the lid of the shoe box and he gave it a tug. The box slid off the shelf, hit him on the head and crashed to the floor. Father Orloff grunted in alarm.

"Sorry," Rolly said. He squatted down to retrieve the shoe box and collect its spilled contents, a dozen or so cassette tapes. As he placed the tapes back in the box, he glanced at the labels. Two of them caught his attention. The first was a Ruby Dean tape, the official release of her first album. The second item was a cassette with the name *OTIS* spelled out in felt-tipped ink on both sides of the casing. He placed the shoe box on the desk but kept the second tape.

"Did you find something?" asked Father Orloff.

"I'm not sure," said Rolly, rubbing his head where the corner of the box had struck him. "It could be something of interest. You don't have a cassette player in the building, do you?"

"I don't think so," said Orloff.

"Maybe there's one hooked up to the audio system?"

Father Orloff pursed his lips and stroked his beard.

"I think it's a CD player," he said.

"Probably," said Rolly. "You don't find many cassette players these days."

Rolly looked at the cassette tape. The more he thought about it, the more important he thought it might be. He didn't have a cassette player at home, but one of his musical friends might still own one. Marley Scratch was a good bet. He glanced up at Father Orloff and wiggled the cassette.

"Can I hold on to this for a little while?" he asked. "I'd like to hear what's on it."

Father Orloff stroked his beard.

"These may be items of a personal nature," he said, after a moment. "I do not feel it's appropriate to release them to you."

"It's only this one tape I want to hear," Rolly said, indicating the OTIS cassette. "I can sign something if you want a receipt."

"I do not know who you are," said the bishop. "Just this card you have shown me. I have no proof you are who you say."

Father Orloff's tone had become less congenial. His posture had stiffened. Rolly wondered if the bishop was concerned about something on the tape or just worried about the legalities of turning over Gerry Rhodes's property to a stranger.

"Did the police go through this stuff yet?" he asked.

"The police have been here, yes," Orloff replied. "They interviewed me."

"Did they go through this box?" Rolly asked, indicating the cassette tapes.

"Not that I'm aware of," said Orloff. "I did not see it myself until you pointed it out."

"Was it Detective Hammond?" Rolly asked. "Bonnie Hammond? Did she interview you?"

"I believe that was her name. Why?"

"I'm working with Detective Hammond, you see," Rolly said. "She'll vouch for me. Perhaps I should call her."

Rolly reached for his phone, but Father Orloff waved him off.

"You may take the tape," Orloff said. "Just the one. There is no need to bother the police about this."

"Thank you," said Rolly.

"Is there anything else?" Orloff asked. "I need to get back to my work."

"No," Rolly said, slipping the cassette into his jacket pocket. It never hurt to bring up the police. Even with priests. "I'm done. Thank you."

Father Orloff escorted Rolly back down the hall, pointing him to the interior door that led back into the church.

"You can let yourself out," he said.

"I appreciate your help, Father," said Rolly, extending his hand. Father Orloff looked bemused but shook anyway. Rolly turned and headed to the door.

"Mr. Waters?" said Father Orloff from behind him. Rolly turned.

"Yes?"

"I've just thought of something. It might be of interest to you, something Gerry told me recently, before he died."

"What's that?"

"He expressed his gratitude for the job, for the accommodations we provided."

"You mean the apartment?"

"Yes. I believe that's what he was referring to. He said he was grateful and that he was going to leave a sizable contribution to the church when he died."

"How sizable?"

"He didn't say. He seemed quite pleased with himself, as if he'd discovered some sort of treasure."

"He said he'd leave it in his will?"

"That was my impression. It seemed like a premonition, as if he knew he would die soon. Is that helpful?"

Rolly rubbed the stubble under his chin. Lucinda hadn't mentioned any sort of will. Did one really exist? Had Lucinda already found it? If so, why hadn't she mentioned it? Gerry

Rhodes appeared to have nothing of value in his possessions when he died. Was there a source of funds they hadn't discovered yet? Did Rhodes really have a claim on the Hendrix guitar?

"Yes," he said. "Thank you for telling me. How much did you pay Mr. Rhodes? What was his salary?"

"Two hundred dollars a week, plus the bungalow. He stayed there rent free."

"How did you come to hire Mr. Rhodes in the first place?"

"What do you mean?"

"Did you post the position somewhere? Did you advertise it?"

"Oh no. It was Mr. Lemotov who recommended Mr. Rhodes to us. I had mentioned to Mr. Lemotov about needing a maintenance person."

"Mr. Lemotov is a parishioner here?"

"Oh, yes. He's one of our biggest supporters."

"I'd like to get in touch with him," Rolly said. He reached in his pocket and pulled out his notebook. "Can you provide me with a contact number?"

"I would not want to do that," said Father Orloff. "Not without his permission. Mr. Lemotov is a successful businessman, very busy. He owns several buildings in the area, including that nightclub up the street."

"Bump's?"

"Yes. He also owns Bunin."

"What's that?"

"A restaurant. Georgian food. Exquisite borscht. Across the street from Bump's."

"What's Mr. Lemotov's first name?"

"Dimitri," said the bishop. "Our parishioners like to call him Uncle Dmitri."

20

THE MODEL SHOP

It was dark inside Bunin, a sharp contrast to the sunny weather of the early afternoon. Rolly blinked his eyes as he adjusted to the change in light. The restaurant didn't look busy. He checked his watch. It was just after one in the afternoon. A man walked out of the kitchen and spotted him.

"Good afternoon," the man said, playing host. "Are you with Svetlana?"

"Excuse me?" Rolly said. The host puckered his lips like a dried prune, then cleared his throat.

"I mean to ask, do you have reservation?" he asked.

"I wanted to talk to the owner," Rolly said. "What did you say about Svetlana?"

"My mistake," the host said. "I think you are other man. Are you selling something?"

"I'm looking for Mr. Lemotov," Rolly said. "Dmitri Lemotov."

"Mr. Lemotov is not here at the moment. May I give him message?"

"My name's Rolly Waters," Rolly said, pulling a business

card from his wallet. He'd decided on a soft approach. "It's about buying a guitar for his niece."

The man stared at Rolly's business card for a moment.

"It says here you are a private detective."

"I'm a guitar player, too. Mr. Lemotov knows me. We met at Bump's, across the street. I was playing there."

The man nodded. He walked to the host station, picked up the phone, tapped a number and informed the person on the other end of the line of Rolly's arrival. He nodded and hung up.

"Mr. Lemotov is next door at the hobby shop. He will send someone for you."

"I can hop over there," Rolly said.

"He would prefer that you wait here."

Rolly nodded and took a seat. He surveyed the room again. Three women, twenty-something blondes, sat at separate tables with male companions, none of whom looked younger than forty. Another blonde sat by herself, looking bored.

The front door opened. Sergei the bodyguard entered the restaurant, tightly wound and intransigent.

"You come with me," he said.

"I'm here to see Mr. Lemotov."

"Yes. The boss. You come with me."

Rolly followed Sergei out the door. They turned and walked fifty feet to the hobby shop next door, its display windows stacked with boxes of model airplanes and cars. The sign on the door said it was closed. Sergei stopped, turned to Rolly and held out his left hand.

"Please to give me your phone," Sergei said. Rolly didn't much like the idea of handing his phone over to Sergei, but refusing would only piss off the taciturn ex-jetfighter pilot. Rolly was in too far to retreat. He handed over his phone.

"All the way to back," Sergei said, opening the front door. "You will find Mr. Lemotov there. I keep phone with me."

Rolly walked into the shop. He passed by shelves filled with model kits—planes, trains and automobiles—and made his way to the sales counter. There was no one at the counter. The fluorescent lights above it cast a dingy blue glow. From somewhere in the back, the terrifying voice of Howlin' Wolf belted out "Smokestack Lightning."

"Mr. Lemotov?" Rolly queried the room, wondering if he should continue. Howlin' Wolf dropped his volume.

"Come in, Mr. Waters," a voice said.

Rolly made his way to the door where the voice had come from and peeked inside. Dmitri Lemotov sat in his wheelchair, staring through a magnifying desk light at a model of a military jet.

"Have a seat, Mr. Waters," he said, scraping at the plastic model with an X-Acto knife. Rolly took a seat on the other side of the desk. Lemotov put the knife down and inspected his work.

"This is MiG-27," he said, indicating the model. "Very important in Soviet military history. What do you think?"

"Very nice," Rolly said for lack of any alternative.

"Did you ever build models, Mr. Waters?" Lemotov asked.

"I tried it a couple of times," Rolly said. "When I was a kid. My dad bought me some kits. Destroyers and battleships. He was in the Navy."

"You did not enjoy the activity?"

"I was more interested in playing my guitar."

"Yes, of course," said Lemotov. "Music is a life's work. You would not have had time for something as common as model-making. There is no glory in it. Music is a noble calling."

"Sometimes," Rolly said. "Some nights, not so much."

Lemotov grunted.

"Before I was injured," he said, "I flew a plane such as this one. A MiG-27. In Afghanistan. I was shot down by the Mujahideen, with a Stinger missile your government provided to them. That is how I came by these injuries, unable to use my legs. I was dismissed from the air force. I could no longer fly. Perhaps that is why I take up this hobby. I have built different models, different MiGs, but I always come back to this plane. Because I almost die in one of these planes."

Lemotov paused to inspect another part of the model. He picked up a piece of sandpaper and rubbed it across the back edge of the jet's tail. Howlin' Wolf continued to sing over the speaker system, pleading for a spoonful of love.

"You wish to discuss a guitar for my niece?"

Rolly nodded. "Yes, but I have something I'd like to ask you about first."

"What is this?"

"I understand you introduced Gerry Rhodes to Father Orloff at the church," he said.

Lemotov finished sanding the back edge of the model and dropped the sandpaper on the desk.

"Yes," Lemotov said. "How is Mr. Rhodes?"

"He's dead," Rolly said.

The briefest of clouds passed over Lemotov's face.

"I am sorry to hear that," he said. "He seemed much improved the last time I saw him."

"When was that?"

"At the church, of course. I attend every Sunday."

"How did you know Mr. Rhodes?"

"He worked for me at one time."

"Doing what?"

"Oh, general things. Technical things. I own many properties in this area. The restaurant, this shop, and the massage parlor next door. The nightclub where I see you last night. I own them all. Mr. Rhodes was good at repairing things, electronics and such. I was fond of him. Did you know he used to work in the music business?"

Rolly nodded. Lemotov continued.

"Such stories. Mr. Rhodes worked with Ruby Dean. And

Jimi Hendrix. Is it not remarkable that one man worked with two such artists? But I must tell you honestly, he was not a dependable employee. He had many troubles with alcohol. But the stories he told, of his days working with musicians. Buddy Guy. Stephen Stills. Roy Buchanan. Did you know he ran monitors for Rory Gallagher's last American tour?"

"I know he worked for Roger Sledge."

Lemotov leaned back in his chair and stared at Rolly for a moment.

"Why do you do this detective work, Mr. Waters? It is a dirty business. Why do you not play guitar all the time?"

"I crashed my jet too," Rolly replied. "A long time ago."

"I do not understand."

"It's a personal thing."

Lemotov tapped his fingers on the desk like a drumroll, going from finger to finger. He leaned forward in his chair and studied the MiG model again.

"I am Russian by birth," he said. "But I grow up in Poland. I was not treated well in Poland during my youth. Every day I defend myself from Polish boys who attack me. But I also learn much about Polish culture and history. Do you know of the Stryzaga?"

"No," Rolly said, wondering how many stories he'd have to sit through before he could leave. Lemotov was not going to be a quick interview. The old man continued.

"In Polish mythology there is a beast called the Stryzaga. It is half-human, half-owl, with gray skin. It is a vengeful creature that flies through air and searches for those who have wronged or deceived it. It descends on their souls and rips them to pieces."

Rolly nodded and pressed his lips together, wondering if this story was a warning or just an old man's rambling. Perhaps it was both.

"When I was fighter pilot," Lemotov said, picking up the MiG model and inspecting his work, "I am like Stryzaga. I search and attack the enemy from above. I tear them to pieces. Sometimes when I was flying, I would think of those Polish boys, the ones who would hurt me. I imagine dropping my bombs on them, tearing them limb from limb. I would be like Stryzaga, getting my revenge."

Definitely a warning, thought Rolly. But he wasn't sure why. He hadn't expected that asking questions about Gerry Rhodes would be dangerous. His palms started to sweat as he recalled Moogus's warning from last night. *That bunch is evil.* The trick now was to get out of the shop with only a warning. He could outrun the old man in the wheelchair, but Sergei was at the front door, waiting for him. He had one more question he needed to ask.

"Did Mr. Rhodes ever tell you about a guitar he owned?" he said. "A Stratocaster that was played by Jimi Hendrix?"

Lemotov looked up from his model plane.

"You know of this guitar?" he asked, his eyes flashing like those of an owl that's detected a mouse. Or a Stryzaga spotting one of its victims.

"I may have found it," Rolly replied, trying not to bolt for the door.

"Where?"

"In Roger Sledge's guitar collection."

Lemotov leaned back in his chair, drumming his fingers again. Rolly suppressed an impulse to say more and waited for a response.

"I am curious, Mr. Waters. Why do you look for this guitar?"

"A client asked me to look for it."

"Does your client have some claim on it?"

Rolly weighed the question a moment. He needed to protect Lucinda.

"Probably not. The transfer from Mr. Rhodes to Mr. Sledge seems legitimate. I just want to tidy up some loose ends."

"I do not understand this term. 'Loose ends.' What does it mean?"

"I want to make sure Mr. Sledge is the rightful owner. I need to check out every possibility."

"Why do you come to me for this?"

"Mr. Rhodes worked for you. I know you do business with Sledge. Perhaps you heard something."

"What would I hear?"

"Something that would change Sledge's story, how he got the guitar, something that would indicate it was still Mr. Rhodes's property. To tell you the truth, I don't like Mr. Sledge. He takes advantage of people. Musicians mostly. I think he took advantage of Mr. Rhodes to get that guitar."

"You are Stryzaga too," he said. "You seek revenge."

"I'd call it justice more than revenge," Rolly said. He wondered if he was doing his job or just using up Lucinda's money, hoping to get something on Sledge. Lemotov stopped his finger drumming and leaned forward in his chair.

"This man Roger Sledge," he said. "He tells me he can get Svetlana contract with big record company. Me, I am happy to support my Solnyshkuh. I pay Mr. Sledge money to help her dream come true. He wishes to marry her, I say okay, as long as she is happy. Do you think Mr. Sledge has taken advantage of me?"

"I couldn't say," Rolly replied. He couldn't explain what Sledge saw in Svetlana, aside from her appearance, the kind of looks that made record label bosses drool. She'd need at least a modicum of musical talent to take the next step. She'd need to soften her Russian accent. To Rolly's ears, on both counts, it felt like a fool's errand.

Dmitri nodded and returned to his model airplane. The interview seemed to be over. Rolly rose from his chair.

"You will not forget, I hope," Dmitri said, twisting the X-Acto knife in his hands. "About my niece? You will help her select a guitar?"

"I won't forget," Rolly said. There was no way out now. "You have my card. Have her get in touch."

Dmitri smiled.

"I will do that," he said.

Rolly turned and walked out the door. Uncle Dmitri continued to bankroll Svetlana's career. Uncle Dimitri was an obstinate man.

21

THE AGENT

Rolly pulled into the driveway between his granny flat and his mother's house. As he stepped from the car, a black SUV pulled in behind him, blocking the driveway. He glanced at the license plate. It had government tags. The driver's-side door opened. A woman stepped out. It was the bartender from the Music Box two nights ago, better known to him as Agent Shelley Goffin of the FBI.

"Good afternoon, Mr. Waters," Goffin said. "We need to talk."

"What about?"

Goffin looked around the yard, then back to Rolly.

"I'd like to talk privately," she said. "How about we go inside?"

Rolly sighed and pulled out his house key.

"Come on, then," he said.

Agent Goffin followed him through the front door.

"Have a seat," Rolly said, indicating the Formica table in the kitchen.

"Thanks, but I'll stand," Goffin replied.

"Suit yourself." Rolly plopped his phone and keys on the

kitchen counter, grabbed a glass from the cupboard, opened the refrigerator and poured himself a glass of orange juice.

"Want any juice, coffee, water?" he asked.

"Sit down, Mr. Waters," Goffin said in terse response. Rolly took a seat at the kitchen table and tried to keep his composure. He'd learned from previous encounters that FBI agents often had more bark than bite.

"Where's your partner?" he asked, remembering Agent King in his navy-blue jumpsuit letting himself in through the gate at the airport café.

"What do you know about Dmitri Lemotov?" Goffin asked, brushing aside Rolly's provocation.

"Russian guy," Rolly said. "Used to be a MiG pilot. Owns property over in Allied Gardens. Goes to church every Sunday. Gives the church money. Also has a niece who's a terrible singer. You would've heard her at the Music Box a couple of nights ago when you were playing bartender."

"I heard her. What's your business with Lemotov?"

Rolly shrugged.

"I'm handling an estate case. The deceased was at one time an employee of Mr. Lemotov's. I hoped he might provide some information for me."

Agent Goffin pulled out a notepad, found the page she was looking for.

"You entered the Bunin restaurant on Waring Road about an hour ago."

"Yes."

"Then you left the restaurant and went into the hobby shop next door. Is that correct?"

Rolly nodded.

"What was your business there?"

"I needed some glue."

"Cut the crap, Mr. Waters," Goffin said, giving him the kind of look mothers give misbehaving children. "Just tell me what you were doing there."

"I was looking for information about the deceased. The family hired me to look for discrepancies in the estate."

"Such as?"

"That's between me and my client," said Rolly.

Goffin's nose twitched, as if a skunk had walked through the room.

"Did you speak with Mr. Lemotov?" she asked.

"Yes, I was able to speak with him."

"Did he provide you with any useful information?"

Rolly shrugged his shoulders.

"Not really. He likes to build model planes and listen to Howlin' Wolf."

Agent Goffin smiled like the crust on a thin slice of Wonder bread.

"And that's all?" she asked.

"No," Rolly said. "He also told me the deceased man used to work for him, that he had to let the man go, but was able to find him a job at the church down the street."

"How did the deceased die?"

"Took a knock to the head," Rolly said, wondering if the FBI agent already knew all this, if she was testing him. "Detective Hammond at the San Diego Police Department can fill you in. You remember her, right? She was involved in that dolphin case with us last year. The Navy SEAL who returned from the dead?"

"Yes, I remember Detective Hammond." Goffin wrote Bonnie's name in her notebook. "What was the deceased's name?"

Rolly considered the question. He had had no reason to withhold the name. Bonnie would give it to Agent Goffin anyway. Sharing information with FBI agents made them friendlier.

"Gerry Rhodes," he said. "He worked in the music business most of his life. He also worked for Lemotov, and then at the Russian church down the road from the restaurant, doing maintenance. He had a history of drinking and drug abuse, got sober, then fell off the wagon just before he died."

"How do you know that?"

"Someone saw him drinking at a bar near the church. How did you know I met with Lemotov?"

It was Goffin's turn to be reticent. She cleared her throat.

"All I can say is the FBI may, or may not, have eyes on Mr. Lemotov's businesses. Your license plate number was entered into our database after you went into the restaurant. I recognized your name when it came back, thought we'd better talk."

"Why are you staking out Lemotov?" Rolly asked. "What's he done?"

"What hasn't he done is more like it," Goffin said, rereading her notes. "Extortion. Racketeering. Dealing in stolen goods. Drug smuggling. Animal smuggling. We're building a case."

"So he's Russian mafia?"

Agent Goffin placed her notebook on the table and took a seat across from Rolly. A lecture was coming.

"The 'Russian mafia,'" Goffin said, making air quotes with her fingers, "is an amorphous entity, not nearly as organized as the press tries to make it. Lemotov is Russian and he's a crook. So yeah, he probably qualifies. But we haven't found any connections to a larger organization. He's done it all on his own."

"A self-made man," said Rolly. "How long has he been in the country?"

"Twenty years. He's naturalized now, took the oath."

"Is this why you were bartending at the Music Box?"

"Could be," said Agent Goffin. "I appreciate your discretion about that."

"Of course," Rolly said. "It was a good look for you. I didn't realize who you were until I got outside."

Agent Goffin gave him another toast-edge smile.

"Let's talk some more about Mr. Rhodes," she said.

"What about him?"

"Do you know anything that might indicate he was still working for Mr. Lemotov? This bar you said he went to regularly, was it Bump's?"

"That's the place," Rolly said.

"How long did he stay at the bar? Are you sure he was drinking?"

"I don't know for sure, I guess. We . . ."

"Yes?"

"Detective Hammond and I found a cocktail napkin in the canyon behind Bump's. There was a number written on it. Two thousand dollars. Gerry Rhodes often walked along the canyon when he went to Bump's."

Goffin scribbled something in her notebook and circled it twice.

"You think that's important?" Rolly asked. Goffin sifted through the information she was willing to share.

"Dmitri Lemotov is adept at moving his money around," she said, after a pause. "Mr. Rhodes might've been one of his mules."

Rolly's theory about the connection between the napkin and the guitar took its last breath and fell dead. Agent Goffin had confirmed his suspicions, which he hadn't shared with Lucinda.

"That would make sense," he said. "Rhodes left an envelope with the bartender every time he went into Bump's."

Agent Goffin scratched out a quick note.

"What else do you know about Mr. Rhodes?" she asked.

Rolly ran through his scattered thoughts, searching for something the FBI agent would find out about anyway. The Hendrix guitar was off the table for now. That was his secret, not a place for the FBI to start poking around. At the very least, he needed to consult with Lucinda before telling them about the guitar.

"Gerry Rhodes killed someone," he blurted.

"When was this?" Goffin asked, her attention surging like a tube amplifier.

"It was years ago," Rolly said. "Detective Hammond's got the case files."

Agent Goffin scribbled in her notebook again. Rolly waited until she'd finished. He had a few questions of his own.

"What do you know about Lemotov's niece?" he asked. "The one who was singing at the Music Box. Svetlana?"

Goffin shrugged.

"Not much," she said. "She's been in the country just over a year. Got a green card. Roger Sledge was her sponsor, then her husband. Probably arranged through the website."

"What website?"

"Svetlana.com. Russian brides. It's one of Lemotov's least criminal businesses."

"Oh," Rolly said. He remembered the host asking if he was with Svetlana when he entered the Bunin restaurant, the young blond women at the tables with older men. The picture was clearer. "You think she's really Lemotov's niece?"

"What do you think?"

"I don't think it matters." Rolly stood up from the table, then went and rinsed his glass in the sink.

"About that building near Gillespie Field, the flight school," Goffin said. "We'd prefer you stay away from it."

Rolly returned to the table and took a seat, remembering his encounter with the policeman.

"Did one of your people call the police on me a couple of days ago?"

Goffin smiled again. The bread crust was getting thinner each time.

"That was Agent King's idea. It seemed like the quickest way to get rid of you without revealing our operation."

"How'd you spot me? That street was deserted a half mile on either side."

"Like I said, Mr. Waters, we have eyes on all of Mr. Lemo-tov's businesses."

"Did your 'eyes' see those people in the Prius? The ones who slapped the sticker on the front door?"

Agent Goffin leaned forward, newly interested.

"What sticker?" she said.

"Round. Purple with white lettering. *PJL*. The passenger jumped out of the car, slapped the sticker on the front door and they took off."

"Can you describe them?"

"Two people. I think." Rolly shrugged. "One driver. One passenger. I didn't get a good look at them."

Agent Goffin opened her notebook again.

"PJL," she said, writing down the letters. "You have any idea what that stands for?"

"I did a Google search," Rolly said, shaking his head. "Found a Pakistani cricket league and some sort of printer file format. That's all I came up with."

"License plate?"

"Sorry," Rolly lied. Agent Goffin gave him a disdainful look, more out of disappointment than suspicion, he thought. He needed to look up the license plate soon, or get Bonnie to do it.

"There are security cameras on either side of the building," he said, trying to sound helpful. "Maybe your tech guys could break into the network."

Goffin sighed, liked she'd heard it before. People saw too many movies. They thought the FBI could do anything.

"It's a closed system," Goffin said. "No internet connection. I might be able to get a search warrant to look through the recordings. Or not. This is the first I've heard of the sticker. I'll need to check with my agents."

"It's probably nothing," Rolly said.

Agent Goffin kneaded her forehead as if trying to relieve a painful thought. She gave up, checked her watch, closed the notebook and rose from the table.

"I need to go," she said.

"Lovely to see you again, Agent Goffin," Rolly said, trying to sound sincere. Agent Goffin rolled her eyes and opened the door. She looked back at him.

"Consider this your warning, Mr. Waters," she said. "Don't do anything stupid. I don't need your private-eye antics screwing up my case. We've got people close to Lemotov. I don't want to have to pull them out because you started flapping your mouth."

Rolly remembered the man in the jumpsuit at the airport café.

"I saw Agent King," he said. "At the airport."

"Yes, he told me," Goffin replied. "We need you to stay away."

"I understand," Rolly said. "I'll be good. Should I be worried about Mr. Lemotov?"

"I don't think so," Goffin said. She smiled in an unpleasant way, as if the crust of the bread had gone stale. "But I wouldn't recommend getting up in his business too often. He might take you seriously."

22

THE CASSETTE

The gate on Sixth Avenue buzzed. Rolly grabbed the handle and opened the gate, then trudged up the stairs. He felt for the cassette tape in his pocket to make sure it was there. The door opened as he reached the landing at the top.

"Hey, brudda," said Marley Scratch.

"What's with all the boxes?" Rolly asked. Things had changed since the last time he'd visited Marley's loft.

"I gotta move out," said Marley.

"When?"

"End of the month. They finally sold the building. The new owners are going to tear it down and turn this place into a shiny tower. Half the space. Triple the rent."

Marley had lived in his downtown loft for as long as Rolly could remember. It was one of the last of the old buildings in the area. The bottom floor had once been the Apex music store, where Rolly's mother had purchased his first electric guitar, a Fender Mustang, when he turned fourteen. The area had always been a little grubby and had become worse over the years, which had allowed Marley to maintain the lease for two thousand square feet of loft space on the second floor for a song. But gentrification had come to the city center of late. Shiny tall office buildings and condominium towers had barged their way in. Marley's building would be one of the last to go. The same gentrification had pushed Norwood out of his original shop. There were a few pockets of resistance left, historical one-story buildings, but the land had become too valuable to support small businesses and bohemian digs.

"Where're you moving?" Rolly asked.

"Not sure yet." Marley shrugged. "I got a line on a place in National City or maybe out in Spring Valley. I'm putting most of the stuff in storage for now."

"That's a drag."

"Tell me about it. You're lucky I still got my cassette player set up. Music is the last thing that'll go. Can't live without it."

They walked past the cardboard boxes to the opposite wall, where Marley had his stereo system set up on wood shelves hung from brick walls. Old school. Marley switched on the power amp and turned back to Rolly.

"You got the tape?"

Rolly pulled the cassette tape out of his pocket and handed it to Marley.

"Otis," Marley said, reading the scrawled label. "What is this?"

"I'm not sure," Rolly replied. "That's why I need to hear it."

Marley opened the cassette player, dropped in the tape and pushed the play button. The leader hissed across the play head. Music came on. It sounded homemade, just a man and his guitar, playing a tune, perhaps his own tune. Otis Sparks. At least that's who Rolly assumed it was, given the name on the label. He'd heard some songs on the website. The voice sounded the same. It was pretty good as demo tapes go, better than most.

"Who is this?" Marley asked.

"His name's Otis Sparks. Played around town back in the seventies. You have a connection to him."

"I do?"

"Mavis Worrell at the Afrocraft Co-op on Market. She said you were selling some instruments there."

"Mavis, yeah, she's cool," said Marley. "But what's the connection?"

"Otis Sparks was her brother."

"No shit."

"He died in 1984. A man named Gerry Rhodes shot him. Got off on a self-defense plea. I'm working on Gerry Rhodes's estate, looking for some things that might've gone missing. I found that cassette in his office."

"This Rhodes guy was white, right? White guys always get to plead self-defense when they shoot a black guy."

"It was an office invasion," said Rolly. "That's all I know."

The song on the tape ended. There was some rustling about in the background and then Otis began his next song, a loose and relaxed number that could become something funky once a good band got a hold of it.

"Mavis never mentioned her brother to you?" Rolly said. "She made a website about him."

"No." Marley shrugged. "I don't remember anything like that."

"What else do you know about her? Other than the shop?"

Marley thought for a moment.

"She has me out once a semester to one of her classes at Grossmont College, to show my instrument collection. The African stuff. Musical Culture in the Black Experience. That's the name of the course. Something like that."

"Anything else?"

"Not really. She's out in the community a lot, involved in social justice things, building up the neighborhoods, Black pride, that kind of stuff. She's one of the good guys. Girls, I mean. Women."

Rolly nodded and continued to listen to Otis Sparks on the cassette tape. There was nothing on the tape yet that would provide any useful information to him. He listened to the sound of the guitar Otis played. It was an electric guitar, somewhat subdued, with a bright slapping sound that could be a Stratocaster. The second song came to an end.

"You get that one, Gerry?" Otis said on the tape. A more distant voice called back to him.

"All good," the voice said. "You wanna redo or move on?"

"I got a new one I want to try."

"Okay."

Rolly decided the other voice must be Gerry Rhodes. He'd been an audio technician, after all. Rhodes and Otis must have recorded the tape in Sledge's studio, with acoustical padding and expensive microphones. That's why the cassette sounded better than most. Otis was demoing songs, putting them out there for other singers to hear and maybe pick up for their own records. Other than touring, the only real money in the music business came from song royalties, which Otis would get if other singers recorded his songs. Perhaps Gerry Rhodes had loaned his Stratocaster to Otis for the session. The tape went silent for a couple of seconds, a clean silence without any studio noise. The mic came back on.

"This one's for you, Gerry," said Otis. "I hope you and Lizzie get back together." He started playing the guitar again, a two-chord jazz pattern, with what sounded like a ninth chord on the second of the two. Rolly couldn't say for sure without his own guitar handy. Otis began singing.

> "Got this feeling I can't describe
> A kind of hunger deep down inside
> Someday I'll get over it
> Someday I'll get over you.
> Blue flame burning deep down in my heart
> Growing colder since we've been apart

Someday I'll get over it
Someday I'll get over you."

"I've heard that song before," Marley said.

"So have I," said Rolly. "With a female voice. It was Ruby Dean's big hit."

"That little gal with the big hair?" Marley said. "She was from around here, right?"

"Yeah. That's the one. I gave her guitar lessons." It was strange to hear Otis Sparks singing Ruby's song—in a different style and register, but clearly the same song. There was something else strange about hearing it this way, but Rolly couldn't put his finger on it. He looked over at Marley. "You got your laptop somewhere? I need you to look up something for me."

"Sure," Marley said. He retreated to his bed, brought back a laptop computer, placed it on the shelf and opened it up.

"*Someday* by Ruby Dean," Rolly said. "That was the name of the album. What year was it released?"

Marley typed in his search, clicked through the website a couple of times.

"AllMusic says it was released in 2001," he said.

"Interesting," said Rolly. "Look up when Ruby was born."

Marley tapped through a few more pages.

"1980," he said.

"Otis Sparks died in 1984," Rolly said. "Ruby would've been four years old."

"Okay."

"Check the credits for the song," said Rolly, remembering the record on Gerry Rhodes's turntable. "Who does it say wrote the song?"

"Dean-slash-Sledge," Marley said when he found the information.

"That's what I thought. So how does a song Otis Sparks wrote and sang when Ruby Dean was four years old get credited to her and Roger Sledge?"

"They're white people," Marley said. "They stole it. He's Black and he's dead."

"That's what it sounds like to me," Rolly said. The song ended. Nothing else came up on the tape. The session had ended. Rolly hit the stop button and rewound the cassette to the beginning. He didn't need to play it again. A story was falling into place.

"I think Mavis Worrell met with Gerry Rhodes the night he died."

"Whoa," said Marley. "You don't think she killed the guy, do you?"

"No," said Rolly. "He was going to help her; maybe he wanted to atone for shooting her brother. I think he was going to give her this tape."

"I see where you're going with this," Marley replied. "If she had the tape, she could prove they stole her brother's song and sue for the royalties."

"Partial royalties, at least," Rolly said. "Maybe Rhodes wanted to make a deal with her so he could have a share of the money. He told his priest that he would leave something to the church after he died. My client thought it had something to do with a Jimi Hendrix guitar, but maybe it was this. He had that record, *Someday*, on his turntable when he died. He told my client that the song had been written for him."

"'This one's for you, Gerry,'" said Marley, repeating Otis's words on the tape. "Who's Lizzie?"

"I think that was his wife," Rolly said, mentally calculating the date. Lucinda would have been a little kid, no more than five years old, which meant Otis had written the song around the time her father and mother separated. It really was written for Gerry.

"Let me get this straight," Marley said. "This Otis guy, Mavis's brother, writes that song for Gerry. And this Gerry guy kills him?"

"That's right. Not that night I don't think, but not much later."

"Then Ruby Dean has a big hit with the song but doesn't give Otis any credit? She and this Sledge guy make all the money?"

Rolly nodded. Marley whistled.

"That's a hell of a story," he said. "You think Mavis could sue her and claw back those royalties?"

Rolly considered the question for a moment, sifting through the possibilities. Did he need to tell Lucinda before he talked to anyone else? It would be better if he could confirm some things beforehand. It was all speculation for now.

"I need to talk to Mavis again," he said.

"You want me to call her?"

"No worries," said Rolly. "I can handle it."

Marley cleared his throat.

"What is it?" said Rolly.

"I'd like to be there if that's okay," Marley said. "I could probably help."

"What're you talking about?"

"I didn't tell you the whole story, earlier, when you asked about Mavis. She called me after you showed up at the store. Wanted to make sure you were legit."

"Nothing wrong with that," Rolly replied. Marley seemed to have something else on his mind, though.

"I didn't know all this stuff about her brother," Marley said, rubbing his cheek. "Never even knew she had a brother."

"I wouldn't expect her to tell you." Rolly didn't understand why Marley sounded so reticent. That wasn't his style.

"Thing is," Marley continued, "I wasn't entirely telling you the truth when you asked about Mavis earlier. We've been seeing each other. We know each other in the biblical sense."

"How long have you been seeing her?" Rolly asked.

"Six or seven months now," Marley replied. "I swear I never

heard nothing about this before, her brother getting shot and all that."

Rolly nodded. Marley and Mavis seemed like a good match.

"Well," he said, thinking it over. "I guess you'd better come along too."

23

THE MEETING

Mavis Worrell opened the front door of her home in the Tierrasanta neighborhood, a ten-minute drive from Bump's Tavern. She was dressed more casually than she had been at the Afrocraft Co-op, sporting burgundy sweatpants and a Grossmont College sweatshirt. Her hair was tied back in a scarf.

"Come in," she said, her eyes red from irritation, either allergenic or emotional, but Rolly suspected the second, her brother's death newly refreshened. When they'd phoned, she'd tried to put off meeting with him, but Marley's tender entreaties won the day, her initial reticence about hearing her brother's voice on the tape overcome by curiosity.

Marley stepped through the door first and hugged Mavis. Rolly followed them into the living room, which had been rescued from its neutral corporate furniture by the bright colors of African blankets spread on top of the sofas as well as the contemporary African art and sculpture that dotted the room. A multi-stringed instrument made from a large gourd and stretched animal hide took up one corner of the room, a kora, if Rolly remembered the name right. He suspected Marley had contributed that piece of decor.

"Would either of you like coffee or tea?" Mavis asked, pointing at a mug of steaming green water on an end table. "I made a cup of rooibos for myself."

Rolly had no idea what rooibos was, but he wasn't much for tea anyway. His mother was always forcing the stuff on him.

"I'm fine," he said.

"Have a seat," Mavis said, indicating the sofas. "Let's hear this tape."

They sat down together on the sofa, Marley taking the seat in the middle and setting up his laptop computer. They'd digitized the cassette recording so they'd have a backup and could protect the original. Rolly pulled the cassette out of his jacket pocket and showed it to Mavis.

"I found this in Gerry Rhodes's office at the Russian Orthodox church in Allied Gardens."

"Otis," she said, reading the label. "And you're sure it's my brother?"

"I think there's a strong possibility, given their shared history. It sounds like Otis, too, at least to me."

"Let's hear it," she said. "I'll know if it's Otis, I'm sure."

Marley tapped on his trackpad to play the recording. The guitar came on first, then the voice. Mavis looked impassive at first, but with each additional note she seemed to soften.

"That's him," she said, about halfway through the first song. "That's Otis."

"Have you heard this song before?" Rolly asked. Mavis shook her head.

"No. I don't think so. I didn't hear everything that he wrote. He moved out of the house the year after he graduated high school."

The first song ended and the second one began. Mavis sipped on her tea, looking contemplative.

"They're good songs," she said. "He had a real talent, didn't he? I know he was excited about making another album, that he was going to make a name for himself."

Rolly nodded. Hearing the songs for a second time, they still held up. The second song ended.

"This is the one I really want you to hear," he said, over the silence. Otis came back on the mic, speaking to his recording engineer. Mavis leaned forward.

"What's that he said?"

Marley paused the recording and set it back a few seconds. Mavis listened intently as he replayed it.

"Who's Lizzie?" she asked. Marley paused the recording again.

"Lizzie was Mr. Rhodes's wife," Rolly explained. "They got divorced."

Mavis nodded. They listened to the song all the way through.

"You want to hear it again?" Marley asked, when it was over.

"No," Mavis said. "I always liked that song, you know."

"You've heard it before?" Rolly asked.

"Of course," said Mavis. "It's that Ruby Dean song. 'Someday.'"

"I think Otis wrote it," said Rolly.

Mavis stared at him a moment, putting together the pieces. Rolly explained.

"Your brother died in 1984. Ruby Dean was only four years old then. Her manager, Roger Sledge, was also Otis's manager. And Gerry Rhodes worked for Roger Sledge. Have you or anyone in your family ever received a royalty check for that song?"

Mavis shook her head.

"No," she said. "Not a dime."

"Otis doesn't get any credit on the album," Marley said. "Those two crackers straight-out stole that song."

"There's one other possibility," Rolly said, thinking of an alternative he hadn't considered before. "Sledge might've bought the song outright. He might've had some sort of work-for-hire contract with Otis."

"You mean like a ghostwriter?" Mavis asked. "When someone pays someone else to write a book and puts their name on the cover?"

"Something like that," Rolly said. "Did Otis ever mention a contract like that?"

Mavis stared into her tea. Rolly waited.

"I remember Otis was upset with Mr. Sledge," she said. "That's why he went out there that night. He was angry. That's what got him killed. My brother was a good man, Mr. Waters. He had a lot of pride. He had a temper, too."

Rolly thought about the voices on the tape, the easy banter between Gerry Rhodes and Otis Sparks. They sounded like friends.

"I still have a hard time believing Gerry Rhodes killed your brother," he said.

"I've learned to accept it," said Mavis. "Good people do terrible things sometimes. Is there any way you can prove this?"

"Prove what?"

"About the song? That my brother wrote it."

"The proof is on the tape. If you get the right lawyer, they might be able to get you a settlement."

"I don't want a settlement. I want my brother's name on that record. I want everyone to know that he wrote that song. That he had talent."

"You should ask for that too," Rolly said. He wondered if Lucinda would care about the tape, if she needed to hear it too. It wasn't the Jimi Hendrix guitar, but it was something about her father she might like to know. It explained why her father felt so connected to the song, why he might have had it on his turntable the night that he died.

Most people would never care that Otis Sparks wrote the song. It was Ruby Dean's hit they'd heard first and that's how it would stay. Nobody but musicians and record store geeks cared about who wrote the songs, and Ruby's recording would be the definitive version. Like Elvis Presley's 'Hound Dog.' Most people didn't know that Big Mama Thornton recorded a great version first, and that two Jewish guys wrote the song before that. People didn't care. Still, if Mavis took Sledge to court, it would make the news. Her brother's story would be made public. A small record label might get in touch, with an interest in re-releasing Otis's first album, along with the demo tape. It was worth pursuing, but it wasn't up to Rolly. It was Mavis's decision to make. Lucinda was Rolly's client and the tape was intriguing, but it had nothing to do with a Stratocaster owned by Jimi Hendrix, as far as he knew. There was one other question he needed to ask Mavis.

"Did you meet with Gerry Rhodes the night before he died?"

"What the hell?" Marley said, stepping in. "Where'd that come from?"

"Eyewitnesses at the bar where Mr. Rhodes was last seen said he was talking to a middle-aged Black woman. They said she was dressed in African garb."

Marley shook his head.

"African garb? You don't have to answer that, Mavie," he said. "He didn't tell me about this."

"No," Mavis said, putting a hand on Marley's forearm. "It's okay. I owe Mr. Waters an explanation. He's done me a great service bringing me this tape. I understand now. I'll tell you both the whole story."

"Do we need to have a lawyer or something?" Marley asked.

"That won't be necessary," Mavis replied. "I haven't done anything illegal."

She leaned forward on the sofa and put her hands together, resting them on her knees.

"Mr. Rhodes contacted me recently. Out of the blue. He called me at the shop. I was flabbergasted at first. It took me a moment to realize who it was."

"What did he want?" Rolly asked.

"He wanted to meet with me. He said he wanted to make up for what he had done, that he had some information that would be in my interest. He said he didn't have a car, but he needed to meet me. I guess I've always wondered what really happened between him and my brother."

"You agreed to meet him at the bar? At Bump's?"

Mavis nodded.

"I made one stipulation. We could talk about whatever he wanted, but he would have to tell me what he remembered from that night when my brother was killed. How it happened."

"And he agreed?"

"Yes. We met at the bar. He wanted to talk about something else, but I made him tell me the story first. He told me he'd been drinking when it happened, snorting coke with Mr. Sledge and another man. He didn't remember my brother coming into the studio. He didn't remember shooting him. He said he must have blacked out, because he could only remember waking up with the gun in his hand and my brother dead on the floor. Mr. Sledge was there, telling him that he'd witnessed the whole thing, that it was a clear case of self-defense, that he'd hire a lawyer."

Rolly nodded. It wasn't unusual for people to black out when something traumatic happened to them. The brain had ways of dealing with emotional traumas, of going around them and tucking them away. Considering Gerry Rhodes's level of drug use and intoxication, it was surprising he'd remembered anything. His brain had reconstructed the story over the years, like everyone's did, subconsciously storing it in ways that might not be accurate.

"Needless to say," Mavis continued, "it wasn't the informa-tion I'd hoped for. It didn't bring me much peace and it didn't fully explain what happened that night. But I'd made a deal with the man, so I stayed and listened to what he wanted to say. I couldn't make heads or tails of it. Not until tonight, when you brought me the tape."

"What did he tell you?"

"He said he had a plan to get me my money, money that Otis had coming to him, lots of it, that he knew Otis would have wanted me to have it. He wouldn't tell me what it was, though, just that he'd found something recently that would help me get the money. Otis's money. That he owed it to Otis, for being his friend. I told him I had enough money, that there wasn't enough of it in the world to make up for what happened to me and my brother."

"How'd he react to that?"

"He asked me why Otis went to Sledge's studio that night. I told him the real reason. It wasn't about contracts or royalties. It was about me."

Mavis broke off her story. She looked over at Marley. He put a reassuring hand on her forearm.

"Whatever it is, Mavie," he said, "you're still my queen."

Rolly waited. She needed a moment to boost her courage, to find the words she wanted to say. Mavis raised her eyes and stared into the corner, avoided looking at either Rolly or Marley.

"I've been carrying this with me for a long time, Mr. Waters. I always felt it was my fault, that I'd done something wrong. That if I hadn't told Otis what happened, he would never have gone over there, to Mr. Sledge's house, that I could have prevented his death."

Her voice faltered. She took a deep breath. Rolly saw something forlorn beneath the smooth surface of her elegant face. Her whole body had hardened like steel.

"I was only fifteen," she said. "I didn't recognize what he was doing, the way that he treated me. How he was grooming me."

"Who?" Rolly asked.

Mavis turned her eyes to Rolly now, full of hurt and fire.

"I told Otis, you see," she said. "The day he died. That's why he went there. That's why he was angry. Roger Sledge raped me."

24

THE BRIDE

The next morning, Rolly sat at the kitchen table with his laptop, perusing the promises of Svetlana.com. Beautiful Russian girls looking for husbands. In their underwear and silk negligees. A crunch of gravel outside caught his attention. He heard the low rumble of an automobile pulling into the driveway. He peeked through the blinds as a black Range Rover came to a stop outside. The driver climbed out, walked around to the other side of the vehicle and opened the passenger door. A woman stepped out, the flesh-and-blood Svetlana in all her glory. Rolly remembered their conversation at Bump's two nights earlier, how he'd put off Uncle Dmitri's request to assist Svetlana in choosing a guitar, then told Dmitri at the hobby shop to have Svetlana contact him. He'd expected a phone call, not a personal visit.

Svetlana smoothed out the wrinkles in her designer jeans, leaned down and checked her face in the mirrored window of the limousine, then turned to look at Rolly's house. She squinted her eyes and flared her nostrils, testing the air, then threw back her shoulders in a way that accented her curves and approached the front porch. Rolly waited a couple of beats to respond after she'd knocked on the door.

"Who is it?" he called.

"It is Svetlana," came the answer. "My uncle Dmitri tells me to speak with you."

Rolly opened the door. In the morning light she looked even more glamorous, in a 1970s *Playboy* magazine kind of way. He pretended not to notice, telling himself she wasn't his type. He wasn't immune to the attractions of a woman like Svetlana, but he'd developed a fair level of resistance over the years.

"You can come in," he said. "But your chauffeur has to stay in the car."

Sergei the chauffeur narrowed his eyelids and snarled, but Svetlana waved him off. She knew she could handle a loser like Rolly all by herself. As she stepped through the door, her side-kick lit up a cigarette and leaned back against the Range Rover. *Good enough*, Rolly decided. He closed the door and flipped the deadbolt into place.

"Have a seat," he said, indicating the couch. Svetlana looked horrified at the thought of soiling her well-rounded derriere with whatever microscopic creatures lived in Rolly's decrepit sofa, but she found her courage and took a perch on the edge of its cushioned seats. Rolly pulled a chair out from the kitchen table, flipped it around and plopped down, putting defensible space between himself and the Russian temptress.

"How can I help you?" he asked. Svetlana surveyed the room.

"You have many guitars," she said. "I am not surprised. Your performance at the nightclub was stimulus to me."

"Thank you," Rolly said. The number of guitars on his wall had nothing to do with his skill level. Roger Sledge had a dozen guitars in his collection, but he couldn't play a note. There was something sad, and just plain wrong, about that.

"My uncle Dmitri has said to me that you work with Ruby Dean," Svetlana said. "She is my idol."

"I gave her guitar lessons," said Rolly. "That's all. Before she hit it big."

"Yes, but to give lessons to someone so rarefied, you must have taught her a great deal."

"Not all that much." Rolly chuckled. "She did most of the hard work herself."

"Mr. Roger Sledge was her manager."

"Yes," Rolly said, not sure if that had been a question.

"He is my manager too. Mr. Roger Sledge. He says I must do everything like Ruby Dean."

Rolly nodded, wondering where the conversation was going.

"How did you meet Mr. Sledge?"

"We meet at my uncle's club. In Moscow."

"Your uncle Dmitri?"

"It is his brother, Boris. I work at the club, you see. I was what you call hostess. This was quite fortunate. Uncle Dmitri arranges with my uncle Boris so I meet Mr. Sledge in person. We have spoken before, on the computer."

"Through that website?" Rolly asked. "Sventlana.com?"

"Yes, that is the one," Svetlana continued. "It was my job to assist Mr. Roger Sledge. When he came to the club. I knew some English, you see, so I could do conversation with him. I learned about what he had done for Ms. Ruby Dean. I told him of my desire to be a musical performer, that I, too, wished to be like Ruby Dean."

Svetlana paused for a moment, as if unsure, or perhaps embarrassed, about what to say next. Rolly spared her the effort.

"As we say in America," he said with an affirming nod, "the rest is history."

He smiled. Svetlana nodded enthusiastically.

"Yes, history. I am going to make history."

It wasn't exactly what Rolly had meant, but he left Svetlana's misappropriation uncorrected. It wasn't important. The relationship between Dmitri, Svetlana and Sledge had become more complicated. He glanced at the front door, thinking about the pilot-slash-chauffeur-slash-bodyguard who waited outside. Dmitri's wingman and the ex-MiG flyboy, Sergei.

"Your chauffeur seems very protective of you."

Svetlana smiled. It was almost a giggle.

"My uncle Dmitri," she said, "he is very, how do you say . . . jealous of me. I think that is the word. I am precious to my uncle. He does not want me to drive car. He says it is dangerous. Sergei has been with my uncle for long time. He is a right-handed man, as you say."

"Right-hand man, I think you mean."

"Yes," said Svetlana, correcting herself. "A right-hand man. It is his job to protect my uncle's assets."

"Like you?"

Svetlana looked like she was blushing, though it was hard to tell under the layers of makeup she wore.

"If I become music star, my uncle and Mr. Roger Sledge will make money too. For their investment in me. They have made contract."

"I see," Rolly said. The two men, Dmitri and Sledge, no doubt had a contract that would pay them both handsomely, assuming a performer of Svetlana's mediocre talents ever made any money. If by some magical intervention Svetlana did become a star, Rolly doubted she'd see a dime of the proceeds.

"How much is your uncle paying Mr. Sledge to manage your career?" he asked.

Svetlana frowned.

"I am not very good with the numbers," she said.

"Just give me a ballpark," Rolly said.

Svetlana's frown got even deeper.

"I do not understand this term, 'ballpark,'" she said. "Is that not place for the athletes?"

"It means 'approximate,'" Rolly said. "An estimate. If you

had to guess, how much did your uncle give Roger Sledge, to manage your career?"

"It is more like what you call loan. I think it is two hundred."

"Two hundred dollars?" Rolly asked. "That's not very much."

"I mean thousands. He loaned Mr. Sledge two hundred thousand dollars."

Rolly leaned back in his chair. Now they were getting somewhere. Roger Sledge had claimed that Dmitri Lemotov paid him to manage Svetlana's career, but a loan was a whole different matter. Breaking a new artist was a complex apparatus with many moving parts. It cost a lot of money to get the machine running—hiring musicians and record producers, paying for touring costs and public relations. Sledge had been in the business a long time. He knew how it worked. His ego or infatuation, maybe both, had inspired this kind of moonshot. Rolly wondered who the sucker really was—Dmitri, Svetlana or Sledge. Or all of them at the same time?

"You're sure it's a loan?" he asked. "Mr. Sledge will have to pay the money back to your uncle?"

"Yes." Svetlana nodded. "That is their arrangement."

A dim light appeared in Rolly's brain and grew brighter as he realized two disparate facts might be connected. Uncle Dmitri admired guitar players. Rob Norwood had been hired to appraise Sledge's guitar collection.

"Did Mr. Sledge put up any collateral?" he asked. Svetlana frowned again, looking confused. Rolly explained, "Collateral is something of value he'd give to your uncle if he couldn't pay off the loan."

"Oh yes," said Svetlana. "There is a collateral. It is the guitars. In the basement. Did you know Mr. Roger Sledge has some of Ruby Dean's guitars in his collection?"

"Yes, I've seen them." Rolly nodded. Uncle Dmitri knew as well as anyone that his niece had little chance of making it in the music business. He was after the guitars. And he'd get them at a good price, assuming Sledge's collection was worth as much as Sledge seemed to believe it was. The Hendrix Strat alone could be worth more than the loan if it was authentic. Sledge had been pressing Rob Norwood to pad the appraisal, to cut corners. Was he trying to pull the wool over Lemotov's eyes to speed up the payment? Rolly felt sure of only one thing. Lucinda would never see her father's Hendrix guitar once Dmitri got a hold of it. If she had a legitimate claim, they'd need more evidence soon.

Svetlana shifted on the sofa. She brushed her pants, then pulled a tissue out of her purse and wiped her cute little nose.

"So it is agreed," she said.

"What's that?" Rolly asked, returning from his ruminations. He'd almost forgotten she was there.

"I wish to be like Ruby Dean," she said. "But I must have guitar. And then you will give me lessons."

"What?" Rolly said, still thinking about Sledge's guitars.

"You must teach me," she said. "The musical lessons."

Rolly tried to remember their conversation at Bump's, if they'd discussed guitar lessons. Between the noise and the Russian accents, he wasn't sure he'd understood everything that had been said, but he felt pretty sure they hadn't discussed any guitar lessons. This was a new ruse.

"Well," he said. "We'll need to buy you a guitar first."

"Yes," Svetlana said. "And you will help me to purchase it. Ruby Dean Model II from the Taybor Guitar Factory."

"You should try it out first," Rolly said. He didn't know the model that well, but it was an expensive choice, an artist limited edition from a boutique manufacturer. "We'll need to go to the factory. To see how it fits in your hands."

Svetlana nodded her assent.

"You will go with me now to the factory?"

"I can't do it this morning," Rolly said, checking his watch. Tomorrow was Saturday, when he'd meet up with Lucinda at the nurses' banquet. He hoped he could have something for her by then.

"Afternoon, then. One thirty," Svetlana said. "We will meet there."

Rolly gave a dazed nod. It was too early in the morning to deal with a woman as brash and glitzy as Svetlana. He'd bought himself a few hours, at least. She stood up and moved toward the door. Rolly jumped to his feet and went to open it. Svetlana leaned forward and kissed him on both cheeks as he held the door for her. The smell of her perfume flooded his sinuses.

"*Spasiba*," she said, which Rolly assumed was a thank you. "I hope this will leave us both very excited."

She stepped out on the porch. Sergei had sloughed off his ramrod posture but straightened up when he saw her.

"Svetlana?" Rolly said. Something was still bothering him.

"Yes?"

"How long have you been here, in the US?"

"It is almost year now, I think."

"Do you have a green card?" he said.

"Oh yes," Svetlana replied. "That was part of the arrangement. Between Mr. Roger Sledge and my uncles."

"Your marriage? Is that what you mean?"

"Oh yes. It was part of the agreement that Mr. Sledge makes with Uncle Dmitri. That we must be married. I wish to do everything like Ruby Dean."

25

THE CONUNDRUM

R ob Norwood looked unhappy, sitting behind the counter, staring down at his phone, so glum that he didn't make any smart-aleck comments when Rolly entered the store. He swiped at his phone's screen, grumbling afresh at each bit of information that came up.

"What's up?" Rolly said.

"This appraisal," said Norwood. "It's gone sideways."

"Sledge's appraisal?"

"Yeah. He keeps pushing me to finish. And pad the numbers. If it was only ten percent extra, I might consider it, but too many of his guitars have that thing on them."

"What thing?"

"Those letters I told you about. *PJL*. It's bugging me."

"Have you asked Sledge about it?"

"No. I'm afraid to."

"Why?"

Norwood stood up and surveyed the shop, as if searching for other customers. There was no one else in the shop.

"These two guys came by yesterday," he said, dropping his voice to a whisper. "They claimed they were Sledge's business partners and asked how the appraisal was going. I don't think they trusted him, like maybe they thought he was pulling the wool over their eyes."

"What did you tell them?"

"I hemmed and hawed a little bit, told them I couldn't say anything until the process was complete. It wasn't like they threatened me, but . . . there was a definite intimidation thing going on."

Rolly considered Norwood's quandary. He had a feeling he knew who the goons were.

"What did these guys look like?" he asked.

"One guy was older, in a wheelchair. The younger guy was smaller than me but built like a cornerback. He was keeping an eye on me all the time, like he was the older guy's enforcer."

"Did they have Russian accents?" Rolly asked.

"Yeah. You know these guys?"

Rolly nodded and scratched his chin. It was an interesting development, more evidence for his theory. Dmitri had loaned Sledge money against the value of the guitars. That funding might have been contingent on getting a fair and impartial appraisal of the guitar collection. If the appraisal turned out to be less than Sledge had borrowed, there'd be consequences. Dmitri would know he'd been cheated. The Stryzaga would need its revenge.

"The guy in the wheelchair is Dmitri Lemotov," Rolly said. "He owns a lot of property over in Allied Gardens, maybe other places too. Sledge is trying to turn Dmitri's niece into a singer, make her a star. Svetlana. She looks like Shania Twain crossed with Ruby Dean, but she sings like a desperate house cat."

"Is that the chick Moogus was playing with?" asked Norwood.

"That's the one. I heard him play with her at the Music Box. It wasn't pretty."

"At least he got paid. We've all done some mercenary gigs in our time."

"Yeah," Rolly said. Moogus was the only one of them who still made a full-time living playing music. He didn't have a side hustle, which meant he took a lot of crappy gigs to pay his bills. But Moogus wasn't fit for any job except drummer, whereas Rolly was either a private eye who played guitar or a guitar player who dabbled in detection. He couldn't say which was more accurate, but right now he needed to work his detective side.

"How can I get in touch with Ruby Dean?" he asked.

Norwood raised his eyebrows.

"You try calling her management?"

"It could take days if I do that. I want her to hear something."

"You trying to sell her a song?"

"No. Nothing like that. It's an old recording, something I came across the other day as part of my investigation. I thought you might have her personal number."

"I'm not giving you Ruby's personal number."

"C'mon. It's just this one thing. I won't bug her about anything else."

Norwood cogitated for a moment, weighing his options. He picked his phone up off the counter.

"I'm not giving you her number, but I'll give her a call. I think she's at her place in Valley Center. What do you want me to tell her?"

"It's about an old recording of 'Someday' that I found on a cassette. I need her to give it a listen."

Norwood nodded, then tapped the screen of his phone and put it up to his ear. He asked for Ruby, gave his name to someone on the other end of the line, then gave Rolly a thumbs-up.

"Ruby?" he said a moment later. "Yeah. It's Rob Norwood . . . No, I haven't sold the guitar yet. The right buyer will show up. I'm sure of it. Listen, I've got somebody here in the shop you might remember. Rolly Waters?"

Norwood glanced over at Rolly as Ruby talked to him on the phone. He chuckled at something she said. Rolly figured she'd made a crack about him. She'd probably asked Norwood if Rolly was sober.

"He's doing okay," Norwood said into the phone. "He's a private eye now . . . Yeah, none of us can believe it either. Anyway, he's got some cassette tape he wants you to listen to. It's a recording of 'Someday' . . . What's that? No . . . I don't know."

Norwood looked over at Rolly again.

"Where'd you get this cassette?" he asked. Rolly considered the question for a moment. He didn't want to say anything that would reveal his suspicions.

"It was part of Gerry Rhodes's estate," he said.

Norwood communicated the message, looked at Rolly again, then handed him the phone.

"She wants to talk to you," he said. Rolly took the phone.

"Ruby?" he said.

"What happened to Gerry?" she asked, a quiver in her voice.

"He died," said Rolly. "He got hit on the head. The police are checking it out."

"Oh, that's sad. Do they think somebody killed him?"

"They're still looking into it. His family hired me to locate some things that were missing from his estate."

"I didn't know Gerry had any family."

"A daughter," Rolly replied. "He was divorced."

"Gerry was always kind of quiet," Ruby said. "But he was a good guy. Not many like him in this business. He never had an agenda."

"I found a photograph of you and Gerry. You inscribed it to him."

There was a pause at the other end of the line.

"Yeah, Gerry was a sweetheart," she said. "What's this about a cassette tape?"

Rolly described the tape to Ruby as best he could, avoiding

any mention of Otis Sparks and the timing of the recording session.

"I guess I could give it a listen." Ruby sighed. "Can you bring it up here today?"

"To Valley Center?"

"Yeah. I'll show you around. I got a mansion on a hill, ten acres of land, two horses, three dogs, two trucks, a secretary and a cook. All the requisite pop star stuff. I'm lonely, too. I'll make you a drink."

"I don't drink anymore," Rolly said.

"So, you made a good choice for once in your life." Ruby laughed. "Like I should talk. Anyway, come on up. Bring the tape. Rob can give you the address. This will be fun."

Rolly glanced at his watch. Eleven thirty. He estimated forty-five minutes to get to Valley Center, a half hour there and another forty-five back. He'd just be able to keep his appointment with Svetlana. Perhaps he'd return with a signed photo for Ruby's greatest admirer. Svetlana would forgive any tardiness if he brought her something like that.

"Okay if I head up there now?" he asked. "I have to be at Taybor Guitars at one thirty."

"No problem for me," Ruby said. "I'll be here all day. Rob's got the address."

"Thanks." Rolly handed the phone back to Norwood, who got the word from Ruby and hung up.

"I guess you're in," he said.

"Thanks for letting me talk to her," Rolly replied.

"You owe me for this one. Did you say you're going to Taybor Guitars later?"

Rolly nodded.

"Do me a favor while you're there," Norwood said. "Talk to Campbell Lange."

"The woman who did Sledge's earlier appraisal?"

"Yeah. She's in charge of Taybor's Premier Customer service," Norwood said. "Working with the big shots." He pointed to a guitar high on the wall behind him. "She worked with Ruby to design that guitar. The Ruby Dean edition."

"That isn't the second edition by any chance?" Rolly asked, remembering the guitar Svetlana wanted to purchase.

"Nah. That's a prototype," Norwood said. "Ruby played it some, early on. Campbell designed and built it. She used to have her own shop, but Taybor offered her a cushy job a while back and she folded it up. More dependable income. And benefits."

"Why do you want me to talk to her?"

"I need to ask her some questions about her appraisal. I've called over to Taybor, but she hasn't returned my calls. If you can find her, tell her we really, really need to talk."

"What if she doesn't want to talk to me?"

Norwood pulled one of his business cards from the top of the counter and wrote something on the back.

"Make sure she gets this," he said, handing the card to Rolly. "I need to know if she's seen those letters before. If they were on any of Sledge's guitars when she did the appraisal."

Rolly read the back of the card. *PJL.* He'd called Bonnie, asked her to look up the license plate for him. He hadn't heard back from her. He looked at the books and papers Norwood had spread out over the counter, and the photographs of Sledge's guitars Norwood had printed out for his report.

"When do you think you'll be finished?" he asked.

"Sledge wants it by Monday," Norwood replied. "I called a couple of the local guys I know. Jerry Rains and Tommy Bee. Sledge has guitars from them both in his collection. They confirmed their guitars were the real thing, that they sold them to Sledge. I asked them about the *PJL* thing. They couldn't remember anything like that."

Norwood rubbed his temples as if the world's largest headache throbbed in his brain.

"It's not just the initials I'm worried about," he continued.

"It's the wear and tear. The guitars are different from how Lange described them in the earlier appraisal."

"Different how?"

"A blemish here, some wear and tear there."

"You said it's been fifteen years since her appraisal," Rolly said. "Someone's probably touched them or played them since then. They're bound to show a little more damage."

Norwood shrugged.

"You'd think," he said. "But it's not more wear and tear that I'm finding. It's less."

Norwood showed one of the guitar photographs to Rolly.

"Take this blond Telecaster, for instance. The wood grain is similar, but it doesn't look right when I compare it to Lange's earlier photograph. It's close, but not the same."

Rolly contemplated Norwood's conundrum for a moment. If blemishes were the birthmarks and scars of a collectible guitar, the wood grain was its DNA. No two were the same.

"That would mean . . ."

"Yeah," Norwood said. "I'm starting to think this whole collection is fake. That Sledge, or someone, replaced the originals."

26

THE CASTLE

Ruby Dean's place was just as she described it: not quite a ranch, but several acres of land on top of a boulder-filled mountain in the backcountry of San Diego County. The house was surrounded by a black security fence. At the bottom of the long driveway there was a gate with a call box, designed to keep salesmen and overly enthusiastic Ruby Dean fans at bay. Rolly pulled up in his old Outback, pressed the button on the call box, fixed his eyes on the security camera and tried to look as much like his younger self as possible. The gates opened. He'd passed the test. When he reached the top of the driveway, Ruby Dean was waiting for him outside the front door of her house. He climbed out of his car.

"Hi, Ruby," he said. She looked older in person than she did in her publicity photos, but she still looked like a star. Ruby grinned at him.

"Holy crap," she said, giving him a big hug. "The one and only Rolly Waters, still alive and kicking. It's good to see you."

"You too," said Rolly.

"Well, come on in," she said. Rolly followed her into the

foyer. Two mutts of an indeterminate breed rushed out to greet them in a barking frenzy.

"Hush, fellas," Ruby said. "Get down now. Don't worry about them, Waters. They're just excited. We don't get many visitors."

Ruby led Rolly into the living room, which featured a baby grand piano, a wet bar and three sofas gathered around a glass coffee table. The walls displayed a collection of western-themed paintings—cowboys and horses set against mountainous backdrops and wide-open vistas.

"You want anything to drink?" Ruby asked. "Beer? Coffee? Juice? I got one of them espresso machines."

"Regular coffee, if that's okay," Rolly said. Ruby turned to a short, round woman who'd appeared at the far door.

"Coffee for my friend here, Ellie," she said. "And I'll have my usual."

Ellie nodded and left the room.

"Have a seat," Ruby said, indicating the sofas. Rolly took a seat on the inside corner of the closest one. Ruby took the other sofa, at the end closest to him. She'd been a teenager the last time Rolly had seen her up this close, pretty but gawky, unsure of herself. She was an adult woman now and a successful one, someone who knew how to present herself. She'd learned how to separate the personal from the professional. She wasn't the rowdy extrovert you'd see in concert or on TV, but she wasn't too far from that, either.

"I'll give you a tour later if you want to see the place," Ruby said. "You look good. Got a few extra pounds on you, but you were way too skinny back then. I still remember those guitar lessons you gave me."

"I don't think I was much of a teacher," said Rolly.

"You were terrible," Ruby said with an enthusiastic grin. "But memorable. I enjoyed just watching you play, trying to pick up some of the things you were doing. And you told me something I've always remembered."

"What's that?"

"Hang on to the good people you find in this business. You were right. There's a lot of bastards out there. I married one of them."

"Roger Sledge?"

"That's the one."

"That's who I came to ask you about. Well, not directly, but I think he's involved in this somehow."

"Is it creepy and dishonest?"

"Probably." Rolly nodded his head.

"Then I'm not surprised Roger's involved in it. Christ, that bastard really messed me up. I guess I owe him something for getting my career off the ground, but I wouldn't recommend it for anyone's health and peace of mind. Have you talked to him? He must be a hundred years old by now."

Rolly nodded but held off from any further answer, as Ellie had arrived with a cup of coffee for each of them and a shot of something golden brown for Ruby.

"Mazel tov," Ruby said downing the shot.

"Yeah, I've talked to him," said Rolly. "Sledge. He's still in the business, has a new girl he's trying to turn into a star. This one'll be a tough haul. She doesn't have half your talent."

"She's good-looking, though, right?"

"Very."

Ruby looked back down the hall where Ellie had come from. She sighed.

"It's part of the business, I guess," she said. "Maybe not as much as it used to be. My biggest regret is letting Roger push me in that direction. I wished I'd held my ground more on the glamour side. A lot of people don't even know I play guitar pretty good."

Rolly clucked in sympathy. It was true. Amongst the general population, Ruby was best known for her big hits and big tits. She was a fine guitar player, though, with a personal style that mixed blues and country licks. The music business might have started to change, become more willing to promote women who could play an instrument, and there were more women playing in bands, but success was still a big mountain to climb if you didn't have the right looks.

"That's why I got out," Ruby said. "That's why I fired him. Why I divorced the bastard. That and the sexual assault. He controlled my life and my music. I wouldn't give up either of them. You married?"

"Came close once," said Rolly. "It wouldn't have worked out. I was still a drunk."

"What made you give up the sauce?"

"I got in a car accident," Rolly replied, wondering if Ruby knew the answer already. "It was a long time ago."

"I guess I'll quit someday," said Ruby. "But I'm not ready yet. Now, what is it you wanted to show me?"

Rolly pulled a USB drive out of his pocket. Marley had copied the digitized song to the drive.

"I need you to listen to this," he said.

"Sure," said Ruby. "I got a laptop right here." She took the USB drive from Rolly and inserted it into the back of the computer on the coffee table, clicked a couple of times and brought the file up on the screen. "'Someday,' huh? Anything you want to tell me about this before I press play?"

Rolly leaned forward.

"Have you ever heard of a musician named Otis Sparks?" he asked.

"No, I don't think so," she said.

"Sledge was his manager, before you came along. Otis and Gerry Rhodes were friends. Then Gerry shot him one night."

"Roger told me about that when we were married," Ruby said. "I didn't remember the guy's name. I still don't believe Gerry could have done something like that. He was a quiet guy, kind of mousy, but he looked out for me, back when I was going through hell with Roger. Should I play this thing now?"

Rolly nodded and Ruby pressed play. They waited in silence until the song had finished. Ruby sighed.

"Yeah," she said. "I remember hearing this. Roger played it for me. He thought I should record it. I'll give him credit for that. I changed the key and rewrote some of the lyrics. It was better than any song I'd written at that time."

"On the record it has your name and Sledge's for song-writing credits. Not Otis Sparks."

"Is that Otis singing on the tape?"

Rolly nodded. Ruby stood up, took her shot glass to the bar and poured herself another one, downed it, poured another, then returned to the sofa.

"I asked Roger about that once," she said. "He told me it was okay, that he'd taken care of the guy who wrote it. I assumed that meant he'd paid for the rights."

"Did he show you any documentation he might have had, about buying the song?"

Ruby shook her head.

"No. I didn't understand how things worked back then. I just knew I wanted to make it in the music business. I didn't care how much Roger had me under his thumb. He took half of all my songwriting credits back then. I was young and stupid."

She chuckled.

"I wonder how my fans will react," she said, "when they find out I didn't write my biggest hit. My platinum record."

"Otis has a sister," said Rolly. "She's still alive."

"I'd better call my lawyer, then," she said. "He'll work out something we can do to take care of her. What are you going to do about Roger? He's the one who should be forking over the royalty payments. He didn't write any part of that song. That was the beginning of the end for me, you know, when I started working on my second album and Roger wanted credit for all those songs I'd worked my ass off to write. That's when I realized he just wanted to control me. That was when he started slapping me around."

Ruby knocked back her third shot and slammed the glass down on the table.

"Dammit," she said. "Just when I think I've got that bastard out of my life he finds a way back in. It'll be my word against his, I suppose."

"What do you mean?" Rolly asked.

"If this woman, the guy's sister, takes Roger to court, they'll want a deposition from me. Roger's lawyer will want me to testify so he can bring up my past, make me look like a pissed-off bitch who's out for revenge."

Ruby rubbed her temples and laughed.

"That's what I am, of course, but I don't want everybody else knowing it. I'm still ticked off about that divorce settlement. I gave up a lot just to get Roger out of my life. Did you know he kept all my guitars? How low is that?"

"Pretty low," Rolly said. Taking someone's guitars was like taking a piece of their soul. It was like stealing their friends.

"You know," Ruby said, waving her hand at the expansive living room, "I didn't want all this. I just wanted to play guitar for a living. Like you."

"Like me?"

"Sure, Waters. You were my hero. I remember watching you play with your band. You were on fire, somewhere so free it was almost like you'd left the room and were flying above the rest of us. I said to myself, 'Now that's a real guitar player.' That's why I wanted to take lessons from you. You blew me away. I had to bug you for months before you were willing to give me lessons."

"I don't remember that," said Rolly. "I hope it was worth it."

Ruby smiled.

"Wouldn't trade it for anything even though it didn't work out. Rob was better for the level I was at then."

"You're a fine guitar player," Rolly said. It was true.

Ruby smiled.

"Not in your class, Waters, but thanks. You want to see the rest of the house?"

"Sure," Rolly said. Ruby stood up, then put her hand back on the sofa arm as if she'd lost her balance.

"Whoa," she said. "How many shots did I have?"

"Three," said Rolly.

"That's at least one too many," she said. She patted her face a couple of times and shook her head. "Even for me. C'mon, I'll show you around."

Rolly followed her into the kitchen, then out to the porch, and onto a large patio with a pool that looked across the hills to a group of buildings that sat near a reservoir. A small airstrip had been built near the reservoir. Ruby showed Rolly the bedrooms and bathrooms and the garage, where a new Porsche, an electric Ford F-150 truck and a Toyota Camry were parked.

"The Toyota is Ellie's," Ruby said as they passed through the garage. "And now the pièce de resistance—my home recording studio."

She opened the side door of the garage and flipped on a light switch, revealing the control room of a recording studio, with a 24-track mixing desk and racks of processing gear on either side. A large window behind the mixer looked onto a modest, but more than sufficient live room. A dozen acoustic and electric guitars, Ruby's tools of the trade, sat on stands in the live room. Rolly inspected the mixer and other gear. Then they walked into the live room.

"Nice," Rolly said, admiring the guitars. One of them caught his eye, a sleek lime-green number.

"Is that a real Stratocaster?" he asked, moving in closer to the guitar. There was no Fender emblem on the headstock.

"It's a copy," Ruby said. "Campbell Lange made that for me."

27

THE LUTHIER

Rolly sat on a leather sofa in the Taybor Guitar showroom, not far from Gillespie Field and Roger Sledge's recording studio. He checked his watch. It was just after two. Svetlana was a half hour late. He had a feeling she wasn't going to show up. The sales rep who'd shown him around when he first arrived decided to check back in.

"You want to try out any other guitars?" the rep asked.

"No thanks." Rolly shrugged. "I think I've been stood up."

"If you want to purchase something for your friend to try at home, we've got a thirty-day no-hassle return policy."

"I'll come back another time," Rolly said. He stood up, then remembered Norwood's request. "Is Campbell Lange around today? Can I talk to her?"

"You'd have to check over at corporate," the rep said, pointing outside. "Out this door, take a right, next building over."

Rolly thanked the rep, exited the building and turned down the sidewalk. It was warm out, the sun burning down through a hazy blue sky. Norwood had floated the possibility that Sledge's guitars were fakes, that there was something fishy going on.

Campbell Lange had done the original appraisal of Sledge's collection. She'd also built guitars for Ruby Dean, including a top-notch copy of a Fender Stratocaster. Did Norwood suspect that Sledge had hired Lange to do the same for his collection? If so, what was the *PJL* mark all about, and what would any of this mean for Lucinda's claim on her father's Stratocaster? He entered the building next door. A woman who looked like everyone's favorite mom sat at the receptionist desk. She transferred a call and hung up the phone.

"Good afternoon," she said. "Welcome to Taybor Guitars. How can I help you?"

"I'm here to see Campbell Lange," Rolly said.

"Do you have an appointment?"

"No," Rolly said. "My name's Rolly Waters. I can wait if I need to."

The receptionist nodded, then picked up her phone and tapped the extension. She nodded a couple of times after communicating Rolly's request, then looked back over at him.

"You're a guitar player, is that correct?" she asked. "You're that Rolly Waters?"

"Yes."

The receptionist repeated the information into the phone, nodded and hung up.

"Ms. Lange will be out to speak with you soon," she said. "Please have a seat."

Rolly nodded and sat down in the reception area, with its cubist nickel-plated chairs and mahogany-topped coffee tables. Taybor Guitar catalogs and corporate reports sat on the tables. The walls were lined with color photographs of their product line, as well as signed photos of famous musicians playing their Taybors in concert. Ruby Dean was there along with the others.

"Are you Waters?" a voice inquired. He looked up to find a short, thick woman shaped like a guitar case waiting for him. She wore a checkered green Pendleton shirt and thick, black-rimmed glasses on her round face.

"Ms. Lange?" he said, extending his hand.

"That's me," she said, without shaking. She turned and headed down the hall. "Let's talk in my office. I've only got a few minutes."

Rolly followed Lange down the hallway and into her office. She closed the door and sat down, indicating for him to do the same on the other side of her desk. He noticed a scar on the left side of her face, running from just under her ear to the top of her neck, a long vertical slice.

"I've got five minutes," she said. "I'm interested, but you'll need to make your case for my bosses."

"Make my case?" Rolly felt confused. He hadn't told anyone why he was here.

"You fall into our seasoned pro category," Lange replied. "Can't do as much for you as for the big acts, but maybe we can work something out."

"I don't understand."

"You want an endorsement deal, right? How are you on camera? You ever done video lessons?"

"No, I. . ." Rolly stammered, then recovered. "I mean I'd love to do an endorsement deal, but that's not why I'm here. Rob Norwood sent me. He's been trying to reach you."

Rolly extracted Norwood's business card from his pocket and placed it on the desk in front of Lange. She picked up the card.

"Don't tell me Norwood wants an endorsement?" she said.

"Rob's appraising a guitar collection," Rolly said. "For Roger Sledge."

"Oh."

"He found something weird."

"Okay."

"You did the previous appraisal. I think it was fifteen years ago."

"Yeah. I did some appraisals back in the day," she said. "I did one for Sledge. So what?"

"Turn the card over," Rolly said. "Read the back."

"*PJL*," she said, reading the letters out loud. "What's that supposed to mean?"

"We don't know," Rolly said, including himself in the review. "Rob said he's finding them everywhere."

"What do you mean, 'finding them everywhere'?"

"On Sledge's guitars. They're inside the neck braces, under the pick guards. Someone's hidden these initials all over the guitars."

Lange leaned back in her chair and ran her finger along her scar, as if checking it was still there.

"That is . . . unusual," she said.

"He looked through your appraisal. There's no mention of the *PJL*s anywhere. He said you always put your initials somewhere on the guitars you made."

"My initials are *CL*."

"He's not saying you put the *PJL*s there. He just wants to know if they were there when you inspected the guitars. They're not mentioned in your appraisal."

"Is Rob challenging my valuations?"

"No. Not exactly. He thinks something may have happened since then, that maybe they're not even the same guitars you appraised. Do you know what those initials mean? Anything you can tell me . . . him, would be useful."

Lange leaned back in her chair and clasped her hands in her lap.

"Has he told Roger Sledge about this?" she asked.

"Not yet," Rolly replied. Lange stared up at the ceiling, searching for answers in the acoustic tiles above.

"It's a scam," she said.

It felt like an accusation. Rolly shifted in his chair, preparing for battle.

"I'm not trying to scam you," he said. "And neither is Rob. We're just trying to figure out what this *PJL* stuff is about."

Campbell Lange grunted.

"I'm talking about Sledge. It's always a hustle with him. He's trying to put something over on someone. On Norwood. On you. Someone else you don't even know."

Someone like Dmitri Lemotov, Rolly thought to himself. Sledge was playing a dangerous game if he was trying to cheat the old man. One guitar in particular would be a big problem if it turned out to be fake.

"Do you remember the white Stratocaster Sledge had in his collection?" Rolly asked.

"You mean the Hendrix Strat? Sure, I remember it."

"You think it's the real thing?"

Lange shrugged and leaned back in her chair again.

"It's hard to know for sure, but it was the right era. Pre-CBS. If I recall, it was a 'sixty-four Strat with no whammy bar. I remember the guy who Sledge got it from had some decent provenance. He'd worked on a Hendrix tour, had some documents to prove it. Had a photo of himself with Hendrix and the guitar. There was a woman in the photo, too."

"Was the man's name Gerry Rhodes?" Rolly asked, wondering where the photograph might be. He hadn't seen it.

"That sounds familiar," Lange replied. "I bet the guy regrets selling it now. Probably worth ten times, maybe a hundred times, what I valued it at then. You could probably retire on that guitar."

"Gerry Rhodes is dead," Rolly said. Norwood hadn't mentioned the photograph. Sledge hadn't provided a copy. He'd call Lucinda. They could go through her father's belongings again. "I'm working for his estate."

"You're a lawyer?" Lange asked, as if it were the most unlikely thing she'd ever heard.

"No," Rolly said. He pulled a business card from his wallet, placed it on the desk. "I'm a private investigator."

"Oh," Lange said. "I thought you played guitar for a living."

"Half a living," Rolly said, not wanting to screw up his potential endorsement deal. "I do this as well."

"I see," Lange said. "You know, Sledge stiffed me on that appraisal job. He didn't make the last payment. That's how I got this."

Lange put her finger on her scar and traced it from top to bottom.

"What happened?" Rolly asked.

"Sledge kept stalling on the payment. I realized he was trying to stiff me. I could have filed small claims or something, but that takes a long time. I really needed the money. I went after him."

Lange crossed her arms and stared at the wall, where there was a photograph of Lange presenting a guitar to Ruby Dean.

"This was back when Sledge was still managing Ruby," she said. "She had a concert, opening for Dwight Yoakam, I think. At ECPAC in El Cajon. I snuck in during the sound check. I knew Sledge would be there. I spotted him backstage, hassling the sound guys like he knew more about concert production than they did. I walked over and started giving him hell, demanding my payment. They were working on the light grid. One of the lights fell. It caught my cheek with the edge and sliced right through the side of my face. If Ruby hadn't yelled, it might had landed on top of my head. She probably saved my life. Of course, if Sledge had paid me when he should have, I wouldn't have been there at all. It wouldn't have happened in the first place."

Rolly looked at the photograph on the wall again. Lange with Ruby Dean.

"You work with Ruby, right?" he said. "You design guitars for her?"

"Ruby Dean Models I and II," Lange said. "I designed and built the prototypes, with Ruby's input. That's my job here, handling prestige endorsements, building and overseeing special editions. There aren't many women in my position in this business. Ruby's always been there for me. She told the company, right from the start, that I was going to design the guitar for her or she wouldn't honor the contract. I think she felt bad about what happened to me with Sledge. She knew how the guy operated. She was married to him."

Lange pushed Norwood's card back across the desk. "You can tell Rob Norwood I don't know anything about this *PJL* thing. And tell him to get his money from Sledge up front, before he hands over the appraisal. That was my big mistake."

"Keep the card," Rolly said. "Call Rob if you think of anything else. I'm just his errand boy."

Lange looked at the card on the desk like it was a foundling left at her door.

"I need to get back to work," she said, disengaging from the conversation. "You can let yourself out."

Rolly stood up and headed toward the door. He turned back to Lange, who was scrolling through her phone screen.

"What about that endorsement deal?" he asked.

"Hmm?" Lange said, without looking up from her phone.

"My endorsement deal?"

"Oh, yeah," she said. "Give me a call. We'll work something out."

Rolly wasn't quite sure how endorsement deals worked, but he expected he would land at the low end of things. He wouldn't get a guitar named after him, like Ruby Dean.

28

THE HANGAR

Rolly sat in the patio of Archibald's café at Gillespie Field and contemplated the menu. He considered ordering the grilled chicken sandwich with steak fries, feeling like he should go with the chef's salad instead. After leaving Taybor Guitars, he'd called Lucinda. She was at the airport, taking a rented Cessna out for a short spin. They'd made an appointment to meet at the café after her flight. He'd eat his lunch and wait there while she flew her plane. He decided to go with the grilled chicken sandwich, with the fruit salad instead of the fries. He took a gulp of iced tea, leaned back in his chair and waited for the waitress. He wished he and Lucinda could meet at a better restaurant. Perhaps they would after this was all over, if he asked her out on a date.

A Gulfstream jet, Dmitri Lemotov's, sat on the apron a hundred feet from the café's fence, its cargo bay and fuselage door open. A man in a gray jumpsuit approached the plane, pulled something out of his pocket, leaned into the cargo bay for a moment, then turned and walked towards the café. He opened the café gate and stepped into the patio. It was the FBI man Rolly had seen the last time he'd been there, Agent King. Rolly checked for spots on his silverware to avoid making eye contact. Agent Goffin had warned him to stay clear of anyplace connected to Lemotov. Agent King crossed the patio and went through the exit out to the street, seemingly unaware of Rolly's presence. King had his cover to keep.

The waitress checked in and took Rolly's order. He turned his eyes back to the Gulfstream, wondering what the FBI agent had been up to. Searching for something? Planting a tracking device? Or had he just been playing mechanic, maintaining his undercover identity? One of the other restaurant patrons got up and walked to the gate. Rolly kept his eyes on the keypad as the man punched in the code. It was an easy pattern to remember, known as The Cross amongst detectives and thieves because the user made the sign of the cross on the keypad: 2-8-4-6. There were other common patterns people used—The Single, The Sequence, The Square—that were more popular, but The Cross was easy to spot. Rolly watched as the man passed through the gate and then walked to the control tower.

A motorized cart pulled up to the Gulfstream jet. Two men, similar in age and appearance to the ones Rolly had seen at Svetlana's concert, climbed down from the cart and began to load the baggage compartment. They transferred three suitcases into the compartment and then started loading guitar cases into the jet. Rolly counted eleven of them. One last guitar case remained on the cart. As one man secured the luggage, the other one grabbed the last guitar, walked up the stairway and entered the jet. He returned empty-handed.

After the waitress arrived with Rolly's order, he turned his attention back to Lemotov's jet. The two men rode away on their baggage cart. The luggage bay had been closed, but the jet's passenger door was still open. Rolly rose from his chair, walked to the gate and studied Lemotov's jet, running through possible scenarios, but they all ended with the same outcome.

Lemotov had foreclosed on his collateral, perhaps stolen it, and Sledge's guitar collection had now been transferred to the jet. Lemotov's men had selected one of the guitars from the collection and placed it in the jet's cabin, the most valuable one perhaps, the Jimi Hendrix Stratocaster. Rolly feared it was headed out of the country to be stashed away in some Russian oligarch's private collection, never to be seen again. He couldn't let that happen. For Lucinda's sake. For his own. The guitar deserved better than that.

He tapped The Cross on the keypad, hoping he'd got the code right. The lock buzzed. He opened the gate and stepped onto the apron. No one accosted him or called out a warning. He couldn't see anyone around Lemotov's jet. Aside from the café, the closest building was at least two hundred feet away, enough distance to give him a head start. He puffed himself up with as much fighter pilot attitude as he could manage and headed for the plane. Once he made it there, he'd have to move fast. Up the stairs, into the cabin, grab the guitar and get out. Then hope for the best. The cavalry wasn't coming. Unless he called them.

Still walking, he reached in his pocket and pulled out his phone, scrolling through the names until he found Agent Goffin. He tapped the name and waited for her to answer. Goffin's voice mail came on the line.

"This is Rolly Waters," he said. "I'm at Gillespie Field, on the tarmac near the flight school. I think Dmitri Lemotov might be leaving the country. They're packing up his private jet. He's taking some contraband with him as well. I'll do what I can to slow him down."

He disconnected and started to put away his phone, then thought twice and entered 9-1-1 on the screen, but didn't send the call through. He'd only connect if something went wrong. If the FBI didn't arrive, he might be able to draw some emergency vehicles to the area, their sirens blazing, making things tricky for anyone who tried to accost him or get in his way. He reached the stairs leading up to the cabin. A wide metal track ran down the center of the stairs, a motorized rail for loading Dmitri Lemotov and his wheelchair into the plane. Rolly took a deep breath, checked his surroundings, then scampered up the stairs and in through the hatch.

He'd never been inside a private jet before. It was narrower than the commercial jets he'd flown on, but somehow felt roomier, like a luxury motor home with wings. White leather seats, dark wood trim, polished black tables, a sofa and a large-screen TV. The cockpit door was open. He glanced inside, wondering if he could do something to disable the plane, but he had no idea which buttons to push. He turned his attention to the rest of the cabin, searching for overhead bins. There were none, another way the Gulfstream differed from commercial jets. He started down the aisle and spotted the guitar case in back, strapped into a seat. He hurried to retrieve it, but as he passed the rear-facing seat across from the guitar, he realized someone was there.

"Good day, Mr. Waters," Dmitri Lemotov said.

Rolly jerked away from the old man, stumbled and fell against the opposite seat, smacking his face into the textured cover of the guitar case. Lemotov chuckled.

"I didn't expect you either," he said.

Rolly lifted himself and backed away, keeping his distance. The old man might be crippled, unable to walk, but he was still dangerous. Men like him always were. Lemotov, the former fighter pilot, the Stryzaga, the half-owl with gray skin who flew through the night in search of revenge. And ripped souls to pieces.

"Where are you taking this guitar?" Rolly asked, his voice quivering like the vibrato on a Fender Twin amplifier.

"That is not your business," Lemotov said. "The guitar is mine now. As are the rest. I think my niece will be pleased to have a guitar owned by Ruby Dean, don't you?"

"Did you steal them from Sledge?"

Lemotov frowned and shook his head.

"I am a businessman, Mr. Waters. Mr. Sledge and I had an arrangement."

"You loaned him money. The guitars were collateral."

Lemotov nodded.

"And Mr. Sledge has honored his contract," he said. "Not enthusiastically, but he has honored it."

Rolly knew he couldn't prevent Lemotov from taking the guitar. He thought of one way he might slow him down.

"Did you get the appraisal?" he asked.

Lemotov shook his head.

"Sadly, no. Mr. Sledge had some trouble with the appraiser. And circumstances have made it necessary for me to leave the country. I am taking them with me. Why do you ask?"

Rolly blurted out the only thing he could think of to give Lemotov pause.

"The guitar in that seat is a fake," he said. "Jimi Hendrix never touched it."

Lemotov's eyes glinted. He cocked his head to one side, accenting his owl-like appearance.

"Is this some sort of trick?" he asked.

"No," Rolly said. "They're not the guitars that you think they are. I thought you were stealing them. Now I think it was Sledge. He knew you would take them, so he replaced them with cheap copies."

"How do you know this?" Lemotov sounded displeased, less in control.

"I know the man Sledge hired to do the appraisal," Rolly said. "I've talked to him. He's worried about the appraisal, says that Sledge has been pressuring him to assign higher values than the guitars are worth."

"Perhaps it is your friend who is cheating me," Lemotov said, squeezing the armrest with a talon-like grip.

"No," Rolly said, realizing he might have put Norwood in

jeopardy. "I've known this guy a long time. He's high integrity, completely honest."

"Perhaps not completely."

"Let's put it this way," Rolly said. "You've dealt with Sledge. You know what he's like. I'd vouch for my friend over Sledge any day."

Lemotov stared at Rolly for a moment, then looked at the guitar case.

"You are sure of this?" he asked.

"I'm not an expert," Rolly warned. "But I did get a chance to play the original at Sledge's house. Just for a couple of minutes."

"You must open the case, then," Lemotov said, a smile like silver mercury spreading across his lips. "And play something for me. A private concert. You will be able to tell me if it is the original."

Rolly looked down the aisle at the open doorway, his only escape. Sergei, or someone, would be coming soon. He needed to leave, but the Stratocaster was too strong an enticement, an irresistible force in his brain, like Gerry Rhodes's last shot of whisky. They'd both made poor choices.

"Okay," he said. He unbuckled the case, flipped the locks open, pulled out the guitar and seated himself across from the old man.

"What do you want to hear?" he asked.

"On this guitar," Lemotov said, "I think you must play 'Little Wing.'"

"Haven't tried that one in a while," Rolly said.

"I am sure you will do it justice."

Rolly tuned the guitar, flexed his hands, played a few chords, and reminded himself of the chord sequence. "Little Wing" was one of those tunes every guitar player tried to conquer, one of the most lyrical guitar performances in the history of rock-and-roll. He took a deep breath, flexed his hands and started the tune. He made his way through the introduction with only a few minor glitches, then started to sing. Dmitri Lemotov closed his eyes and leaned back in his chair. The Stryzaga had been tamed. At least for now.

As Rolly made his way through the song, he considered the guitar in his hands. It was just a white Stratocaster. There were thousands of them in the world, old and new. But this one might be special, imbued with a kind of magic passed down through a master's hands. Had Jimi Hendrix really played this guitar? It didn't take him long to decide. It wasn't the same guitar he'd played in Sledge's basement. The wear was different along the neck and frets. The action wasn't as smooth. He said nothing and played to the end of the song.

"Very nice," Lemotov said when Rolly had finished. "What do you think? Is it real?"

"I think so. My friend, the appraiser, could tell you for sure."

"We cannot wait," Lemotov said. "Certain parties have made it difficult for us to remain."

"Is Svetlana leaving with you?"

"Of course. She is family."

"What about her musical career?"

Lemotov winced as if someone had stabbed him in the heart with a tiny pin.

"May I ask you something, Mr. Waters?" he said. "Your professional opinion?"

"Sure." Rolly glanced through the windows. He hoped Agent Goffin had received his message by now. Lemotov was stalling.

"You were there at the club that night," Lemotov continued. "At the . . . what does Mr. Sledge call it . . . a showcase?"

"Yes. I was there," Rolly replied.

"What did you think of my Svetlana's performance?"

"She looked good up there," Rolly said, doing his own kind of stalling.

"Of course. But her singing, what do you think?"

"I think . . ." Rolly said, choosing diplomacy. "I think it needs some work."

Lemotov chuckled and shook his head.

"She is not very good," he said. "I know this, but I do anything for my Svetlana. I gave her chance. There will be no more singing."

29

THE JET

Rolly had lied to Lemotov. The Hendrix Stratocaster wasn't on this plane. It had been replaced with a fake. Which meant Lucinda Rhodes might still be able to claim her father's inheritance.

The playability and feel of the guitar weren't the only things different from the one he'd played in Sledge's basement. There was a tiny round sticker, with three tiny letters, pasted onto the neck mounting plate. Whoever, or whatever, PJL was, they'd left their mark. Rolly placed the guitar back in its case, strapped the case into the seat, put on his most sincere face and looked Lemotov in the eye. He needed his lie to hold up. He needed to get out.

"You've got yourself something special there," he said, wondering how long it would take the FBI to arrive, if they even showed up. "I'm sorry to have bothered you."

"There is a saying we have in Russia," said Lemotov. "Work is a wolf. It will not run away to the woods."

Rolly had no time for an old man's aphorisms. He heard voices approaching, outside the plane.

"Yes," he said as he stood up. "Thank you for your time."

Lemotov slammed his cane down across the aisle as Rolly tried to leave, blocking his way. The light in the doorway flickered as someone entered the cabin. It was Svetlana, wearing oversized sunglasses and toting a Gucci bag.

"What are you doing here?" she asked, sniffing like a thoroughbred at a stable dog. Another shadow passed through the plane's open door. Sergei.

"You should have run away to the woods, Mr. Waters." Lemotov cackled.

Rolly tried to pull out his phone, but the old man was too fast for him. He grabbed Rolly's wrist like a vulture tearing at a dead body. The phone dropped from Rolly's hand, bounced against the seat and fell on the floor. There'd be no 911 call. Rolly grabbed Lemotov's cane and shoved it aside, catching the old man in the face with his elbow. Lemotov's grip loosened, allowing Rolly to break free and move toward the front of the plane. Sergei stood blocking the aisle, awaiting his master's voice. Rolly stopped, kept his distance.

"You okay, boss?" Sergei asked, his eyes riveted on Rolly.

"Bring him to me," Lemotov croaked.

Sergei grabbed Rolly by the front of his shirt and shoved him to the back of the plane, then gave an extra push that deposited him in the seat across from Lemotov, next to the guitar.

"Seal the cabin," Lemotov ordered. "We are leaving."

Sergei walked to the front of the plane, closed the cabin door and entered the cockpit, leaving it open in case he was needed again. Svetlana stared at Rolly a moment as if she might say something, then seated herself in the front of the cabin. Rolly looked at Dmitri.

"You can't do this," he said. "I'm an American citizen."

"Work is a wolf, Mr. Waters," Lemotov said. "Work is a wolf."

"Yeah, you told me," Rolly replied. "What the hell does that mean, anyway?"

"It means what it means," Lemotov continued. "For myself, I say sometimes the wolf must hide in the woods. He must wait. So that he may hunt again instead of being the hunted."

Muffled vibrations surged through the cabin as Sergei started the engines.

"Where are you taking me?" Rolly asked.

"That depends on what you tell me," Lemotov replied. "If it is the truth, you may join us at my home in Havana. You may stay there as many days as you wish. I will pay your return fare. If you do not tell the truth, you will be dropped into the Gulf of Mexico from a very high altitude."

"I'll tell the truth, then," Rolly replied, trying to match Lemotov's coolness, at least enough to hide the cold panic surging inside him. "What do you want to know?"

"Do you work for the FBI?"

"No," Rolly said. That was an easy question to answer. He didn't know if Lemotov would believe it, not without further explanation. "But the FBI came to my house. An agent interviewed me."

"What did they want?"

"They told me to stay away from you."

Lemotov chuckled.

"You did not run away to the woods."

"No," Rolly replied, beginning to understand the aphorism Lemotov had quoted. Rolly's work had taken him by the throat. He hadn't heeded the warnings. Now came the consequences. He couldn't hide in the woods. The engines revved and the plane lurched forward. He wondered if he could make it to the cabin door, open it and jump out before Sergei could extricate himself from the pilot's seat. He doubted it.

The plane turned and rolled forward. He saw the control tower pass outside the window. They taxied out toward the runway, passing parked planes, then came to a stop. The engines dropped to an idle. Lemotov checked his watch.

"Sergei!" he barked. "What is happening?"

"There is a plane in our way. I must wait for it."

"Is it *politsiya*?"

"No, boss. A little Cessna that taxied directly into my path. I can't get around it."

"Run over it, then."

"I cannot do that, boss. We might damage our plane."

A light glimmered through the sickly fear in Rolly's mind.

"Who's in the Cessna?" he asked. "Who's the pilot? Can you see them?"

"It is a woman," Sergei said. "She is waving at me."

Lemotov checked his watch again, more agitated this time.

"We do not have time for this," he said. "What does she want?"

"I don't know."

Rolly leaned forward in his seat.

"I know the pilot," he said. "She's a friend of mine. She's not moving that plane until you let me go."

"You are lying," Lemotov said.

"Let me go and I'll have her move the plane out of your way."

Lemotov stared at Rolly, storing up his contempt for future revenge.

"Go," he said. "Go."

Rolly stood up and started toward the front of the plane, then stopped and looked back at the guitar case on the seat.

"Can I take the guitar with me?" he asked, still pretending it was the original.

"Do not push your luck, Mr. Waters," Lemotov said. "The guitar stays."

Rolly nodded, deciding not to test his good fortune, not for a fake Hendrix Stratocaster. He walked to the front of the plane. Sergei turned around in the pilot's seat, watching him the whole way. Svetlana didn't look up from the *Vogue* magazine she'd retrieved from her Gucci bag. She still had her sunglasses on. Rolly turned to the door hatch.

"How do you open this thing?" he asked, glancing over at the cockpit. Sergei glared at him, then rose and went to the door, opened it and lowered the staircase. Rolly stepped through the open hatch, half-expecting Sergei to boot him down the stairs. He considered making some smart remark as he departed, like private eyes did in the movies, some withering jest, but his brain had dried up like an old sponge. He'd never wanted to get out of a place as much as he wanted to get out of this jet. He bolted down the stairway and ran toward the Cessna, made his way past its slowly spinning propeller and opened the passenger door.

"Get in," Lucinda said.

Rolly climbed into the cabin and buckled himself in.

"You okay?" she asked.

Rolly nodded and took a deep breath.

"I'll tell you what happened later," he said. "Let's get this thing out of here."

Lucinda flicked some switches on the control panel and cranked the steering wheel. The propeller spun faster as they turned away from Lemotov's jet and taxied out toward the runway.

"Where are we going?" Rolly asked.

"I'm going flying," Lucinda said. "I already used a chunk of my rental time waiting to see if you'd leave that Gulfstream. I'm not going to waste the time I've got left. No one's going to give me a refund for saving your ass."

"How'd you know I was in there?"

"As I was taxiing out to the runway, I saw you walking across the apron and up into that jet. I couldn't figure out what the hell you were doing. Especially after they closed the hatch and fired up the engines. You and I had an appointment to meet at the café. It felt like you were either bailing on me or you were in trouble. I didn't like either option. Then I remembered you asking me about the Stryzaga Flight School, like you were suspicious. I had to find out. I saw a chance to get in the way."

"I'm glad you did," Rolly said, feeling the adrenaline in his body begin to drain. "There's a guitar on that plane. I thought it might be your father's."

"Was it?"

"It's a fake," Rolly said. "It's not the real one."

They continued down toward the end of the airfield.

"Are you really taking off?" Rolly asked, hoping Lucinda might reconsider her priorities.

"Nothing to worry about," she said. "You can tell me the whole story while we're up there. I got a half hour left on the rental."

They turned onto the runway. Lucinda checked in with the control tower and, after some questions about what had happened with her plane and the Gulfstream, got her clearance. Rolly's palms began to sweat as they rolled down the runway and lifted into the air, but he didn't object. He was a lot safer with Lucinda than he'd been in Lemotov's jet. His stomach twisted as he thought about Lemotov's threat to drop him into the Gulf of Mexico. Between Sergei and his boss, he had no doubt they would have pushed him out the door. And Svetlana would have sat there in her designer jeans and sunglasses, sipping a spritzer and watching them do it. The Cessna gained speed and rose into the air.

As they continued to climb, Lucinda banked the Cessna to the right, allowing Rolly to look down on the brown land below. They crossed over a freeway and then leveled off. He felt safe now. Lucinda knew what she was doing.

A huge noise shook the cabin as a shadow zoomed over them, shaking the little Cessna like a pile of empty beer cans in a trash bag. Rolly saw the Gulfstream jet soar out in front of them, roiling the air in its wake. The Cessna shuddered in the Gulfstream's turbulent slipstream. Lucinda cranked the wheel and dove toward the ground. She aimed toward the freeway, then leveled off a hundred feet above it. The plane had stopped shaking. They started to climb again.

"Shit!" Lucinda said. "That guy almost hit us. What the hell was he thinking? We all could've died."

"He knew what he was doing," Rolly said. "He used to fly MiGs."

30

THE VIEW

L ucinda turned off the runway and taxied the rented Cessna in toward the café. A half-dozen black SUVs were parked on the concrete apron, along with several police cars and an armored truck, cordoning off the area.

"Holy cow!" Lucinda said. "What's going on?"

"It's a raid," Rolly said. "An FBI raid."

"They're after those Russian guys, aren't they?" Lucinda asked. "Those guys who were going to throw you out of the plane?"

Rolly had told Lucinda everything while they were up in the air—about Dmitri, Sergei and Svetlana, Roger Sledge and Otis Sparks, the stolen guitars, the website where men went to meet Russian brides, the FBI and the cassette tape with Ruby Dean's song on it. Everything he'd learned in the last week.

"They're too late," he said, realizing why Dmitri Lemotov had kept checking his watch, and why he'd let Rolly go. Rolly's phone call to Agent King might have accelerated the timeline, but the FBI raid had already been planned. The old man had known it was coming. Someone had tipped him off, allowing him to escape along with his two lieutenants just before the hammer came down.

"What should I do?" Lucinda asked.

"Keep going," Rolly replied, realizing the FBI agents would want to talk to him. Agent Goffin knew he'd been in the area. She might have seen his car in the parking lot.

Lucinda continued down the taxiway, passing by the control tower and away from the hullabaloo.

"Is it okay if we go in over there?" she asked, pointing to a hangar with a "SoCal Flying Club" sign over the door. "That's my rental place."

Rolly glanced back to check if they were sufficiently removed from the FBI raid.

"That'll work," he said.

Lucinda turned off the taxiway onto the apron and parked the Cessna between two other planes that looked like the one they were in.

"What're you going to do now?" she asked.

"I'm going to talk to Roger Sledge," Rolly said. "I want to find out what he knows about this."

"You think the FBI arrested him too?"

"That's one of the things I plan to find out," Rolly said. A thought had occurred to him, a new theory about Sledge's guitar collection, but he'd need to confront Sledge first and ask him some questions. He opened the door, climbed out and looked back at Lucinda, another capable woman who'd saved his ass. It was a grace he wasn't sure he deserved.

"Thanks for taking a chance like that," he said. "You saved my life."

"I'm a nurse," Lucinda said. "It's my job."

Rolly reached for his phone, then remembered it was on Lemotov's jet.

"What is it?" Lucinda asked, seeing the look on his face. Rolly ran through his options, but didn't find many. He looked at Lucinda.

"I need another favor," he said.

THE GATE to Roger Sledge's driveway was open when Rolly and Lucinda arrived in Lucinda's car a half hour later. Rolly climbed out of the car, thanked her and walked toward the front door. Lucinda drove off. She had a hospital shift starting soon.

He rang the bell, heard a voice call "enter" from inside the house. Rolly opened the door and stepped into the foyer. No one greeted him, but he saw a man seated in a chair in the living room, silhouetted in front of the picture windows. Rolly walked into the living room. The man in the chair turned to look at him.

"Oh, it's you," Roger Sledge said, looking surprised. "I wasn't expecting you."

"Who were you expecting?"

"Just an old friend. A business acquaintance."

Rolly walked up next to Sledge and looked out the window. In the distance, he could see the Gillespie airfield and the ring of law enforcement vehicles surrounding the building that housed Sledge's recording studio and the Stryzaga Flight School. A helicopter hovered in the airspace above the building.

"It's been a good day, Mr. Waters," Sledge said, shaking the ice in his whisky glass. "An excellent day overall. Can I get you a drink?"

"What are we celebrating?" Rolly asked.

"A load off my back. In more ways than one."

"You knew the raid was coming, didn't you?" Rolly said. The FBI raid had been too big, too organized. It wasn't an impromptu response to his phone call. "You talked to the FBI."

Sledge put his drink down on the carpet and lifted a pair of binoculars to his eyes, surveying the faraway crime scene.

"I'm an escape artist, Mr. Waters," he said, placing the

binoculars back in his lap. "I always find a way out. Now, what can I do for you? Why are you here?"

Rolly turned from the window and surveyed the room.

"I'd like to see that Jimi Hendrix guitar again."

"You'll have to talk to Mr. Lemotov about that," Sledge replied, pointing out the window. "He's down there somewhere."

"Dmitri Lemotov's on his jet," Rolly said. "He escaped. With his chauffeur and your wife."

Sledge jerked his head away from the window and looked at Rolly, a glimmer of confusion, perhaps even fear, in his eyes.

"How do you know that?" he asked.

"I got on the plane with him. Fortunately, I got off."

Sledge shrugged and turned back to the window. He finished his drink.

"That's a disappointment," he said. "I'd hoped the FBI would be able to retrieve my guitars. Win some, lose some, I guess. There's still the insurance money."

"Which will be based on Rob Norwood's appraisal?"

"Mr. Norwood refuses to sign off on his work. It's a minor glitch in my plan. I should have hired someone more accommodating."

"He says there are some problems with your collection."

Sledge turned in his chair again and frowned at Rolly.

"What kind of problems?" he asked.

"He says your guitars aren't worth as much as you think they are."

"I'll have to talk to Mr. Norwood about that."

Rolly paused, considering his options.

"Where's the other set of guitars?" he asked. "The real ones?"

"What?"

"I think you had the originals replaced and allowed Lemotov to steal the copies."

Sledge laughed.

"You have quite an imagination, Mr. Waters," he said. "Lemotov took my guitars, just like you said. There aren't any other ones. Be my guest. Have a look in the basement."

Rolly turned toward the kitchen. The house was too quiet. He stopped.

"Where's your assistant?" he asked.

"Christy? She quit this morning."

"How long did she work for you?"

"Longer than most. I'll give her that. That young lady wouldn't be half bad-looking if she had some tits. I offered to buy her some, but she turned me down."

"Is that why she quit?"

"None of my assistants last long." Sledge shrugged. "I'm a demanding boss."

And a lousy one, Rolly thought. He couldn't imagine anyone working for Sledge more than a week. Especially women.

"How did you find her?" he asked.

"What's that?"

"Your assistant. Christy. How did you find her? Was it through an agency?"

"An old acquaintance, who works in the business, recommended her. Christy was hot to come work for me. I'm still a big name in this business, you know. I make people stars."

"Is that what Christy wanted?"

"I don't know what that girl wanted. She was just an assistant. They're dispensable."

"Not like Svetlana," Rolly said. "You can't afford to get rid of her, right?"

Sledge stared at him a moment, weighing Rolly's words. His eyes were defiant, a cornered animal still intent on escape.

"I'm a promoter, Mr. Waters," he declared. "A damn good one. Svetlana will go a lot farther with me than she will on her own. Just like Ruby did."

The man's arrogance and self-deception squished through Rolly's thoughts like toxic sludge. Ripping off other criminals was one thing, but Sledge had done harm to people who didn't deserve it, especially musicians and women. Rolly had one thing even the escape artist couldn't escape.

"I found a demo tape in Gerry Rhodes's belongings," he said. "I think he recorded the session. A songwriter named Otis Sparks."

"Never heard of him."

"You were his manager."

Sledge turned to face Rolly and gave him a hard-eyed glare.

"Okay, smart guy. I was Otis's manager. For a couple of years. Until he came to my studio hopped up on angel dust and tried to kill me."

"Why?"

"I don't remember. It was a long time ago. He was angry at me about something, incoherent."

"And Gerry Rhodes shot him."

"That's right. Gerry put a couple of holes in the guy. He saved my ass. It was self-defense. The jury agreed."

"There's a song called 'Someday' on the tape. Did Gerry ever play it for you?"

"Gerry? No."

"But you've heard the tape, haven't you? It's the same song as Ruby's big hit. Otis Sparks wrote that song. And you stole it."

"You're talking to the wrong person, here. Ruby must have stolen it."

"I talked to Ruby," Rolly said. "She changed the key and added a verse. The original came from this tape. She said you gave her the tape."

"Of course she'd say that," Sledge grunted. "That bitch is still out to get me."

"Your name's on the record, Mr. Sledge. You took song-writing credit."

"Producer's imperative," Sledge said. "You should understand that as well as anybody, Mr. Waters. That's how the business works."

"Yeah, I know exactly how it works," Rolly said. "But the fact remains. Otis Sparks wrote ninety percent of that song and never received a dime in royalties."

"That's unfortunate," Sledge said. "If it's true. But you can't prove any of this."

Rolly paused for a moment, disgusted and somewhat awed by Sledge's sense of entitlement.

"Otis had a sister," he said. "I know what you did to her."

Sledge stared at Rolly, running through strategies, looking for his escape.

"Get out of my house," he said.

Sledge was guilty, but he wouldn't budge. Mavis Worrell would have to take him to court to get any justice.

"I'd like to see your guitar collection," he said.

"I told you. There aren't any down there. Lemotov's men took them."

"I don't believe you. I want to see for myself."

"No one's stopping you," Sledge replied, waving his arm toward the kitchen, indicating Rolly could go where he pleased. Christy was gone. Svetlana was gone. As far as Rolly knew, there was no one else in the house. He stared at Sledge for a moment, then stomped off toward the kitchen, preparing for the possibility that Sledge might be telling the truth. Why else would he let Rolly inspect the basement? He got in the elevator and took it down to the basement, stepped into the room and flipped on the lights. The walls were bare. The guitars were gone.

Someone rang the doorbell upstairs. Rolly turned off the light and ducked his head back into the elevator, listening to find out who it might be. Sledge's voice boomed across the room. A woman's voice answered, a voice that sounded familiar.

"FBI, Mr. Sledge," Agent Goffin said. "You need to come with us."

THE LAWYER

Rolly stood in Roger Sledge's basement, listening for voices, any indication that someone was still in the house. He hadn't heard anything since Sledge and the FBI agents left the house. The FBI hadn't known Rolly was there, and Sledge had either forgotten to tell them or decided he didn't want them talking to Rolly.

The guitars might be gone, but Rolly had a plan for finding out what had happened to them. He grabbed a chair, moved it to the corner of the room, climbed onto the seat and inspected the security camera. There was a tiny slot in the back of the camera and an even tinier button next to it. He pressed the button and a memory card popped out. He squeezed the card between his thumb and index finger and extracted it from the camera. So far so good. Now he needed a way to view the files on the disk. He didn't have a computer and there weren't any in the room. He climbed down from the chair and took the elevator back up to the kitchen. He felt uneasy walking around in Sledge's empty house, worried that someone would show up. He might have noble intentions, but he was still a thief. He walked through the kitchen and into the living room, searching for a laptop computer, any gadget that could display the files on the disk. He had no phone, no ID and no way to get home outside of calling a cab or someone he knew. This was the stupidest thing he'd done since sneaking onto a plane owned by a Russian gangster.

Light flashed through the windows on either side of the front door. Someone had pulled into the driveway. He stashed the memory card in his pocket and looked for a place to hide, then decided hiding would only make things worse if the FBI or the police showed up. It seemed unlikely that Sledge had returned so soon. He took a deep breath, faced the front door and waited to greet whoever came through it. If he got lucky, it might be a package delivery. Maybe the house cleaners. Footsteps approached from outside. The doorbell rang.

"Come in," he said.

The door opened and a man walked into the room. Rolly stared at the man. The man stared at Rolly. Both were dumbfounded, unable to speak.

"What are you doing here?" they said in unison. Rolly answered first.

"I was just leaving," he said. "I was talking to Mr. Sledge."

"Is Roger here?" said Sledge's lawyer, Stan Gabriel—the craft-brew-sipping, record-spinning ex-DJ.

"The FBI came by the house," Rolly said. "They took him away."

"Christ," Gabriel said, shaking his head. "What did Roger do this time?"

"It's about Dmitri Lemotov," Rolly said.

"Who?"

"He's a Russian gangster. Gets around in a wheelchair?" Gabriel shook his head.

"Never heard of him."

"You know Svetlana, though, right? Sledge's wife?"

"I've met her. What's she got to do with this?"

"Dmitri Lemotov is her uncle, maybe. Svetlana and

Lemotov are on a private jet, headed to Cuba, along with their pilot and Sledge's guitar collection. They made it out just ahead of the FBI raid on Lemotov's business, at Sledge's old recording studio."

"They stole Roger's guitars?"

Rolly nodded.

"Either that or they collected on a debt. Lemotov loaned Sledge money to promote Svetlana's singing career."

"I didn't know she was a singer."

"That's up for debate."

Gabriel sighed. He looked tired.

"Is there anything else?" he asked.

"I think there's a connection to Gerry Rhodes's death."

"What makes you say that?"

"The FBI thinks Gerry Rhodes was Lemotov's mule, helping him launder money."

Gabriel cleared his throat. He looked like he might spit on the floor but swallowed his irritation instead.

"There are a lot of things Roger doesn't tell me," he said. "I'm only his lawyer, you know, not his friend."

"Are you sure about that?" Rolly said.

"Quite sure. Roger doesn't have any friends."

"Then why are you here?" Rolly asked. Gabriel sighed.

"I made a deal with the devil," he said. Gabriel looked like a man whose flight had been cancelled. Again and again. "I guess I'll go find him, see what I can do. You need to leave, or I'll have to report you to the police."

Rolly remembered the memory card in his pocket. It wasn't something he wanted to share with the police. Not yet.

"I don't have a car," he said. "It's at the airport in El Cajon. I don't have my phone."

Gabriel took his phone out of his pocket.

"I'll call you an Uber," he said.

"Maybe you could give me a ride," Rolly said, angling for a few more minutes with Gabriel, a little more time to break through. Gabriel still hadn't told him why he was there. "My car's in a parking lot there. In the middle of the FBI raid. I'm hoping things have cleared up."

Gabriel dropped the phone to his side.

"Christ," he said, rubbing his forehead with his free hand. "What did Roger get himself into?"

"I'll tell you everything I know," Rolly said, realizing there might be a way to keep Gabriel talking as well as avoid the FBI. "If you give me a ride to my car."

Gabriel put his phone back in his pocket.

"All right, Mr. Waters," he said. "You win."

They left the house, climbed into Gabriel's BMW and headed out to the street.

"Spill the beans," Gabriel said as they headed down the hill.

Rolly started spilling. He told Gabriel everything he knew about Svetlana's singing career and Sledge's financial arrangement with Dmitri Lemotov, the website for Russian brides and the FBI's warnings to stay away from it all. He told Gabriel about the guitar collection, Lemotov's escape in the Gulfstream jet, his own escape from Lemotov and the FBI raid that followed.

"Is that all?" Gabriel chuckled when Rolly had finished.

"That's everything I know," Rolly replied.

"Roger's really outdone himself this time, I have to say."

"I guess so," said Rolly. "There's one more thing. 'Someday.'"

"Someday what?"

"The song. Ruby Dean's big hit. Sledge gets half the royalties. Did you have anything to do with that?"

"Me? I might've filed the copyright papers or something. Roger would have given me the information, so that's what I would've sent in."

"Sledge didn't write that song. He had nothing to do with it."

"Ruby wants full credit now?"

"Ruby is open to sharing her royalties. But not with Sledge. Otis Sparks wrote the original song."

The car swerved to the right as Gabriel glanced over at Rolly. He jerked it back to the middle of the lane.

"Did Ruby tell you that?" he said.

"No. *I* told her. I played her a recording from a cassette tape Gerry Rhodes kept in a shoe box, a recording of Otis Sparks singing that song. Otis died when Ruby was four years old. He wrote the song."

Gabriel stared at the road ahead, thinking his dark lawyerly thoughts. They turned off Cuyamaca Street onto North Marshall. Rolly could see the Gillespie Field control tower ahead of them. The café's parking lot, and his car, were close by. He needed to lean on Gabriel a bit more, break through his lawyerly professionalism. There was something personal, an abrasion between the two men, Sledge and Gabriel. Rolly could feel it.

"Has Sledge told you anything about the night Otis Sparks was killed? Why Otis was there? Why he was angry?"

"You think it's got something to do with this copyright thing?"

"Maybe. Did you know Otis Sparks had a younger sister?" Rolly asked.

"No. I didn't know that."

"She lives here in town. She's a college professor."

"Have you played her this tape?"

"Yes, I played it for her. She confirmed it's her brother."

"I could probably find her some money if she's willing to negotiate."

"She wants justice more than anything. She wants her brother to get his due. She wants her brother's back royalties. And she wants his name added to the copyright and Sledge's removed."

"I doubt Roger would be willing do that."

"Then she'll take him to court. Her brother's death was the

worst day of her life. It destroyed her family. She wants her brother to get the credit he deserves. The tape is pretty strong evidence."

They'd arrived at the café. Rolly pointed to the spot where his car was parked. Gabriel pulled up behind Rolly's Outback, put his BMW into neutral and stared out the front window. The FBI presence had dwindled.

"You say Gerry Rhodes made this recording?" Gabriel asked.

"Yes," Rolly said. He figured he had another thirty seconds. He needed to give Stan Gabriel one last push, even if it meant revealing Mavis Worrell's dark secret. Gabriel wasn't Sledge. There might still be a half-decent human being inside him.

"There's something else about Otis and Sledge. Why Otis went after Sledge the night he was killed."

"I guess you'd better tell me that too."

"Otis wasn't angry about their business dealings. It was personal."

"What is it?"

"Sledge raped Mavis Worrell. She was only fifteen at the time."

Gabriel rubbed the top of his stomach as if he were trying to pull something out from inside him, a heavy and poisonous guilt.

"I'm an old man," he said. "I'm tired of Roger's escapes. Of his gaslighting and lies. It's exhausting."

He looked out the window again, his shoulders slumped. His age seemed to have overtaken him, as if he'd heard a voice calling from the grave.

"I was there," he said with a quiet relief. "At Roger's studio. The night Otis died."

The confession caught Rolly off guard, rearranging all his theories. He remembered something Bonnie had told him, something in the police reports.

"There was a police report," he said. "From that night. A

man who ran across the airfield and climbed over a fence. That was you, wasn't it?"

Gabriel closed his eyes and rubbed his forehead, kneading the crease of his skull.

"Yes," he said, his voice like air escaping a tomb. "That was me."

A thought glimmered in Rolly's mind, a reason why Gabriel had put up with Sledge all these years.

"Did you kill Otis Sparks?" he asked. "Is that why you ran?"

Gabriel looked at Rolly. There was something weary and desperate in his eyes, an animal that had exhausted itself in a trap.

"No," Gabriel said. "I didn't kill Otis."

He stared out the front window of his expensive automobile.

"But it was my gun."

32

THE LIE

"I made a deal with the devil when I was young," Stan Gabriel said, gripping the leather steering wheel of his BMW as if he were driving the last hours of Le Mans instead of idling in the café parking lot. "We'd been doing drugs—Roger and Gerry and me. Gerry was out cold."

"Gerry Rhodes was asleep?" Rolly asked.

"Practically comatose," Gabriel replied. "Gerry mixed his narcotics a lot. He had a real problem. We'd all been drinking, too. We were totally fucked up. I went to the bathroom. I had a gun tucked in my belt."

"Why did you have a gun in the first place?"

"We dabbled in dealing, Roger and I, selling drugs. That was how Roger originally financed the studio. This was back in my DJ days, before I went to law school. I'm not proud of it, but there it is. I started carrying a gun, thinking I was a gangster. It was a snub-nosed revolver, one of those Saturday night specials, so I could defend myself if it became necessary. The gun was unregistered. I bought it off a guy in Spring Valley who had a garage full of the things."

Gabriel paused, searching his thoughts, retrieving and

weighing the sins of his youth. Rolly knew what it was like, confronting that weird mix of exhilaration, shame and relief that flashed through your memories like the pages in a photo album. You couldn't focus on any one page too long. You'd forget there were other, maybe better, parts of your life.

"So you went to the bathroom," he said, prompting Gabriel. "What happened then?"

Gabriel broke from his trance, looked at Rolly and resumed his story.

"I was in the bathroom when Otis showed up. I heard someone yelling, screaming at Roger. Said he was gonna cut off his balls. I pulled my gun and ran out to the living room. I saw this Black guy . . . I didn't know it was Otis. I'd never met him. I thought it was some gang guy coming in to steal our dope. I just wanted to scare him, to make him back off. I . . ."

Gabriel's voice trailed off.

"You shot him?" Rolly asked.

Gabriel dropped his hands from the steering wheel.

"The gun went off," he said. His voice had become cold and declamatory. "I guess I shot him. Otis wasn't dead when I last saw him. He was still breathing. I'm sure of it. He was lying on the floor, groaning. I wanted to call the police, but Roger stopped me."

Rolly's thoughts spun like the lights on an out-of-control Ferris wheel. Gabriel had confessed to something he didn't need to, a secret he'd been holding onto for almost forty years. He might've shot Otis Sparks. But he hadn't admitted to killing him.

"Why did Sledge stop you from calling the police?" Rolly asked.

"He said the cops would arrest us, that they'd have us up on a serious drug rap. I'd been arrested before, for possession. I got off with community service and probation, but I was dealing now. I had my gun and an eight-ball of dope on me that I wasn't about to flush down the toilet. Roger said I'd go to jail for sure if they caught me. He said he'd take care of things, that I should go out the back way via the airfield. That's what I did. I wasn't thinking clearly. We were all high."

"What about Gerry Rhodes?" Rolly asked. "What did he do?"

"Gerry was still comatose, completely sacked out on the sofa. He might've been coming around, I don't know, with all the noise. I got the hell out of there, out the back, ran across the tarmac and climbed over a fence. I heard sirens coming down the road maybe five minutes later. I hid in an alley until they passed. Then I walked home. Six miles. By the time I got home I was sober. At least straighter."

The FBI helicopter zoomed past overhead, but the raid seemed to have settled down. Gabriel surveyed the parking lot like a nervous sheepdog, but any FBI vehicles that had been there appeared to be gone. Rolly mulled over the story Gabriel had told him. He wanted to make sure he'd heard it right.

"You're sure Gerry Rhodes was unconscious?" he asked.

"That's right." Gabriel nodded. "That's what I thought, anyway. Later, I wasn't sure. I called Roger the next day. He said not to worry, that he'd taken care of things. I didn't know what he meant, not until I heard about Gerry, that he'd been arrested."

"Did you go to the trial?"

"I sat in the back row a couple of times. I couldn't take it, thinking that Gerry might go to jail on my account. I got nervous that someone at the trial had seen me that night, that they'd recognize me or that my conscience would make me jump up and confess. Then Gerry won on that self-defense plea. Roger was right. It would all be okay. I stopped worrying about it."

"You were never called to the stand?"

"No. No one knew I'd been there except Roger and Gerry."

"Did Gerry testify?" Rolly asked.

"No. They kept him off the stand. For his own good. Because of the drug stuff."

Rolly scratched his cheek and considered the information. Was Gabriel really telling the truth?

"Sledge was the only witness to testify?" he asked.

"Pretty much," Gabriel said. "There were the cops, and a neighbor who heard shots, the same one who saw me running across the tarmac. Roger lied on the stand. He said that Otis had an accomplice, that two men broke into the building. He said the other one ran away after Otis was shot. The defense made a big deal out of that, that the two guys were working together when they came to the place, that they had premeditated criminal intent. It made the self-defense angle more credible."

"But it was all Sledge's story, right? In court. It was his version of things?"

"Pretty much."

"He framed Gerry Rhodes," Rolly said. "To get you off the hook?"

Gabriel nodded.

"I went along with it. And Roger had something on me forever."

"Why did Gerry Rhodes go along with it?"

"Gerry didn't remember what happened. He only knew what Roger told him. And they found Gerry's prints on the gun. He must've picked it up at some point. Or Roger put it into his hands before he called the police. You have to understand about Gerry, his personality. He'd give the shirt off his back for somebody else, but he'd never stand up for himself. He was too self-effacing. He didn't have any ego."

Rolly remembered the banter Otis and Gerry had exchanged on the cassette recording. They sounded amiable, relaxed with each other. They sounded like friends. Gerry Rhodes had walked an uneven path in his personal life and his career, detoured by drugs, debts and divorce.

"If Gerry thought he'd killed Otis," Rolly said, "he must've felt guilty about it the rest of his life."

"I would have if I were him," Gabriel said, looking down at the dashboard as if checking his speed. Except the car wasn't moving. "I've felt guilty about what I did ever since, and I didn't do anything wrong."

"It was your gun," Rolly said. Gabriel was still resisting responsibility. "And you left the crime scene."

Gabriel's mouth twitched. His face looked like it might crumble to dust.

"Fuck Roger Sledge," he said. "Fuck him."

"Why do you think he pinned it on Gerry?" Rolly asked. "Why did he send you away? It would have been a case of self-defense for you too. It might not even have gone to trial."

"You don't understand a guy like Roger," said Gabriel. "He likes to have a hold over people, to have something on them. He likes to control them. He's been holding this thing over me my whole life. He might've used it against Gerry too, paying a lawyer and telling Gerry he'd back him up the whole way. I think Gerry felt like he owed Roger something. He thought Roger saved him from going to jail. Which he did, except Gerry should never have been on trial in the first place. This other thing, about Otis's sister. That explains a lot too. Roger didn't want that coming out in a trial."

"Mavis never told her parents," Rolly said. "She's always felt guilty about what happened, as if she were responsible."

"It's too late for a criminal case," Gabriel said, returning to lawyer mode. "The statute of limitations has expired. But that doesn't mean she can't use it for leverage. In a civil suit. With the cassette. If this gets out in the papers, on the internet, Roger won't be in control anymore. I think that's the way to negotiate Ms. Worrell's interest."

"By threatening to expose Sledge?"

"Yeah. It's the only thing Roger understands. He certainly won't do it out of charity."

"Would you help her out with that?"

"I couldn't be her attorney, for obvious reasons, but I'm willing to tell Roger what I know and recommend a course of action. That's all I can promise. He'll do what he wants to do. She won't get much money from him. Especially now that those guitars are gone. Roger's ego and hubris are about all he's got left."

"What about the house? And the recording studio. They must be worth a lot."

"Not with double mortgages on both of them," Gabriel said. "The alimony payments from Ruby ended last year."

"You're saying Ruby paid Sledge alimony?"

Gabriel nodded.

"I'm a good lawyer, Mr. Waters," he said. "And Roger is a pertinacious man. He won't let go of something until he gets what he wants. He wears people down. Like me. He wore Ruby down and she's as tough as they come."

"He's got a history with women, doesn't he?" Rolly said. "I looked up the court records and found several women had filed lawsuits."

Gabriel laughed.

"'Several' is an understatement," he said. "Those are just the ones who filed papers."

"Did he rape any of them?"

Gabriel scratched the side of his face, just below his right ear.

"I can't tell you that, Mr. Waters," he said. "I'm still Mr. Sledge's lawyer. Attorney-client privilege. I'd be disbarred if I told you. Though, at this point in my career, I couldn't care less about that."

"Were there any others who were that young? Fifteen years old?"

"Not that I'm aware of. That was abominable, even for Roger."

The two men stared out the windshield. It was a sunny day

with a smudge of dirty air on the horizon. Smog had settled over the valley.

"It's a shame, really," Gabriel said. "Roger's made a lot of money in his life, but he's lost most of it, because of his appetites, his utter lack of shame and morality. Roger likes to say he's old-fashioned, but it's really an unfettered id that he's never been able to, or even tried to, control. Money, lies and aggression. That's all there is for him. I think the escape artist may have come to the end of the road, though. He might lose everything."

"He's got the money Lemotov loaned him."

"Which, given the FBI's involvement in this matter, will be impounded if it hasn't been already. He'll have to declare bankruptcy. Roger's done it before, escaped his debtors, but I don't know how he's going to do it this time."

Rolly nodded. He grabbed the handle and opened the car door. Something had bothered him about Gabriel's story, something he'd filed away to ask later. Now was the time.

"You said 'shot,'" Rolly said.

"What's that?"

"You said you fired one shot. But the neighbors testified they heard *shots*. Plural."

"I heard them too," Gabriel said. "That's how I know I didn't kill Otis. I heard more shots as I was running out of the building."

33

THE VIDEOS

Rolly sat at the dining room table in his mother's house, looking at the security video from Roger Sledge's basement, hoping to find out what had really happened to Sledge's guitar collection. He'd driven straight home after his conversation with Sledge's lawyer, Stan Gabriel, cogitating on Gabriel's confession about the night Otis Sparks died, wondering if he should share the information with Bonnie, if new evidence in an almost forty-year-old shooting death would get any traction from the police or the district attorney. It seemed unlikely. Gabriel's confession didn't change the essential facts of the case. Someone had fired those additional shots, the ones that killed Otis. It could've been Gerry Rhodes. It could've been Roger Sledge. If it was Sledge, then Sledge had framed Rhodes. Had Sledge killed Gerry Rhodes too? Did he know about Gerry's meeting with Mavis Worrell? It was all speculation and not much to go on. It was probably best to tell Bonnie and let her worry about it. He needed to stick with his original assignment.

Lucinda Rhodes had hired him to find a white Stratocaster her father once owned, a guitar Jimi Hendrix might have once played. Rolly felt sure the guitar was still out there, that Lemotov didn't have it. Sledge didn't have it either, which was why Rolly sat at his mother's table, using her digital camera to search the memory card he'd snatched from Sledge's basement security camera, hoping there was something on those videos that revealed what had happened to the original Stratocaster.

The video files were time-stamped and dated. He watched them in reverse chronological order but found no surprises. The most recent video showed Sledge's former assistant, Christy Carpenter, alone in the room, staring at the blank walls where the guitars had once been. It was dated the same morning she'd quit Sledge's employ. The next video, from the evening before, showed Lemotov's men, including Sergei, taking the guitars down and packing them up for the transfer to Lemotov's jet. There was a long stretch with just an empty room and then Norwood showed up, taking guitars down from their hooks, placing them on the pool table and inspecting each one, scrutinizing the details and taking notes on his laptop computer. Rolly continued through the files to the dates before Norwood started his appraisal. There wasn't much on them—Sledge or Christy, sometimes both, but they were rarely in the room for more than five minutes. On one occasion, Christy Carpenter took photographs of the collection, most likely to send to Rob Norwood to start the appraisal process. But the guitars never left the room, not until Lemotov's men took them away.

Rolly's mother entered the room.

"You're cutting it rather close, aren't you?" she said.

"What's that?"

"Your move. The construction crew's starting next week."

Rolly leaned back in the chair, sorting through the videos. Something was missing.

"It won't take me long," he said to his mother. "I don't have that much stuff."

"I'm just reminding you in case you've forgotten. Goodwill's coming to pick up the furniture on Monday. I'd like some time to clean up the place."

"Why do you need to clean up? They're going to tear things apart anyway."

His mother looked as if she might scold him.

"I'm not going to argue," she said. "I want to clean things up."

"Okay, okay," Rolly said. "I promise I'll get it done soon. I just need . . . wait a minute."

His mother frowned, as if expecting some sort of plea or excuse, but Rolly wasn't thinking about moving his stuff. He knew what was missing from the video files. His mother continued to frown at him, arms crossed, preparing for an argument.

"I'll get started as soon as I check on this," Rolly said, indicating the camera's screen. "Can I use your phone?"

"Where's *your* phone?" his mother asked.

"On a plane," Rolly said. "It's a long story."

Rolly's mother dropped her arms, changing her posture from defensive to something more maternal and protective. She'd seen her son through difficult times and could change her disposition at the drop of a hat when she knew he needed help, even if it was only by letting him borrow her phone.

"I'll get it," she said, and went out to the kitchen. Rolly scrolled through the list of file names on the memory card. Every day of the week was there except one. Six days of files. One day of the week with no files, consistently for the last month. His mother returned to the room and handed the phone to him.

"Thanks," he said. He ran a search for Norwood's Mostly Guitars, then tapped the number that came up in the listings. His mother took a seat at the table, keeping an eye on things in case Rolly misplaced her phone as well. She'd always be vigilant, looking for signs of moral failure and intemperance.

"Norwood's Mostly Guitars," said a voice at the other end of the phone.

"Rob," Rolly said. "This is Rolly."

"Why does your caller ID say Judith Waters?"

"I lost my phone. I'm using my mom's. I need to ask you something, about that appraisal you're doing for Sledge."

"*Was* doing," said Norwood. "He fired me."

"When did this happen?"

"Yesterday morning. That assistant, Christy, called me and said Sledge wanted to cancel the contract, that my services weren't needed anymore."

"Someone stole all of Sledge's guitars," Rolly said.

"No shit," Norwood replied in dry amazement. "I guess that would explain it."

"Yeah," Rolly said. "It was those guys who came to see you at the store. The Russian guys."

"They didn't get much for their trouble."

"That's what I wanted to ask you about. I think I've figured it out. You still think those guitars were copies, right?"

"I know they weren't the guitars Sledge claimed they were, not the same ones Campbell Lange did the original appraisal for. Not the ones they were supposed to be. I'm sure of it."

"You remember those women who came in to clean the place?" Rolly said.

"Sure. They came once a week."

"On Wednesdays, right? The same day I saw you there."

"Yeah. That's right. I think it was Wednesdays."

"They're not on the security video," Rolly said. "You're on there. I'm on there with you. Sledge and his assistant are on there and the guys who took the guitars are on there. But not the cleaners. There are no Wednesdays on the security camera's memory card. Someone deleted the files for those days."

"I always went to lunch when they were there," Norwood said.

"Exactly."

"How'd you get a hold of Sledge's security videos, anyway?"

"You don't need to know about that," Rolly said. "Just tell me anything else you remember about the maids being there."

"Let me think," Norwood said. "There were two of them and . . . here's something I always thought was weird. That hotel cart they brought with them, the supply cart. Have you ever seen anyone use those things outside a hotel?"

"No," Rolly said. It seemed so clear now, so obvious. "They could probably fit a guitar in there, maybe two."

"That's what I'm thinking now, too," Norwood said.

Rolly stared at the file names listed on the camera screen. It all fit together, but it didn't make sense. Why had the maids stolen the guitars? Were they planning to sell them? Was anyone else involved in their plan? Had they stolen the documentation as well, the files in Sledge's office that would establish provenance and make the guitars more valuable? Did someone else steal the papers for them?

"You still there?" Norwood asked, interrupting Rolly's thoughts.

"Yeah, I'm here," Rolly said. "Do you remember the maids' names? Maybe a company name?"

"Nope," Norwood said. He chuckled. "Maybe it's that PJL thing."

"What about Sledge's assistant? Christy?"

"You think she had something to do with it?"

"She provided all the documentation for you, right? She had access to Sledge's files."

"I see where you're going with this."

"*PJL*. It's three letters. And three women, if Christy's part of the plan."

"There's no C in *PJL*."

"It has to mean something, though," Rolly replied. Christy Carpenter had access to the security cameras. She might have deleted the files. She and the maids had worked together. He felt sure of it. If he could find them, he might be able to get

Lucinda's guitar back. Unless Sledge found them first. But Sledge wasn't looking for them. Sledge thought Dmitri Lemotov had stolen his guitars.

"Don't tell anyone else about this," he said. "I'll try to figure things out."

"Good luck," Norwood said.

Rolly ended the call and handed the phone back to his mother. It rang.

"Is that Norwood?" he asked, assuming Rob had remembered something and called back.

"No," his mother said, looking perplexed. "It says your name. Your phone's calling me."

She turned the screen toward Rolly. He saw his name on the display.

"Let me answer," he said. His mother handed him the phone. He tapped the connect button and held the phone to his ear.

"Hello?" he said. No one answered. He heard a dull roar in the background, some sort of scuffling, angry curses in Russian, a whooshing sound like the wind, a thump and then silence. Footsteps. A rustle as someone picked up the phone.

"Hello?" Rolly said. "Is someone there?"

"Who is this?" a woman's voice inquired.

"It's Rolly Waters," Rolly said. "How'd you get my phone?"

"Oh, the guitar man." It was Svetlana. "The *durak*. *Do svidaniya*, goodbye."

She ended the call before Rolly could respond. He tapped the screen and tried to call her back, but no one answered. The doorbell rang.

"I wonder who that is," his mother said. She rose from the table and headed toward the kitchen. Rolly stared at the phone and tried to figure out what had just happened. Perhaps the phone call had been a mistake, an accidental tap on his mother's name in the directory. It sounded like Svetlana was still on Lemotov's jet. But what were the other sounds he'd heard on the call, the whooshing noise, the yelling and cursing?

He heard his mother talking to someone in the kitchen, another woman's voice responding, asking questions, saying his name. The voices moved toward him. His mother entered the room, followed by her visitor. Rolly put down the phone.

"Hello, Agent Goffin," he said.

"Hello, Mr. Waters," Agent Goffin said. "I'm glad to see you're alive."

"What makes you think I wouldn't be?"

"I understand you lost your phone."

"How'd you know that?" Rolly nodded. He knew what the answer would be.

"We've been tracking your cell signal," Goffin said. "Along with Lemotov's jet. They seemed to be moving together. I was concerned for your safety."

"I appreciate that."

"We assumed you were with your phone until Roger Sledge told us you showed up at his house. You were gone by the time we went back. What were you doing there?"

"Can I ask a question first?" Rolly said.

"What is it?" Goffin said, assuming the FBI's standard take-no-shit stance, something they taught day one at the academy.

"Why did you arrest Roger Sledge?" Rolly asked.

"We haven't arrested Mr. Sledge. We wanted to question him."

"What about?"

"As you know, we raided Dmitri Lemotov's properties today. Mr. Lemotov escaped, along with two of his companions. We're not happy about it."

"I'm sure. But why are you questioning Sledge?"

Agent Goffin unfolded her arms, ready to deal.

"We think Mr. Sledge might've tipped someone off and helped them escape."

34

THE FEDS

A gents Goffin and King sat across the table from Rolly in a room in the Federal Office Building downtown. It wasn't an official FBI interrogation room, more like a small conference room the agents had commandeered for the interview. Agent King asked for Rolly's permission to record the meeting. Rolly gave his consent. King pressed a button on the cassette recorder he'd placed on the table. Rolly had played this game with them before. Agent Goffin would ask most of the questions while Agent King sat by her side like a coiled German shepherd. King was the muscle. Goffin was the brains.

"Have you heard of the Small Dark Aircraft project, Mr. Waters?" Goffin asked.

"No."

"The Small Dark Aircraft project," Goffin continued, "was developed by the FBI and Homeland Security to address a hole in our anti-smuggling efforts, namely the use of small aircraft to bring narcotics and other contraband into the country."

"Like Lemotov's jet?"

"Exactly. The cartels, and other criminal entities, employ highly trained pilots to smuggle in contraband by flying low and complex routes through the mountains, using evasive maneuvers to avoid our tracking."

"Lemotov told me his pilot used to fly MiGs."

"Many of these pilots are ex-military."

"What's this got to do with me?"

"How did your phone end up on Mr. Lemotov's plane?"

Rolly sighed. One good thing about telling Goffin and King the stupid things he'd done was that they had no trouble believing him. He told the agents about seeing Lemotov's men packing the guitar cases into the Gulfstream's cargo hold, how he'd managed to sneak onboard, his encounter with Dimitri Lemotov, the arrival of Svetlana and Sergei and the loss of his cell phone. He fudged the details of his escape, leaving Lucinda out of the story, suggesting that the small plane that had blocked their path was a matter of divine intervention, distracting Sergei and allowing Rolly to make a break for it. The agents were silent for a moment after he finished. Rolly refined the question he'd asked them earlier.

"Are you going to arrest Roger Sledge?" he asked.

"We'll ask the questions, Mr. Waters," Agent Goffin said.

"I'm not answering any more questions unless you answer mine."

The two agents exchanged glances. Agent Goffin clasped her hands together on the table and tapped her thumbs.

"Mr. Waters," she said. "This is an ongoing investigation. We cannot comment on it, especially to a private detective with a history of drug abuse and what seems to be an excessive addiction to risk."

Fair enough, Rolly thought to himself. He needed to explain his actions, help the agents understand why he'd been so foolish.

"One of those guitars could be worth a lot of money," he said. "A whole lot."

"How much?"

"Jimi Hendrix might have played it."

Agent King whistled.

"There was a Hendrix guitar that sold for two million dollars," he said. Rolly nodded. King had demonstrated some knowledge of electric guitars in their previous encounters. FBI hard-asses needed a hobby too.

"I don't think it's worth as much as that," he said. "But it could be plenty. I think Sledge was using it for collateral."

"Collateral for what?"

"A loan from Lemotov. Sledge arranged with Lemotov to promote his niece's singing career. He married her, too. It might have been part of the deal."

"Lemotov married his niece?"

"No. Sledge did," Rolly replied, surprised at the agent's ignorance. "I think it's a green card thing. The relationships are kind of confusing. At any rate, I've heard Sledge is almost bankrupt."

"We've heard that too." Goffin snorted, reclaiming the FBI's competence.

"This guitar might be the only thing of substantial value Sledge has got left," Rolly said. "He used it for collateral. It all makes sense, except for one thing."

"What's that?"

"There are two guitars that look the same. One of them is a fake."

Agents Goffin and King stared at Rolly for a moment, then glanced at each other.

"Are you thinking what I'm thinking?" Agent Goffin asked King.

"It's pretty creative," King replied. "Even for Dmitri."

"What are you talking about?" Rolly asked. Agent Goffin turned back to him, tilted her head and focused on a spot near Rolly's right elbow before returning her head to its natural position and her attention to him.

"Money laundering," she said. "Mr. Lemotov owns a half-dozen businesses through which he launders the money from his illegal operations. The restaurant, the hobby shop, Bump's nightclub. The flight school. He even laundered money through his church."

"That Russian church near Bump's?"

Goffin nodded. Rolly remembered Bishop Orloff describing Lemotov as the church's biggest supporter. In more ways than one, apparently. And Gerry Rhodes had once worked for Lemotov.

"We arrested the bishop," Agent Goffin said, as if reading Rolly's mind. "He's confessed. He told us that Gerry Rhodes was a mule. Lemotov made a large cash donation to the church each week. The bishop gave Mr. Rhodes the money, minus a percentage for the church. Rhodes delivered the rest to Bump's bar, which put the money back in Lemotov's pocket. All scrubbed and cleaned."

Rolly mulled over the new information. It was another sad story about Lucinda's father he'd have to share with her. Lucinda could take it. She was resilient, like a lot of children of divorce. Like Rolly.

"Does this have anything to do with Gerry Rhodes's death?" he asked.

"Mr. Rhodes's case is being handled by the San Diego Police Department. They are, of course, keeping us advised."

"You still haven't answered my original question," Rolly said. "About Sledge. Are you going to arrest him?"

Goffin looked over at King, who gave her a what-the-hell, go-for-it shrug.

"Mr. Sledge was working with us," Goffin said. "He was our informant. He came to us, offering to share information about Lemotov. It seemed like an opportunity, but now we think it was Sledge who warned Lemotov about our raid. He knew when it was coming. He told someone, maybe his wife. That's why we've detained him."

"Has he confessed?"

"Mr. Sledge denies it. That's why we're talking to you. Did

Lemotov or either of his underlings say anything that might implicate Sledge?"

"No," Rolly said. No one on the plane had said a thing about Sledge. "Not that I can remember."

"Is there anything else you can remember?" Goffin asked. Rolly parsed through vivid memories of his terrifying venture aboard Lemotov's jet. Fear had a way of enhancing their colors.

"Lemotov kept talking about a wolf in the woods," he said. "Some sort of Russian aphorism. He kept checking his watch."

"Did Mr. Lemotov seem anxious about the time?"

"He definitely wanted to get out of there."

"And he told you they were going to Cuba?"

Rolly nodded. Someone knocked on the door. Agent Goffin stood up, walked over and opened it. A dull-looking man in a dull suit waved a piece of paper in her face. Goffin snatched the paper from him, first glancing at it, then over at Rolly. She left the room, closing the door behind her. Agent King frowned.

"What was that all about?" Rolly asked.

Agent King shrugged.

"Just be glad you're not dead," he said.

"I am," Rolly replied. "You know, I saw you at the café. In that jumpsuit. I figured you were working undercover. That's why I didn't say hi."

"You want a medal or something?"

"I saw you hide something inside the cargo bay of Lemotov's jet. What was it? Some sort of tracking device?"

Agent King shrugged.

"Just something new the bureau has in its arsenal."

"Did it work?" Rolly asked. "Do you know where they are?"

"We will soon," King replied.

The door opened and Agent Goffin entered the room. She handed King the piece of paper and sat down. King glanced at the paper and grunted. Agent Goffin resumed her questioning as he continued to read.

"Are you sure Mr. Lemotov was on the plane when you left, Mr. Waters?" she asked.

"I couldn't be surer of anything. The guy threatened to drop me in the Gulf of Mexico."

Goffin cleared her throat and glanced over at Agent King. He lifted his eyes from the paper and nodded at her. Goffin turned back to Rolly.

"We've captured Mr. Lemotov's jet," she said. "It landed at the airport in Nogales. Across the border from Tucson."

"Lemotov told me they were going to Cuba. I swear."

"Yes, well," Goffin said. "We may have had something to do with the change in flight plans. Some new technology we've been using. They may have landed earlier than expected for mechanical reasons."

"I see." Rolly glanced over at Agent King, remembered him reaching into the Gulfstream's cargo bay. King said nothing. King never blinked.

"We're working with the PF on this," Goffin continued. "The Policía Federal in Mexico. They made the arrest."

"Good. You got 'em. Now can I get out of here?"

"According to the PF," Goffin continued, "they only arrested two people. There were only two people on the plane."

Agent King flipped the sheet of paper around and pushed it across the table. Rolly read through it, then looked back up at the agents.

"Svetlana and Sergei," he said. "What happened to Lemotov?"

"That's what we'd like to know."

"You think the policía are telling the truth? Lemotov might've bribed them."

"I've talked to our agent there. He confirmed the arrests. He only saw two people come out of that plane."

"Maybe Lemotov's hiding in a secret compartment, someplace they use for stashing drugs."

"That's unlikely for someone in Mr. Lemotov's condition,"

Goffin said, annoyed by Rolly's amateur speculations. "Is there anything else you can think of, some reason Dmitri Lemotov wasn't on that plane?"

Rolly stared at the report in front of him. He remembered something he hadn't told the agents. It seemed important now.

"They called my mother," he said. "From the plane."

"What's that?" Goffin asked, confused by the seeming non sequitur.

"Just before you arrived at the house, my mother got a call from my phone. I think it was accidental, a butt dial or something. My mom's number is the first one on my speed dial. I answered the phone and I heard this roar, like inside a plane. There was this scuffling sound. And screaming, like cursing in Russian. I heard a thump and then things went quiet. Svetlana picked up the phone, like maybe she'd found it on the floor."

"Did she say anything to you?"

"She asked who I was. I told her. She called me something . . . I think it was *durak*? Then she said *do svidaniya* and goodbye and hung up the phone."

The agents stared at Rolly for a moment, then turned to look at each other. Agent King snickered. Agent Goffin chuckled. A moment later, they were laughing out loud. Rolly just stared at the two agents. He wasn't in on the joke. Their laughter began to subside.

"Didn't see that one coming, did we?" Goffin said, addressing her partner.

"Nope," Agent King concurred. "But I gotta say, it feels kinda good."

"What is it?" asked Rolly. He had an idea now of what might have happened. It didn't seem all that funny to him.

"Sergei and Svetlana," Agent Goffin replied. "Working together. All this time we've been focused on Lemotov. We had him nailed. In prison for the rest of his life. We were sure of it. And then those two threw him out of a plane."

"*Do svidaniya*, Uncle Dmitri," Agent King said, waving a

hand in farewell. "This time you're the *durak*. The idiot. You lose."

Both agents laughed again, a bitter laugh like warmed-over coffee. Then they grew silent.

"How soon can I get my phone back?" Rolly asked.

The two agents looked at each other and started laughing again.

35

THE BANQUET

Lunchtime the next afternoon, Rolly found himself sitting at a large round table in the banquet room of the Mission Valley Marriott, feeling self-conscious. He hadn't attended many hotel banquets, not as a guest, but he'd often been in the band playing after the dinner—visiting the bar on his breaks, using any drink tickets the hosts had provided in lieu of better payment. There was an old joke about a guitar player who arrives at the Pearly Gates for judgment. Saint Peter welcomes other souls in line ahead of the guitar player—a doctor, a lawyer, a priest—and sends them in through the front door. After some questioning, Saint Peter allows the guitar player into heaven as well, but tells him to go through the service door, then past the kitchen, take a right at the janitor's office and then down the hallway to get there. Musicians always had to use the service door, even in paradise.

Lucinda sat next to Rolly at the table, along with four other nurses. He was the only man at the table and didn't remember any of the nurses' names. He hadn't slept much the night before. He still felt exhausted from yesterday's travails. In the morning he'd started moving his belongings into his mother's house, adding a different kind of stress to his week. The dullness of the banquet felt like a soothing tonic around him, pleasant bubbles subduing the mind-burning terror of his recent adventures. The food at the banquet wasn't bad, but it wasn't going to win the chef any Michelin stars, either. He ate it without tasting it, a reticent zombie flashing weak smiles. Lucinda noticed the difference in his demeanor.

"Are you okay?" she asked.

"Just tired, I guess," Rolly replied. "I didn't get much sleep."

"I didn't sleep much last night either," Lucinda said. "I felt bad about what happened to you yesterday, those guys in the plane. It's my fault, isn't it? I got you into all this."

"You didn't make me get on that plane."

"No. But that guitar did. You couldn't leave it alone. And I'm the one who asked you to find it."

Rolly nodded. Lucinda was right. If he'd never known about the guitar, he never would have gone looking for it. But it was his own recklessness and stupidity that had put him on that plane, like all the other bad choices he'd made in his life. Once the hook got set in his brain, be it drugs, alcohol, sex or saving a Jimi Hendrix Stratocaster from Russian thugs, he couldn't get rid of it. The hook would only set deeper. Agent Goffin had called it an addiction to risk. Rolly hadn't come through for his client. He hadn't come through for anyone in his life.

"I appreciate what you did for me," Lucinda continued. "I know you tried. I mean, gosh, those guys were going to kill you. It's not worth it."

"That guitar was worth a lot of money."

"I always felt cheated," Lucinda said. "Not having my dad around when I was a kid. That's why the guitar was important, I think, his leaving it to me. He was trying to do something for me, to show me he loved me. That's why I cared so much. Not that I wouldn't appreciate having the money. I'll stick to nursing, I guess. And renting my little Cessnas."

"Do you really want to become a professional pilot?"

"I think it would be fun flying people around. I'd get more respect."

"People respect nurses."

Lucinda sighed and glanced around the room.

"Sometimes they do. I like it, though, being up in the air. So free. No one can harass you up there."

"Flight attendants might have something to say about that."

"Well, yeah, but no one's going to bother a pilot while they're working. You're flying the damn plane."

"You've got a point there."

"Speaking of which . . ." Lucinda said. She pointed at a man making time with the nurses three tables away. "That's him. That's the guy."

Rolly studied Lucinda's harasser. The doctor was handsome in a kind of square-jawed, well-manicured way. He looked like the kind of person for whom everything had been easy, oblivious to the unease he created in the women around him, taking the nurses' deference for the adulation he thought he deserved, a more urbane and educated version of Roger Sledge, without the outward boorishness. A profanity wrapped up in an attractive package.

"Is he married?" Rolly asked, seeing the flash of a gold ring on the doctor's left hand.

"Yeah, he's married," chimed in the nurse next to Lucinda. "Dr. Delusion doesn't wear his ring when he's on duty, says it's unsanitary."

"What did you call him?" Lucinda asked.

"Dr. Delusion. Acts like he's God's gift to women. Even if they're not interested. *Especially* if they're not interested. The more you resist, the more he'll pester you to go to bed with him. I transferred to another department to get rid of him."

"He propositioned you, too?" Lucinda asked. The other nurse nodded. Lucinda sighed.

"That's a relief, I guess," she said. "I thought it was only me."

"Oh no, honey. We've all had to deal with him at some point. Have you reported him to HR?"

"No. I was afraid to. I've only been working here three months."

"It's tricky, 'cause he doesn't really do anything wrong. Not physically threatening. He pretends it's all a joke if you try to confront him. You should file a report, though. They'll move you to another ward if you want."

"I don't want them to move me. I want him to stop."

"Good luck with that," said the other nurse. "He's one of the top three heart surgeons in the state. His dad was a surgeon, too. On the hospital board. They'll give him a warning, but they won't get rid of him."

"Will he stop bothering me if I report him?"

"He might," the nurse said. "For a little while. You learn to live with it, file another grievance if he starts up again."

"I don't want to live with it," Lucinda replied.

"You could sue him," said Rolly. "I know a lawyer who might be able to help."

"I don't want to file a lawsuit, either. I just want him to stop bugging me."

Rolly leaned back in his seat. He wanted to help Lucinda, but he wasn't sure what he could do. Physical intimidation wasn't his strongest suit. Even if he was capable of it, Lucinda wouldn't want him to beat the guy up. Escorting Lucinda to the banquet and flashing his private detective business card might put off Dr. Delusion for a while, but guys like him would keep coming back. He was an escape artist. Not unlike Roger Sledge.

"Let's talk about something else," Lucinda said, turning back to the table. "Did I tell you all that Rolly plays in a band? He gave Ruby Dean guitar lessons."

"What kind of music do you play?" the other nurse asked.

"Blues mostly," Rolly replied. "Rock-and-roll, funk, a little country, a little jazz."

"Where do you play?"

"Wherever they'll have me," Rolly replied. "We have a regular Sunday night gig at Patrick's downtown. Winston's in Ocean Beach. We open for touring bands sometimes at the Belly Up."

"Do you ever play at the Casbah?"

"Not lately. I had a band called The Creatures. We used to play there a long time ago."

"I like to go to the Casbah sometimes. And the Soda Bar."

Rolly nodded. Both of the clubs had a more youthful crowd than he usually played to these days. The bands there had names like Crack Patrol or Hip Hop Battle Bot. Punk, alternative rock, rap metal. Aggressive and loud, like The Creatures had once been. Young bands on the make, trying to move their way up. Most of them would be gone in a year, disbanded, the members moving on to other bands or quitting the business to go back to college or get a straight job. His mind drifted as Lucinda and the other nurse continued the conversation, comparing notes on music and venues.

Before they'd let him go, the FBI agents made it clear that the agency would impound Lemotov's plane and everything they found on it, including Rolly's phone and Sledge's guitar collection. They weren't going to give them back. Sledge might have the rest of his assets confiscated as well, if the FBI decided he'd aided or abetted Dmitri Lemotov's criminal activities. The Escape Artist would need a good lawyer, a new one, Rolly guessed, if he wanted to claw back his property from the government, and if he wanted to divorce his young Russian wife.

The sound of Lucinda's laughter caught Rolly's ear, sparked by something the other nurse had said to her.

"What was that you said?" he asked.

"You got his attention with that one," Lucinda said. She laughed again.

"I was telling Lucinda about this local band I like," the other nurse said. "A female band. They wear comic book outfits, kind of like KISS, but they're all about girl power. I told her she should check them out. It's good therapy if you've been dealing with Dr. Delusion all day."

"What was their name?" Rolly asked. "You said their name."

The other nurse gave a furtive glance around the room. She seemed a little embarrassed.

"Pussy Justice League," she said, with a soft giggle. "Have you heard them?"

"I don't think so," Rolly said, becoming focused and alert. It felt as if someone had jabbed a needle full of caffeine straight into his brain. *PJL*. Pussy Justice League. There had to be a connection.

"Like I said," the nurse continued, "they're all about girl power and women's rights. They're hardcore, but they're fun, too."

"How many girls in the band?" Rolly asked.

"Guitar, bass and drums. They're a trio."

"Three girls?"

"Yeah, three. That's what a trio is. They're playing at the Casbah tonight."

Rolly put his hands on top of his head. It was going to explode if he didn't contain the crazy thoughts bouncing around inside it. He thought of the sticker the young woman in the Prius had pasted on the warehouse front door. License plate *PJL1234*, the numbers like a band counting off the tempo before starting a song. And the tiny letters Norwood had found on Sledge's guitars. It couldn't be a coincidence. The two maids plus Christy Carpenter. A trio.

"What's going on?" Lucinda asked, looking at him as if he'd just told her aliens had landed outside the hotel. "Are you okay?"

"You remember those letters I told you about? *PJL*?"

Lucinda stared at him a moment, working her way through it. She put her hand over her mouth.

"Oh my God," she said.

"It's them," Rolly said. "Pussy Justice League. They're PJL."
Lucinda leaned back in her chair and gave a loopy laugh.
"I guess I know where we're going tonight," she said.
Rolly nodded.
"We're going to get your guitar back."

36

THE CASBAH

The Casbah nightclub sat directly under the flight path of jet airliners flying into San Diego International Airport, which made it an excellent place to present rock-and-roll concerts. It sat on the corner of a busy intersection two blocks from the edge of the airport's runway. If you stood on the roof, you could almost touch the landing gear of the arriving planes. Their jet-fueled exhaust drifted down on the building, creating a sticky gasoline-like atmosphere. Fully packed, the room could handle two hundred people.

Rolly and Lucinda sat out in the patio, waiting for the next band to go on. PJL. Lucinda had changed clothes since the banquet, going grunge in ripped jeans, Doc Martens and a Pendleton shirt. She looked like a different woman from the one Rolly had first met at the hospital. She wasn't different, of course; it was just two sides of the same person. He liked this side too.

"Thanks for letting me tag along," Lucinda said. "I've wanted to check out this place, even before Amy told us about it. You used to play here?"

"With my old band," said Rolly. "We were more power-pop,

new wave back then. It's not the right venue for the stuff I play now."

"Yeah," said Lucinda. "I don't know much about blues. It starts with Nirvana for me. And Pearl Jam. I like Tori Amos and Sleater-Kinney, too."

"Yeah, they're good," said Rolly. "They're the real thing."

The real thing? He couldn't believe how dumb he sounded. He was at least twenty years older than the Casbah crowd and felt out of place. Lucinda was older than most of the crowd, as well, but she fit in better with her clothes and musical affinities. Rolly was wearing a sport jacket, for Christ's sake. He hadn't changed from his banquet attire. Still, it was nice to be at a music club with a woman he found attractive, who wasn't too young for him, who could carry on a conversation like an adult. It was reassuring to know Lucinda had rock-and-roll musical tastes, more palatable then if she'd expressed an undying enthusiasm for *American Idol* or sleepy smooth jazz. He couldn't seriously entertain having a relationship with anyone who liked that stuff.

"Did you really give Ruby Dean guitar lessons?" Lucinda asked.

"Yeah. For three months. I was a terrible guitar teacher."

Lucinda laughed.

"I need to come and hear you play sometime."

"You might be disappointed," said Rolly. "We don't play any Nirvana."

"Maybe I'll get into the blues."

Rolly smiled and nodded. Lucinda was quietly assertive and seemed without artifice. It was a rare combination in anyone, but especially in the women he'd dated over the years. He'd always fallen for looks and coy flirtation over steadiness and common sense, for women who thrilled him in the bedroom but rarely outside of it. It was a weakness, he knew, one he hadn't yet conquered or fully renounced. He'd managed his drinking problem better than his relationships. It might be time to work on them too.

"Do you know anything about this band?" Lucinda asked.

"Only what your nurse friend told us. If I'm right about who they are, I think we might still find your father's guitar."

"You think they'll be playing it?"

"That would make things a lot easier," Rolly said. Christy and her friends were too smart for a stunt like that. They'd been patient. They had a plan. It was still possible, of course, that the three of them weren't in the band. They might just be fans. Or using the same initials. He'd know soon enough.

"If there's a mosh pit," Lucinda said, with a teasing look in her eye, "I might join in. Just letting you know."

"Thanks for the warning," Rolly said. He smiled. A two-tone flyer for PJL had been posted outside, three women holding their instruments. They looked familiar, but their costumes, makeup and the two-tone resolution of the image made it hard to be sure.

"I might have another beer," Lucinda said. "I've got the day off tomorrow."

Rolly stood up, acting as if it were a request.

"I'll get it myself," Lucinda said, waving him off. "I need to pee. You want anything?"

"I'm good," Rolly said, shaking the remnants of soda and ice in his glass. He took a sip and watched Lucinda as she walked through the back entrance of the club and headed for the bathrooms. He surveyed the patio and wondered if it was just some weird coincidence. Three initials. Three women. A band.

A woman appeared at the back door of the club, surveying the patio. She wore a short black dress and tall boots. She'd painted her face in bold stripes of black and white, which made it hard to make out her features. The woman caught Rolly's eye, held it for a moment, then disappeared back into the club. Lucinda appeared in the doorway, a bottle of beer in her hand. She walked back over to where Rolly stood.

"I think they're about to go on," she said. "We should probably get inside if we want to find a good spot."

"Yeah," said Rolly, still thinking about the woman who'd appeared at the door. The patio patrons had started to filter into the club. Lucinda and Rolly joined the crowd as they bunched up outside the door, jostling against each other as they tried to get in. The room filled up fast.

"Here," Rolly said, offering his hand as they squeezed through the door. "So we don't get separated."

Lucinda took his hand. It felt good. They made their way into the club and found a space against the back wall, which gave them a good view of the stage while avoiding the physical press that would occur once the band started playing.

Onstage, the three women of PJL were fine-tuning their instruments, adjusting mic stands and checking their set lists. Guitar, bass and drums. They wore short skirts and tall boots, pigtails and comic-book makeup—KISS meets Harley Quinn. And, like the members of KISS, it was hard to tell what they looked like under the makeup. Still, something about them seemed familiar to Rolly, something in the way they moved on the stage, the bass player most of all.

The house lights went out, plunging the club into darkness. The stage lights came on, shrouding the women in shades of blue. The bass player moved to the front of the stage and screamed into the microphone.

"We are PJL!" she shrieked. "The Pussy Justice League. Shredding the patriarchy and rocking your world!"

The band launched into their first number. It was loud, aggressive and slightly off-key. The crowd reacted instantly, cheering and raising their arms. A few of them began to pogo in place. Rolly was glad he'd stayed at the back of the room. As he contemplated the crowd, he realized there were more women than men in the audience, perhaps twice as many. They varied in personal style, from buzz-cut baristas to slacker secretaries. Rolly looked at the stage again, focusing on the bass player before giving his attention to the other two musicians. He felt sure of his theory now and turned to Lucinda with a satisfied smile.

She leaned in and spoke in his ear, but the band was too loud to hear what she said. He nodded his head, assuming she'd asked about the women onstage. Then Lucinda handed him her beer, plunged into the crowd and started thrashing around with the rest of them. Perhaps she'd asked his permission to join the fray. He would've nodded, either way.

Pussy Justice League forged on with their set, cranking out one strident tune after another, sounding like an amalgamation of Hole, Joan Jett and Sonic Youth. It wasn't pretty, but it was effective. He could make out an occasional fragment of the lyrics, something about *shutting down daddy* and a chorus that got the audience singing along: *Cancel the creep. Cancel the creep.*

Lucinda extricated herself from the mob and rejoined him at the back wall. Her hair was matted and her face glistened with sweat, but she seemed enlivened, as if she'd recaptured some part of her youth. Rolly felt himself rejuvenated as well. His world was less wobbly. His life was less of a failure. The band played three more songs, left the stage and returned for an encore. They left the stage again after the house lights came up, then returned to break down their equipment. It was a ritual that kept every club band humble. After the glory came the mundane, the packing and load-out and the drive back home. Younger musicians might try to keep the high going by partying with their fans, catching a meal at an all-night diner or hitting the bottle, all of which Rolly had done in his youth. These days, he drove home after a gig and went straight to bed.

"I want to talk to the band," Rolly said as the crowd headed to the back patio to cool off.

"They were great," Lucinda said. "And this place is great."

They made their way to the front of the stage. The bass player knelt on the floor, loading her instrument into its case.

"I liked your music," Rolly said. The bass player looked up at him.

"Thanks," she said, with the cautious detachment musicians often use when dealing with fans—not unfriendly, but hardly enthusiastic. Too many Stagedoor Johnnys and just plain drunks wore you down with their tedious ramblings. Sometimes they'd offer you drugs. The bass player acted cool for another reason. Christy Carpenter knew why Rolly was there.

"I heard you quit working for Roger Sledge," he said.

"Yeah, I quit," she said, sounding frosty, waiting for Rolly to drop the boom.

Lucinda broke in, expressed her enthusiasm for the band and asked about finding their music online. Christy responded politely but kept staring at Rolly.

"I gotta get going," she said, after answering Lucinda's questions. Members of the next band were already placing their equipment on the stage. Clubs like the Casbah expected a quick turnaround, to keep the crowd going. There was no time to waste.

"What did you do with the guitars?" Rolly asked.

"I don't know what you're talking about," Christy replied.

"Where are they? Why did you steal them?"

Christy grabbed her guitar case, stepped off the stage and headed toward the exit. Rolly pursued her.

"What's going on?" Lucinda shouted, following him.

Christy took advantage of her small size and the blunt force of her guitar case to slalom her way through the crowd. Rolly chased after her but got blocked by a knot of men and women bunched up at the exit. When he made it to the sidewalk outside, the crowd had dispersed. He glanced both ways down the street, spotted Christy a block away and gave chase, running through the intersection just as the light changed. Drivers honked at him. Christy turned at the end of the block.

Rolly chased after her. She was younger than he was, and faster, but handicapped by her bass guitar case.

He reached the corner, turned and looked up the side street. It was darker there, without any streetlights. Christy was gone, but she couldn't be far, perhaps hiding in an alcove or driveway. He made his way to the end of the block but couldn't find anyone.

He turned to head back down the street. Something moved. A flat panel of black vinyl rushed in toward his face. He tried to duck, but it was too late. The guitar case caught him on the side of the head. He stumbled and fell against a parked car, then slid down onto the street. As he lay on the asphalt, he heard footsteps running away. Lucinda's voice called from a distance.

"Is that you, Rolly? Are you okay?"

He lifted himself up off the street and waved to indicate he was fine, then started back down the street toward Lucinda. The blow hadn't done much damage, but he wouldn't catch Christy tonight. That was okay. He'd confirmed his suspicions. The girls in PJL were the guitar thieves. He only hoped they hadn't sold the Hendrix guitar yet.

37

THE FLIGHT

A Cessna airplane lifted off from Gillespie Field, banked to the right and climbed to three thousand feet. Headed north. The pilot, Lucinda Rhodes, leveled out the wings and turned to look at her passenger.

"You okay, Waters?" she asked.

Rolly nodded. He loosened his grip on the armrest and gave Lucinda a tight smile. She smiled back.

"I hope this flight's smoother than the last one," she said.

"I hope so too."

Rolly peered out the passenger window, down at the buildings and streets, across the horizon to the brown hills against the powder-blue sky. Lucinda wasn't his client anymore. They were friends, testing the waters before they dove in. Testing the air, in this case. Lucinda had come to see Rolly play with the band a couple of times, once with her nurse friend and once on her own. They'd had dinner together, shared stories from their personal history. It was starting to feel like a relationship, although a tentative one. Lucinda had pressed him to fly with her again, but it wasn't until yesterday that she'd made a specific suggestion. He'd accepted the invitation. He owed it to

Lucinda for saving his life. He owed it to himself to let her know she couldn't scare him away.

It had been a month since the PJL performance at the Casbah when he'd tried to chase down Christy Carpenter and question her about Sledge's guitar collection. The little bits of information he'd managed to dig up about the band members since then—phone numbers, possible addresses—had led to dead ends. The band had cancelled all its appearances. The Toyota Prius with the license plate *PJL1234* had been discovered at a ramshackle used car lot. Christy and her two bandmates seemed to have disappeared from the earth. The search for the Hendrix Stratocaster had gone cold. And Gerry Rhodes's death had been officially classified as an accident by the police. The blood on the rocks had come up a match. He'd fallen down into the canyon.

Roger Sledge was out on bail and fighting the Feds, suing them for the return of his assets. He'd declared bankruptcy and was looking for new legal representation. Stan Gabriel was out. He'd resigned as Sledge's lawyer. It was rumored that Gabriel had made some sort of deal with the Feds. The DOJ's lawyers were slowly building a concrete legal bunker around Sledge, something even the escape artist wouldn't escape.

As for Svetlana and Sergei, they were tucked away somewhere so deep in the federal penitentiary system that they'd never see the light of day. Uncle Dmitri wasn't around to bail them out and no one else cared. More than one of the Svetlana.com girls and a couple of Lemotov's foot soldiers had made deals and started to squawk. As for Lemotov himself, it was unlikely his body would ever be found. It was food for fishes off the coast of San Felipe. His wheelchair sat somewhere at the bottom of the Gulf of California, collecting algae and calcium carbonate on its way to becoming part of a reef.

"Somebody left this for me at work yesterday," Lucinda said, interrupting Rolly's wandering thoughts. She handed him a thin manila folder. Rolly frowned and took the folder. Lucinda's name had been written on one side. Across the metal clasp on the back was a torn *PJL* sticker that had been used to seal the envelope.

"What is it?" Rolly asked.

"Have a look," Lucinda said. "Then we can talk. I'll do whatever you say."

Rolly undid the clasp and opened the envelope. He pulled out a black-and-white photograph. It was a white Stratocaster perched on a guitar stand. The photograph had been tightly framed so that little else was visible. The background was blurred.

"Look on the back," Lucinda said.

Rolly flipped the photograph over. There was writing on the back, three sets of numbers. The first one was today's date with a time listed as well. He checked his watch. Five minutes from now. He stared at the other numbers, two numerals with six digits after the decimal point.

"Are these coordinates?" he asked Lucinda.

"That's right," she said. "Latitude and longitude. I looked them up."

"Where is it?"

"As best I can tell, it's an airstrip near Lake Wohlford. Don't worry. We won't land if I don't think it's safe."

Rolly leaned back in his seat and ran through the names of lakes and reservoirs in the county, trying to remember which one was Lake Wohlford, five minutes north by Cessna flight.

"Who left this for you?" he asked.

"No idea," she said. "The receptionist said it was a messenger service."

"Did you find out which service?"

"No." Lucinda shrugged. "The receptionist said it was someone new."

"Man or woman?"

"The receptionist?"

"No, the messenger."

"I think it was a woman. I'm not sure. I'm not a detective like you. I don't remember to ask all those questions. I'm sorry. I should've shown you this stuff before we got on the plane. Are you mad at me?"

Rolly sighed. He wasn't mad, just confused. He'd put aside the puzzle of the missing Stratocaster, but its mysteries rushed through his mind again like a dam breaking loose. His zealous pursuit of the guitar had almost got him dropped out of a plane. Was this the same Stratocaster, reappearing like a conjurer's trick? And why had the magician contacted Lucinda instead of him? Was it all some elaborate ruse?

"Whoever sent this to you," he said, "they might not want to see me."

"I'm not dealing with this person unless you're included," Lucinda said. "I don't know anything about guitars. How will I be able to tell if it's a fake one or the real thing? None of this would have happened without you."

Rolly leaned back in his seat and looked out through the windshield. He knew someone who lived near Lake Wohlford. He'd been to her house a month ago. He'd seen an airstrip in the distance, down by a lake. He didn't share his thoughts with Lucinda, though. It all seemed obvious now. And crazy, too.

Lucinda adjusted a lever on the control panel. There was a mechanical grinding noise outside the plane. They began to descend.

"Don't worry," Lucinda said, as Rolly subconsciously tightened his grip on the passenger door handle. "I need the flaps down if I'm going to land at that airfield. It's a short runway. We'll do a flyover first."

Rolly nodded, not even hearing her. He was too busy trying to figure out what the hell was going on.

Lucinda flew above the airstrip, tilting the wings toward the passenger side so they could look down at it.

"See anything?" she asked. Rolly shrugged.

"It's just a long strip of asphalt to me," he said. "A couple of planes and some buildings." He pointed. "There's an *R* at that end."

"Yeah," said Lucinda. "That means we land from that end."

She leveled the wings again and flew on past the runway, then banked steeply to her side of the plane, turned a full 180 degrees and leveled out again as she pointed the plane toward the big *R* at the end of the runway.

"Ladies and gentlemen," she said, "fasten your seat belts and put your tray tables away. This is our final descent into Lake Wohlford International Airport."

"Do you need to call the control tower?" Rolly asked.

"No tower here, Waters. We're all on our own."

They descended toward the end of the runway, passed across the big *R* and touched down. Lucinda throttled the engine down and taxied down the runway. She turned off the runway and onto the packed gravel beside it, then guided the plane toward a group of tin buildings with white-painted roofs. There was no one in sight.

"Wonder what we do now," she said.

There was a hill behind the buildings and a dirt road that came down the rise to the airport. A car appeared on the road, headed their way.

"Maybe that's them." Rolly pointed.

Lucinda nodded. She parked the plane at the edge of the gravel apron and cut the engine. They climbed out of the plane and watched the car come down the hill. It was a gray sedan of some sort, a Toyota Camry. The car stopped at the edge of the airfield, twenty yards away. It idled there for a moment. The driver climbed out of the car, stood behind the door and called someone on her phone. She nodded, put her phone away and waved them over.

"Looks like our ride is here," Lucinda said.

"Looks like it," Rolly concurred.

They started across the gravel toward the car. Rolly felt a creeping anxiety as they approached, the way he'd feel sometimes before stepping onstage, the same uncertainty people felt when they got called into the boss's office, unsure whether they were about to receive censure or praise. His mind hesitated, but his feet kept moving. There was nothing dangerous here, just bewilderment. He'd met the driver before.

"Hello, Ellie," he said to Ruby Dean's housekeeper. "You must be waiting for us."

38

THE LEAGUE

E llie dropped her charges off at the front door of her employer's house and continued on to the garage. There were a dozen other cars in the driveway. Ruby Dean opened the front door.

"Hey, Waters," she said. "I had a feeling you'd show up."

"What's the occasion?" Rolly asked, indicating the cars in Ruby's driveway.

"Just a little party I put together. For some special friends."

Ruby paused, as if she expected something from him.

"You going to introduce us?" she asked, nodding at Rolly's companion.

"Oh, yeah," Rolly said, his mind racing a hundred miles ahead of him. "This is Lucinda. Gerry Rhodes's daughter."

"Very pleased to meet you, Ms. Dean," Lucinda said. Ruby took Lucinda's extended hand and pulled her in for a hug.

"Just call me Ruby, dear," she said. "I'm real glad to meet you too. Your pa was a good man. I'm sorry he's gone."

The two women broke their clinch. Lucinda looked dazed, as if they'd been driving for ten hours instead of ten minutes. Perhaps she was starstruck at meeting the real, live Ruby Dean.

"What's going on?" Rolly asked, feeling the creep in his nerves again. A strange story had started to unfold in his mind, but it was only a rough draft.

"All in good time, Waters," Ruby replied. "All in good time. Lucinda, would you like to see my recording studio?"

"Sure," Lucinda said, sounding less sure of herself than Rolly knew her to be.

"C'mon, then," Ruby said. She closed the front door and escorted them to the garage. Rolly trailed both women. Ruby paused outside the door to her studio.

"You're going to want to ask me some questions," she said, "after you see what's inside. Let's hold off on that until you meet the folks in the house."

Lucinda caught Rolly's eye, a silent inquiry, asking if he knew what Ruby was talking about. Rolly shrugged. Ruby opened the door, led them into the control room and turned on the lights. She grabbed an envelope that was lying on top of the recording console.

"This is for you, honey," she said. Lucinda's hand trembled as she took the envelope.

"My dad called me Lucy," she said, reading the name scrawled on the front. "Is this from him?"

"You'll know when you open it."

Lucinda broke the seal on the envelope and pulled out a piece of paper. A photograph fell out of the paper and onto the floor. Lucinda reached down and picked it up. She studied it for a moment, then handed it to Rolly. It was an old photograph, three people standing together. One of them was Jimi Hendrix.

"Is that your mom and dad?" Rolly asked. Lucinda nodded. Lucinda's mother wore her hair down to her waist, along with a tie-dyed skirt and granny glasses, maximum hippie chic. She didn't look a day older than sixteen. Gerry Rhodes looked like a young man in love. Hendrix stood between them. As in almost every photograph of Hendrix that had ever been taken, he was holding a guitar, in this case a white Stratocaster. Hendrix had signed the photograph. *To Gerry and his beautiful lady. Peace and Love. Jimi.*

"This must have been before they were married," Lucinda said. "On that tour when my mom ran away with my dad."

"I never knew your mom," Ruby said. "They were divorced before I met Gerry."

"Where did you get this photograph?" Rolly asked.

"Like I said, I'll answer questions later," Ruby replied. "Let's continue the tour."

Ruby opened the door to the live room and escorted them inside. Something in the shadows felt different to Rolly, something new in the room. Ruby turned on the lights. A dozen guitars were arranged in a semicircle in the center of the room, propped up on stands. The guitar in the middle was a white Stratocaster.

"Oh my God!" Lucinda said. "Is that it? Is that my dad's guitar?"

"What do you think, Waters?" Ruby asked.

Rolly walked over and knelt in front of the guitar. He felt more numb than surprised, that this moment had been inevitable, but he didn't understand how it had arrived. He studied the guitar, picked it up and held it in his hands. Something wasn't right about it. He ran his hand over the pick guard, flat and smooth, which meant it was printed instead of hand painted. He pulled out his reading glasses and scrutinized the design, found the three letters he was looking for. He stood up.

"This isn't the Hendrix guitar," he said. "It's a copy."

"Damn," Lucinda said. The delight in her eyes faded at the treasure not found.

"Good work, Waters," Ruby said. She nodded toward the corner of the room. "Grab that guitar case over there."

Rolly walked to the corner, picked up the rectangular, hard-shell case and returned to Ruby.

"Open it up," she said.

Rolly placed the case on the floor, knelt beside it, flipped the latches and opened the lid. A second white Stratocaster lay against the felt lining. He reached down and ran his hand over the surface. He pulled the guitar out of the case and held it in his hands, played a few licks. He looked over at Lucinda and smiled. She put her hand over her mouth as if she might scream.

"Oh my God!" she said. "Oh my God! How did you . . . how did this happen?"

"It's a miracle," Ruby said. "That I can't explain. For legal reasons mostly. Maybe Waters wants to take a shot at it."

Rolly placed the guitar back in the case. He stared at it a moment, feeling a strange sense of relief. All was right in the world again. He might not fully appreciate the details, but he admired the genius of the plan.

"You and Christy came up with the idea, didn't you?" he asked. "You got her that job working for Sledge."

"I'm neither confirming nor denying here, Waters," Ruby replied. "But you keep talking if you want to. If you got some-thing you want to get off your chest."

Thoughts rubbed against each other in Rolly's mind, sending off sparks. A conflagration of coincidences flared up in his brain.

"Christy brought her two friends into it," he began, building up steam. "From the band. They pretended to be maids. They figured out a way to remove the guitars, once a week, one at a time. You replaced them with a guitar that looked like the origi-nal, a copy. The copies didn't need to be perfect, just good enough that Sledge wouldn't notice. Which wasn't that hard. Sledge doesn't know a Les Paul from an SG. He never touched the things. The same color and shape would do, the same type of wood and similar hardware. You needed someone who could look at a photograph and build a guitar that looked just the same . . ."

He paused for a moment, working his way through his thoughts, making connections.

"Campbell Lange," he said. "She designed the Ruby Dean model at Taybor. She's your rep there. She's your friend. She built the fakes, didn't she?"

Rolly looked at Ruby for confirmation, but she wasn't giving any. He continued anyway.

"At first, I'm guessing here, it was about getting your own guitars back, the ones Sledge took from you in the divorce. It worked like a charm. It was so easy you decided to go for the rest, because you hate Sledge."

"Everybody hates Roger," Ruby said. "It's not just me."

Rolly nodded. He couldn't disagree. There was poetic justice here even if it wasn't legally so. He continued with his hypothesis.

"It was all working fine," he said. "Until Sledge decided to use the guitar collection as collateral and hired Rob Norwood to do the appraisal. You knew Rob would report the discrepancies to Sledge, tell him the guitars weren't what they were cracked up to be. Sledge would get suspicious. He'd figure it out. You had one last shot. You went for the most valuable guitar in the collection and replaced the Hendrix Stratocaster. Then you got lucky. The Russians came in and took Sledge's guitars, all the copies you'd made. Christy fired Norwood the next morning. Sledge would never find out they were fakes. If the Russians found out, they'd blame Sledge. If the guitars were returned, Sledge would blame them."

"Is it true what he said?" Lucinda asked. "Is that what happened?"

Ruby smiled like a sphinx.

"Sometimes it's better to be lucky than smart," she said.

"What are you going to do with them now?" Rolly asked.

"That's why I invited Lucinda over today," Ruby said. "Let's go into the house."

They followed Ruby out of the garage and into the main house. Female voices, tipsy with exhilaration and alcohol, came from inside. Ruby led her two charges into the living room and gave a whistle. The chatter went silent as a dozen women looked up from their seats.

"Okay, everyone," Ruby began. "This is Lucinda Rhodes and, for those of you who don't know him, a guy who gave me guitar lessons a long time ago. Rolly Waters."

"Congratulations, ladies," Rolly said, feeling like a dog at a convention of cats.

He spotted some familiar faces in the group. Christy Carpenter and her bandmates. Campbell Lange. Joan and Bonnie. Otis Sparks's sister, Mavis Worrell. He didn't know the rest of the women by sight, but he expected their names would match up with the names on the cover pages of the lawsuits against Sledge, the pages Max Gemeinhardt had sent. A roomful of Roger Sledge's victims reveling in a moment of shared schadenfreude. The Cyclops had been blinded. The serpent defanged.

"I don't get it," Lucinda said. Ruby cleared her throat.

"These ladies," she said, expanding her arms to take in the crowd, "are part of our organization dedicated to equal justice. For rapists, sexual harassers and misogynist pigs. Finding ways to make them pay when legal entities fail. We call it the PJL."

"I thought that was the name of a band," Lucinda said.

"The Pussy Justice League is more than a band," Christy responded. "It's empowerment. Women working together to bring about sexual justice where society and the legal system have failed us. Sisterhood."

"It was just a crazy idea at first," Ruby interjected. "Christy and I started talking after a couple of drinks one night. Things snowballed from there. I helped Christy get the job with Roger. She started going through his files. That's where that photograph came from, by the way, the one with your parents and Jim Hendrix. We brought in my friend Campbell to make the guitars. Christy explained the idea to the rest of her band. They offered to work as maids and make the switch. We found other women who'd been mistreated by Roger and invited them into the group. I didn't know about Mavis until Waters showed up with that tape. I called her, told her about your visit and asked if she'd be willing to meet, just the two of us. We had a good talk. About Roger. And 'Someday.' My lawyers are going to make Roger an offer, try to keep this out of court."

"What if he refuses the offer?" Rolly asked.

"Then she'll sue. I'll pay for the lawyers. In the meantime, I'm going to record some of her brother's songs, put at least one of them on my next record, with proper attribution. Who knows, maybe we'll strike gold again. Even platinum."

Ruby cackled at her little joke.

"Anyway, Mavis and I kept talking. She told me what Roger did to her. That's why I invited her to be part of the group."

"So why were we invited?" Rolly asked.

"You weren't, Waters," Ruby said. She turned and spoke to Lucinda. "I invited you, Lucinda. That Stratocaster was your dad's and your dad was a good man. We'll let you walk out of here today with the guitar if you want to. We got what we wanted, and you will too."

"What's my other option?" Lucinda asked, knowing there was more.

"The PJL is about more than Roger Sledge," Ruby said. "We'd like to keep this thing going. There are other creeps out there getting away with stuff. I can't bankroll this thing forever. I've got a buyer for that guitar if you're willing to sell it. They'll be discreet. We wondered if you'd be willing to donate part of the profits, maybe join our little organization."

"Gosh," Lucinda said, looking thoughtful. The rest of the room waited. "If it weren't for you, those Russian gangsters would have stolen it."

She looked over at Rolly for confirmation. He nodded his head.

"They saved it," he said. "I did my best, but they're the reason it's here."

Lucinda nodded and turned back to the group.

"We should give Rolly something," she said. "In addition to what I already owe him. Some kind of hazard pay."

"Okay by me," Ruby said. "He deserves it. Campbell, you think you can work out an endorsement deal for my old guitar teacher?"

"I can throw something his way." Campbell Lange nodded. "Some kind of retainer."

"Will that work for you, Waters?" Ruby asked. "Is it a deal?"

Rolly looked over at Lucinda. She was a knockout.

"What about Norwood?" he said. "Won't he figure it out?"

"Don't you worry about Norwood," said Ruby. "I covered his appraisal costs. I told him I had some more guitars he could sell. The question is what are you going to do about this?"

"Me?"

"Yeah, you."

Rolly scanned the faces looking at him, each of them abused in some way by an arrogant dirtbag named Roger Sledge. The escape artist. The rapist and criminal. He thought of his mother and the Navy officer who'd beleaguered her with his menacing attentions. The nurses and Dr. Delusion. He thought of that old song Harry Belfonte had sung. The Grateful Dead had covered it too. *Man Smart (Woman Smarter)*. He gave everyone his best smile, a sincere expression of awe and admiration. That's right the women are smarter.

"Nothing," he said. "I'm not going to do a damn thing."

A breathy sound fluttered through the room as everyone exhaled, like feathered wings freed from cages.

"There's one other thing," Lucinda said. "It's personal."

"You name it," said Ruby.

Lucinda winked at Rolly and then turned to the group with a glint in her eye.

"I know a doctor who's in need of your services."

ACKNOWLEDGMENTS

Thanks to Cornelia Feye at Konstellation Press for continuing to support the adventures of Rolly Waters. She is a pleasure to work with. As are my editor Celia Johnson and copyeditor Lisa Wolff. And to my wife, Maria, whose critical input always makes each book better. That's right, the women are smarter.

And an overdue acknowledgment to all my guitar-playing friends, especially those who had to pass the audition–Tom, John, Paul, Matt, Ken, Andrew and Ian. Rolly Waters is a richer character for my having known and worked with each of them.

ABOUT THE AUTHOR

Corey Lynn Fayman has done hard time as a musician, songwriter, and interactive designer, but still refuses to apologize for it. His hometown of San Diego, CA provides the backdrop for his mystery novels, including the award-winning *Desert City Diva* and *Ballast Point Breakdown.*

"As an independently published author, I rely on the recommendations of enthusiastic readers to help spread the word. If you enjoyed this Rolly Waters mystery, please consider posting a review on Amazon or Goodreads. A couple of sentences and a good rating are much appreciated!"

Sign up for Corey's newsletter at Sunburned Fedora, https://www.coreylynnfayman.com, follow him on Facebook https://www.facebook.com/coreylynnfayman/ or his Amazon author page https://www.amazon.com/stores/Corey-Lynn-Fayman/author/Boo2BMEHDG for news, giveaways and special offers.

ALSO BY COREY LYNN FAYMAN

Black's Beach Shuffle

"A terrific start to this series and readers will be looking forward to Rolly's next mystery."

Mystery Review

Border Field Blues

"A powerful new voice on the crime-fiction scene, Corey Lynn Fayman delivers a potent dose of sex, drugs, and rock 'n' roll."

ForeWord Reviews

Desert City Diva

"Fans of wisecracking California crime solvers will enjoy this working-class PI with a poet's soul"

Booklist

Ballast Point Breakdown

"A refreshing and contemporary remake of the classic P.I. Genre, including a thrilling and diverse group of supporting characters and suspects."

Chanticleer Reviews

Made in the USA
Las Vegas, NV
28 April 2023

71270094R00162